LOVE THY SISTER

Maria Grazia Swan

LOVE THY SISTER
Copyright © 2013 Maria Grazia Swan
Second Edition

Printed in the United States of America

* * *

All rights reserved, which includes the right to reproduce this book or portions thereof in any form whatsoever except as provided by the US Copyright Law.

This is a work of fiction. Names, characters, places, and incidents are either the product of the author's imagination or used fictitiously. Any resemblance to actual events, locales, organizations or persons, living or dead, is entirely coincidental and beyond the intent of the author and publisher.

* * *

Front cover designed by Neta Nolan Childers

Formatting by Debora Lewis
arenapublishing.org

ISBN-13: 978-1481963671

ISBN-10: 1481963678

To my sisters:
Annica, Augusta, and Fiordalisa.

PROLOGUE

Crawling away from the pain. She had to get up from the floor. Her mouth foamed. She felt like her chest was exploding.

"One big explosion, followed by a smaller one. Just as pleasurable but not as powerful," the man had said last night in the bonding anonymity of the dark motel room, his voice an oily whisper.

What was that smell? Maybe decaying food the other girls left behind. She concentrated on the noises from below. A door slammed somewhere in the building. She didn't care who saw her, she needed help.

Air, she had to get some air. She grasped the front of her smock until it ripped. Her long black hair fell over her breasts.

"One big explosion...."

Was it last night or just a few hours ago?

Footsteps on the stairs, measured steps, getting louder. Her head jerked up. The thumping grew louder, quicker. No, it was her own heartbeat. Now her whole body was one pounding muscle. Her skin could no longer contain it.

She struggled to stand, wobbled on her stiletto heels. Last night. The music, the writhing bodies....

Her ankle gave way. She lurched for the top of the stairs, grabbed the handrail. Her foot tore free, and she pitched down the stairwell.

That noise again. Her heart, she thought, as the bridge of her nose cracked on the edge of the concrete step. Strange, no pain, no resistance.

Her body slowed as it tumbled down, thoughts fled past her, faces of strangers lying in sheeted battlefields.

Tumbling, remembering, whipping the last with the first, *mi querido.*

She inhaled the smell of her blood and the dust from the concrete. No longer would she wage nocturnal wars to keep morning dreams alive. Nor would she hide in the musty darkness, waiting for a secret rendezvous.

Her fingers relaxed, letting go. The marks impressed by her fingernails looked like tiny half moons on her colorless palms.

Blood slowly soaked the black mane covering her once-pretty face.

All was quiet now around the low mound on the landing.

Quiet and dark, yet the stillness had no threat. And the only possession she left behind was the red shoe at the top of the stairs.

CHAPTER 1
November 1989

Six years. *Dio mio*. Six years since her parents' deaths.

From under thick brown bangs, Mina stared at a blank spot on the wall. A calendar used to hang there. A pretty calendar with pictures of flowers. Not just flowers, flora. *Si* that was the word, flora from various regions of the United States of America. Her mother had a calendar like that, with flowers, or flora, from Italian regions.

Mina tried to focus, remembering the kind of flowers. Memories came hurling back, gnawing at her soul. She shook her head to rid herself of the disturbance, then went back to stare at the wall. Whatever happened to her mother's calendar? She knew what had happened to her mother; she lay next to her father, below thick quarry slabs.

Mina closed her eyes, clearly picturing in her mind's eye the flowers from her mother's calendar, yet not her mother's face. It wasn't the first time, either. She would try to recall the smile, the color of her eyes, the tenderness of her hand holding hers. Time after time, she could only recapture her mother's image as she appeared in the framed photograph on the night table.

The calendar would be six years old now, hardly useful. A tear sneaked from her eyes, landed on her hand. Mina glimpsed at the round, wet spot, and then quickly wiped it against her jeans. She was barely sixteen with little knowledge of English when she arrived in Southern California.

If they could see me now—they who? She hadn't kept in touch with any of her friends back home. Sort of a blessing really. She was almost twenty-three and although older, as the saying goes, she wasn't much wiser. Had she changed? Her fingernails were as stubby as ever, her hair the same shoulder length. Okay, her jeans were genuine Levi's, the kind hard to find in Italy. She still wore the same size clothes, five junior, on top too, disgusting. According to her sister Paola, maybe her brain kept pace with her body, stayed junior, that is.

Huddled in the faded Naugahyde chair, absently studying the reception room of her sister's software company, Mina hated life in general and this place in particular. Such a depressing sight! Drab walls and second-hand office furniture. Paola described West Coast Software's decor as 'Spartan but functional.' *Spartan*? To Mina, the word brought images of glistening bodies, athletic prowess of glorious heroes from the past. Sort of a "Mount Olympus Male Sampler." *Not* some beat-up furniture from the pages of the local *Penny Saver*.

How could anyone *function* in such a depressing environment? *Like a bee in a silk flower shop*. But no one asked her, the younger sister, about decorating ideas. Ideas, the one thing she had *abbondanza* of. And dreams, yes, dreams, too.

What she hated most about the place was the silence, the dead silence of this office on weekends. It reminded her of other silences, other places. Old terrors crept up her spine; she instinctively turned to look behind her. No watching eyes, no threatening stares, only silence.

The phone rang and Mina nearly fell off the receptionist's chair. She stared at the red light blinking on the switchboard. It was Michael Davies' line. On a Saturday? It had to be Paola.

Mina picked up the phone. "Hello?"

"Who the hell is this?"

She recognized Michael's voice.

"It's me, your favorite sister-in-law."

"You mean my only sister-in-law. Why the hell are you answering the phone? Where is Paola?" He pronounced it *Paula*.

Mispronouncing your spouse's name should be grounds for divorce, Mina thought, as if anyone cared about her opinion.

"Home in bed. It's her back, as usual. She sent me to get some papers."

"From my office?"

She sensed fear in his voice. *Why?* "I'm not in your office. Never mind. When are you coming back?"

"Tonight. I don't need a ride. Tell Paola."

"You tell her." *Why was she being so nasty to him?* "Do you have a cold?" His voice did sound raspy.

"What do you expect? It's another goddamn November in goddamn Chicago." He hung up without a good-bye.

What a jerk. Mina didn't understand how her sister could still love him. They hardly talked any more. The less Paola talked, the more Michael cursed. Was there a common denominator? And why was Michael flying to the windy city so often? On business or pleasure? That would explain why he didn't want to be picked up at LAX. Husband-stealing Rachel Fernandez probably went to Chicago with him.

What time was it anyway? A hideous clock hung on the gray wall, its electronic buzz, like a nest of wasps, set her on edge. Twelve-thirty. How long had she been daydreaming?

Her sister must be furious by now. Mina could almost hear Paola's perfectly manicured nails tapping away on the nightstand, one tap for each minute she'd been gone.

Her growling stomach reminded her of the missed breakfast, and now a postponed lunch, just to run errands for her sister. Better get going. She swiveled in the chair. Let's see, Paola said the folder was in her in-box, on the file cabinet behind the desk.

Something glittered on top of the white folder. A chocolate-covered cherry in gold foil, Paola's favorite candy. Mina's, too. Michael must have put it there before he left for Chicago. One of their stupid love rituals, maybe the only one left. To hell with Paola, Michael, and their love games. Her mouth watering, she stripped the wrapper off the candy and lifted the mound of dark chocolate to her lips.

Somewhere in the warehouse, a door slammed. She jumped and the motion sent her chair wheeling. It hit the full wastebasket, which toppled and spilled everything under the desk.

"Maledizione!" Six years in America and she still responded in Italian to every unexpected event. Mina put down the chocolate and crawled under the desk to pick up the trash. Good thing Paola couldn't see her scrunched under the desk collecting garbage. Definitely not ladylike behavior.

Sounds came from the direction of the warehouse, sharp little noises, like high heels tapping on a tile floor. The sound reminded her of a late, late-night TV movie—sinister footsteps right before an ax murderer surprised the naive heroine.

Mina ordered her heart to stop the impromptu *tarantella*. How stupid. It was probably Elena, coming to clean the office like she did every Saturday. Someone entered the reception area.

"Hey, Elena? It's me, Mina. I'm under the desk."

No answer, no more footsteps. Only silence. But in the few inches between the desk's modesty panel and the floor she could see a pair of pointed red patent pumps.

Relieved, Mina whistled. *"Mamma mia*, dancing shoes to clean the office? Bet you didn't go home last night."

The shoes moved, beating a staccato rhythm across the tile floor.

"Hey, wait, I was only kidding." Mina crawled out from under the desk, hitting her head on the top corner in the process. "Ouch!" She got up, rubbing her scalp. The office was empty.

"Fine, I'm going home." Mina grabbed her purse. "Stop hiding, Elena, I'm out of here, you can pick up the rest yourself, I've had enough of this." No answer. "Ask Paco to lock up when you're through. He's in the back, doing inventory. *Ciao*."

She was halfway around the desk when her stomach rumbled loudly. She looked for the chocolate-covered cherry. Gone.

"Okay, Elena, where are you? And where's my chocolate?"

The door to the restroom opened and Elena stepped out. Like Mina she was in her early twenties, petite and slim. Elena's black hair was short and curly, while Mina wore her brown hair shoulder length.

"*Buenos dias*, Mina."

"Did you take the chocolate that was on the desk?"

"Chocolate? *No comprendo*."

"Come on, cut it out, we both know you *comprendo*." Mina looked down at Elena's feet. "Hey, what happened to your red shoes?"

"No chocolate, no red shoes." Elena tapped her forehead. "Maybe Mina *loca* today."

Mina stared at Elena's white Reeboks and shook her head. "Maybe I am. Oh well, this *loca's* going home." She hoisted her purse back onto her shoulder and pointed a finger at Elena. "I'll bet you have chocolate breath."

Paola's folder under her arm, Mina left through the front entrance.

Before coming to California, Mina had pictured West Coast Software as a tall, shimmering glass building, with elevators, marble floors, and all kinds of ultra-modern gizmos that opened and closed doors, greeted visitors—the works. Another fantasy from watching too many American movies.

Instead, West Coast Software's squat one-story building was as gray and unattractive on the outside as inside. Hard to think of her silk-stockinged, pearl-wearing sister working there, yet Paola owned and operated the whole business.

Mina got into her yellow ragtop VW Bug, drove out of the business complex's empty parking lot and onto an almost deserted Harbor Boulevard. This short stretch of road was actually less traveled on weekends—while ten miles to the north, buses and vans with license plates from every state of the Union filled Disneyland's parking lot to the limit.

Here, business parks similar to the one occupied by her sister's company lined both sides of the wide road. Most of the buildings were built long before the little Orange County Airport became the glitzy John Wayne Airport.

"The rent's right and there's plenty of blue collar help," Paola had said.

Blue collar, white collar, the kind of Americanisms that drove Mina crazy. As if you could categorize workers by the color of their shirts.

Driving past the three-story high Marriott Suites, Mina thought of another three-story place, the one where she lived for the first sixteen years of her life. The *casa* her great-great-grandfather had built stone by stone at the foot of the Italian Alps.

Mina loved to brag to her American friends about the three-story-house she left behind. Of course, she never mentioned that it consisted of three square rooms stacked one on top of the other. Her great-great-grandfather was no architect, yet the stone walls of that house had exuded a sense of stability and continuity. Even after her parents died and she knew she would have to leave, she looked upon the *casa* as her link to her past, to her roots.

The house had outside walls so thick, the window formed a niche wide enough for her to sit on. In the summer months, late at night, Mina would curl up on the windowsill of her bedroom, to dream and to wait. She waited for the night breeze to come and blow away *l'afa,* the hot, humid air blanketing the valley from mid-July to September.

From her third-floor perch, the surroundings below took on a whole new look in the night stillness. The tall trees became Ulysses, Hercules, her sentinels lying in wait for the armies of fireflies, tiny soldiers invading their branches. And the sweet-smelling wisteria became Medusa's hair, creeping toward Mina's window.

An occasional *motorino* disturbed the nocturnal peace. A young man and his noisy scooter back from a late date. Then all would be quiet again. Quiet, not silent. She missed all that. Sadness came from deep inside, the longing, the memories.

Mina slowed down at the last intersection before the freeway. Just in time too. Ignoring the changing light, a red Thunderbird turned left onto Harbor with a squeal of tires. Whoa, that was close! She shrugged, released the tension of her hands on the steering wheel. Some people liked to fly low. She glared after the vanishing car and its driver, a woman with long, tangled— Wait a minute. That looked like Paola's dark mane.

Nah, Paola was in bed with a bad back. Too late to try to see the license plate. Still, how many red Thunderbirds...

The light changed. Mina headed for the San Diego Freeway south, and home.

Mina parked on the quiet Mission Viejo street and headed straight for the mailbox, piled magazines, junk and personal mail on top of her folder. Maybe there was a letter from Patrick. She unlocked the side door and threw it open. "Paola, I'm back. I have your papers."

The automatic icemaker was the only sound she heard. Her arms still filled with mail, Mina climbed the stairs to her sister's room.

"Paola, did you hear from Michael? He called the office."

The double doors to Paola's room were open, the huge bed neatly made up. *Boucheron*, Paola's favorite perfume, lingered in the air. Mina dropped the load of mail on the white silk moiré coverlet and went to the closed bathroom door.

"Paola, are you in there?"

She opened the door. More floral French fragrance filled her nostrils. Neatly displayed cobalt bottles of perfume were the only bright spot on the white marble countertop. They looked like enormous rings, made for a giant's hand, and through the skylight above, the shy November sun set their golden caps ablaze. But the bathroom was empty.

Mina ran downstairs to the garage. The red Thunderbird wasn't there; but the front end of Michael's gleaming black Corvette seemed to sneer at her.

She kicked one of the tires.

"Maledizione!" She had to stop cursing. She'd promised Paola. To hell with promises. She slammed the garage door and went back into the kitchen to check the notepad by the phone. No messages, nothing tacked on the refrigerator door. This wasn't like Paola.

Maybe Michael called and she had to run an errand for him. Or maybe she went to the doctor. Hmm, either way, she'd have left a note.

Her rumbling stomach reminded Mina she hadn't eaten lunch. She slapped some peanut butter on a slice of bread. Well, Paola would show up. And she'd better have a good excuse.

As usual, when the smell of peanuts reached her nose, Mina wondered how she could have lived the first sixteen years of her life without peanut butter and sliced bread. She took a bite of the sandwich, leaned back against the kitchen counter with a sigh of pleasure. And pleasure reminded her of Patrick.

She ran back upstairs to her room, elbowed the books off the night table to make space for her lunch, then went back to Paola's room and rifled through the mail. With a small cry of triumph she carried Patrick's long, lavender envelope with its U.K. postage to her bedroom.

The familiar handwriting made her forget everything else.

". . . The hours on the beach are past. Was there an ocean? Did the sand support us? I remember only you . . ."

She lay on the bed, eyes closed, and let the letter drift to her lap. Patrick... His words brought him close, so close she could almost feel his fingers stroking, stirring the heat within her. She missed his hands, the scent of his skin that lingered on her body after—

"Mina, I'm home!"

"Where have you been? I'm in my room. Come talk to me."

Her sister stopped at the open door, probably to survey the clutter level. Framed by the doorway, she reminded Mina of a fascinating blend of famous women, the beauty of a younger Elizabeth Taylor, the spunkiness and grooming of the everlasting Cher.

Tall and perfect, but not very happy judging by the frown on her face.

Mina waited. Would it be the speech about tidiness, the one about discipline, or the one about taking charge of your life? She could almost recite them from memory. Did all older sisters preach so much, or just the Italian-born?

"At least no one will ever attack you in the middle of the night." Paola said. "They'd trip and break their neck before they ever got to you." Her eyes fell on the letter. "Don't tell me. The purple poet strikes again."

"It's not purple, it's lavender—soft, romantic lavender."

Paola leaned against the doorframe and crossed her arms. "Mina, are you in love with this man?"

"In love?" Passion, yes. Excitement, definitely. But love? Tough question. "I don't know. Maybe." Right now the only thing she knew she wanted for sure was for Paola to leave her alone.

"If you don't know, then you're not." Paola picked her way across the room as if she were negotiating a minefield. She sat on the edge of the bed, pushed her tight gabardine skirt up so as not to wrinkle it. "And a good thing, too. Men are all the same—selfish, uncaring."

"One of *those* days, is it? What happened to your bad back?"

Impeccable Paola. Mina didn't know anyone else who spent hours combing her hair to make it look, well...uncombed.

"So," Paola tapped the letter with a glistening red nail, "how goes the romance with your French traveling salesman?"

"Patrick isn't a salesman; he's a marketing genius. He scouts the best locations for the chain of trendy restaurants he—"

"Never mind the reasons, the man travels. Probably has a girl in every city. Bet he inputs those flowery letters into his computer, then all he has to do is add the woman's name and *pronto*, the printer spits out half a dozen every minute."

"This isn't printed, look." Mina wet a finger in her mouth and smeared Patrick's signature. "See?

Plain ink from an old-fashioned fountain pen, a family heirloom. I've seen it. Are you happy now?"

"And you are not in love?"

Mina sighed. "What were you doing in Santa Ana? Your back sure got better fast."

"Did you find the papers?" Paola fingered the single strand of pearls she always wore. They shimmered against her silk blouse, the same shade of violet as her eyes. That color must have come from the father's side, Paola's father of course. Paola and Mina were half-sisters, sharing the same mother, and *Mamma* had brown eyes.

Mina envied her sister's eyes. Once she tried on colored contact lenses that, according to the ad, were guaranteed to make her generic brown eyes blue. Instead, they looked like the reflection of a dark sky in a puddle.

Right now her sister's eyes looked far away. "The papers, right." Mina paused. "I flushed them down the toilet."

Paola didn't flinch. "Fine. I'll look at them later."

"By the way," Mina picked up Patrick's letter. "I think Elena ate your chocolate. Actually, I unwrapped it, but she ate it. I'm telling you now so you don't raise hell on Monday morning."

"What?" Paola's hand hit the lavender paper, sent it flying.

"Calm down, will you? Maybe it fell on the floor when I knocked over the trash. It's just a damn candy, Paola, I'll buy you a box at the store."

"Is she all right?"

"Who?"

"Elena."

"Of course she's all right. What do you think I did, beat her up?" She smoothed out Patrick's letter, now crisscrossed with wrinkles. "Not that I wasn't tempted."

"Mina, listen to me. After Elena ate the chocolate, what happened?"

"How would I know? She hid in the ladies room, hope she got Montezuma's revenge." She caught a glimpse of Paola's expression. "I didn't mean it. Anyway, when she came out she said I was *loca*. Why? Is she allergic to chocolate or something?"

Paola's eyes glittered. "I'm sorry. I'm overreacting. It's this whole mess with Michael and the business."

"You sure don't have much luck when it comes to husbands."

"I don't know what you're talking about. They were both college graduates. *Mamma* approved." Paola gave a rueful laugh. "*Povera Mamma*, impressed with a lousy piece of paper and a black robe."

"Or a wimple," Mina said. "She actually wanted me to be a nun."

Paola grinned.

"Don't laugh," Mina said. "In her mind it was the ideal occupation. It would have kept me out of trouble and on that side of the Atlantic. She couldn't stand the idea of me leaving home to join you."

Paola reached over and stroked Mina's cheek.

"Do you miss her?" Mina asked.

"I miss the person she was before..."

"Go ahead. Say it—before she married my father. As if I didn't know."

"I didn't mean that the way it sounded. Besides, I was already fourteen by then, almost ready to leave the nest." Paola hugged her younger sister.

"Help, help!"

"I wish you'd stop that childish nonsense." Paola said. "You're old enough to face your emotions instead of hiding behind jokes. Is that what you say to your Frenchman in tender moments? Help?"

Mina gave her a wicked grin. *Tutto bene.* "We don't spend our tender moments talking."

"I know you. That's impossible."

"You're right, Paola. We exchange recipes while taking off our clothes."

"Mina! What ever happened to acting like a lady?"

"You mean like this?" Mina stuck out her tongue and flapped her hands next to her ears. "Good," Mina said. "That got you laughing." She patted her sister's head.

"Watch it, you're ruining my hair!"

"You call *that* ruining your hair? Wrong. *This* is ruining your hair." Mina pushed her fingers into Paola's mane, rumpled it, then sprang off the bed and ran for the door.

Paola hopped after her, brandishing her sandal. "I'll get you for this!"

The telephone rang.

"I'll take it in my room," Paola said, still laughing. She hobbled toward her bedroom. Mina headed downstairs. Almost three p.m., could it be Patrick?

"Is it for me?" Mina called, halfway down.

No answer. She hurried back upstairs to find Paola standing pale-faced in the doorway of her bedroom, the sandal still in her hand. "Michael wasn't on the plane," she whispered.

CHAPTER 2

"Mina, would you kindly remove your feet from the dashboard?" Paola weaved in and out of traffic, a flashy red shark in a pool of guppies.

Mina hoped there were no cops on the freeway tonight. "Okay, *va bene*." Mina's feet dropped to the plush tan carpet with a thud. "God, you can be a pain! What's the big deal? Michael has missed planes before."

"You don't understand. He didn't miss the plane. He disappeared at the boarding gate. He must have noticed Brian following him."

Mina snickered. Brian Starrs, would-be detective. She could hardly believe her sister had hired a college kid to follow her sneaky husband. "Where did you find this guy, anyway?"

Paola's eyes were glued to the freeway, but a muscle twitched at the corner of her bright red lips. Bathed in the amber glow from the dashboard, her perfect profile was highlighted against the flash of city lights.

For years, Mina had asked her mirror the same question; why was Paola the one with the face, the body, the class? Their mother never said it out loud. There were times when Mina had felt her mother staring at her. She'd ask why, but Mother would shake her head and turn away. Yet, the silences left no doubt.

Mina had no inclination for complicated cosmetic routines. She figured what you saw was what you got. After she moved to America, her sister taught her the one and only makeup habit she practiced. Mina and her black mascara were inseparable. She kept her face natural, but thickened her long eyelashes with *Rimmel,* the mascara that gave her large, round eyes a sensual kind of secrecy. At least, that's what she told herself.

"I can't believe this traffic. Where is everybody going?" Paola said.

"We'll get there. The restaurant isn't going anywhere, and your private eye is on the meter." She carefully avoided saying *sleuth*, which, with her lingering accent, always came out *slut*. "He won't care if we're late. How did you hook up with him, anyhow?"

Paola switched lanes again. "Adams, my lawyer, introduced us. And please, don't call him a private eye—he's just a nice young man trying to earn extra money to finish school."

Mina shrugged. "Why go through all this trouble to prove Michael's been unfaithful? Doesn't California have a no-fault divorce law?"

Paola's voice dropped an octave. "This has nothing to do with infidelity."

"Really? Then what's going on? Why did Michael go to Chicago? I'm your sister, you know. You could let me in on what's happening."

"That works both ways, *signorina*," Paola said. "You never told me you quit your job. The third one in six weeks." Paola called her *signorina*, only when she was really ticked off.

Mina shrank down in the seat. "This time it wasn't my fault." Some choice they gave her: Work on Halloween night or be fired. Working meant missing the ultimate costume party. She knew she could get another waitressing job anytime. It occurred to her that, like Thanksgiving, Halloween didn't figure into Italian calendars. Neither did the Fourth of July.

"Watch it," Mina sat up as the sign whizzed by them. "You'll miss the exit. Brookhurst is next. So, how can the snoop—"

"I wish you'd stayed home!" Paola whipped off the exit and through a green light.

"Well, I didn't. How can your nice-young-man-earning-extra-money phone you from Chicago at two-thirty in the afternoon and be in Orange County the same evening? Slow down, I see the Coco's sign. No, no, left!"

Paola made the turn on two wheels. Brakes screeched from the oncoming traffic.

"You're getting really good at this," Mina said. "Ever consider racing professionally?"

Her sister didn't answer. She parked the Thunderbird, checked her makeup in the rearview mirror and, pointing a finger in Mina's direction, said, "Remember, you promised to behave."

"Yes, Mother."

Paola, halfway out of the car, turned and gave her a strange look. "Just don't embarrass me in there." They entered the restaurant. Paola ran her fingers through her hair. "Maybe I'll go freshen up," she said. "I think we beat Brian here. I didn't see his car in the parking lot."

She turned to go when a man in his late twenties, wearing jeans and a bulky sweater over a denim shirt, rushed from one of the telephone booths off to the side of the waiting area.

"Paula! I was about to call you." He took Paola's hand in his. "Where is your car?"

Mina resented the way he pronounced her sister's name. "We parked in the broom closet."

Still holding Paola's hand, he seemed to notice Mina for the first time.

Paola introduced them. "Brian, this is my sister, Mina."

Mina looked pointedly at their hands touching. Paola quickly let go and, flushing, asked the hostess to seat them.

Following her sister and Brian to the table, Mina felt like a child trailing along behind the "big people." She always seemed to get swept along in Paola's wake.

At least the view was good. Brian's buns were bound to garner him more than a mere honorable mention in the Levi's Hall of Fame. He was the same height as Paola, but then she was wearing heels. That would make him about five ten. His blond hair, straight and thick, came to a point in the back of his neck, low enough to meet his shirt collar. Mina wondered what it would feel like to run her fingers through it. Slowly, all the way to where the last strand of hair met the warmth of his skin. And for no reason whatsoever, the word *Spartan* crossed her mind.

He flashed a quick smile as he slid into the booth across from her. *Sorriso Durbans*, she thought, remembering the popular slogan for the Italian toothpaste, marketed as the one America likes best, although she never found that specific brand in Californian supermarkets. Brian's smile would be perfect for the toothpaste ad. His smile had the openness she so often found in certain types of American men, the kind her friends called WASP. Yes, he was definitely worth *un peccatino*, a trip to the confessional.

After they ordered, Brian said, "Michael went through the security check, then grabbed his briefcase and carry-on, and practically sprinted to the gate. The flight was already boarding. My turn came and, of course, the buzzer went off. I took the keys out of my pocket and tried again. No go. Next I tried the watch. The thing still went off. By then I was—"

"The gun!" Mina interrupted.

"What gun?"

"Your gun. You know, that's what set off the alarm."

"Why would I have a gun?"

Mina opened her mouth, but a sharp kick from under the table changed her mind. "Never mind," Mina mumbled. "Paola just explained it to me, *grazie*."

A yawning waitress brought their order. Only Brian had ordered food. Mina had a chocolate milkshake, her sister, iced tea.

"You were saying, Brian?" Paola smiled.

Mina took a sip of milkshake, *latte sbattuto*, in Italian it sounded like milk from an abused cow. Speaking of abuse, Mina reached down and massaged her sore ankle. It didn't look bruised—yet.

When she looked up, Brian's head was bent close to Paola's. "Is your iced tea okay?" he asked. Next to her sister's dark hair, his was so light it almost looked bleached.

Could he be any more protective? Mina wanted to throw up.

"Fine," Paola said.

"My milkshake's a little runny," Mina volunteered.

Paola ignored her. "So, tell me, what happened next?"

"We finally figured it out. It was the souvenir spoon I bought for my mother."

"How sweet," Paola said.

"Are you kidding?" Mina moved her leg out of her sister's range.

Brian glanced over at her. Their eyes caught, held. *Mamma mia!* They were the bluest eyes she had ever seen.

"Are you wearing colored contacts?" she blurted.

He smiled.

"Brian." Paola's voice held irritation. "About my husband?"

"Oh yes, Michael. I stepped into the plane and they shut the doors behind me. I went to my seat. By the time I realized he wasn't on board, we were airborne. I phoned you from Houston during a stopover." He sipped from his soda. "Did you hear from him?"

Paola shook her head: "He called the office this morning, but that was before the flight took off. Where do we go from here?"

"Not too far, if I'm driving. My car broke down on the freeway."

"We can give you a ride home," Paola said.

"It'll be a crowded broom," Mina mumbled.

The waitress appeared just in time to divert the under-the-table kicker.

"Aside from the airport, what else went on?" Paola asked.

"Paula, this may sound strange." Brian spoke between bites of fish and chips. "But everything went according to the schedule you gave me. I can read you my notes." He began to search his pockets.

"Later," Paola idly stirred the tea. "I wonder where he is. Maybe we should stop by the office on the way home. I'd love to give Michael a little surprise."

Mina finished the shake and wondered who would pick up the tab. On cue, the waitress came by and dropped the bill on the table. Amused, Mina watched them reach for it at the same time.

"I'm your boss, remember?" Paola took the check. Brian smiled, laid his napkin on the table and got up. He helped Paola from her chair, and then turned toward Mina, who was already on her feet.

Outside, a strong wind blew through the moonless night. Brian sat in the front with Paola. Mina, in back, leaned forward and propped herself between the seats, determined not to miss a word. It was after nine, and, instead of taking the freeway, Paola drove on surface streets.

"So, you're a friend of Adams?" Mina asked Brian.

He half turned in the seat. In the fleeting carousel of streetlights, his eyes were bright as lapis lazuli. "Actually," he said, "I'm a friend of his daughter."

"You go to college with her?"

He hesitated. "No."

"Oh, I get it. You go with her."

"*Signorina*, would you kindly sit back, buckle your seat belt and shut your mouth?" Paola said.

Mina sank back in the seat. "Yes, Mother dearest."

Brian chuckled, a friendly sort of sound, not mocking in the least. Well, not friendly, exactly. Tolerant maybe, or at least comfortable, unfazed by her attempts to shock him.

Mina knew something was wrong when they pulled onto Harbor Boulevard. She saw the blaze of lights through the trees, and scooted forward on her seat again. "Look," she said. "The cops must have nabbed somebody."

Paola turned left into the business complex. West Coast Software's parking lot looked like a carnival gone mad. Flashing lights—red, blue, white—greeted them from the dozen Santa Ana Police cars parked at odd angles in front of the entrance.

"Paola, do you think you've been robbed?" Mina asked.

Pulling as far as she could into the lot, Paola turned off the engine. People—cops and, behind the barricades, onlookers—crowded West Coast Software's entrance.

Paola got out and hurried toward the building without even closing the car door. Brian followed her. Mina crawled out of the back and locked the car.

She couldn't believe she was being the model of caution while her sister rushed ahead, but then it wasn't her company. Mina ran to the entrance. She lifted the yellow police tape, tried to slip under it. A uniformed policeman stopped her.

"Sorry, Miss. You have to back up, please."

"I'm with them," she pointed toward West Coast Software. "That's my sister's company."

"Well, right now you must move back, make room."

"Make room for what?" She stood on tiptoe to look over his shoulder. Two white-coated men were pushing a gurney. As they came closer, she saw that a body lay on the gurney, shrouded in a white sheet.

She backed up, stiff as a marionette.

A voice behind her said, "Move to the side, please, out of the way."

Mina turned. The coroner's white wagon was backing up to the entrance, its back door yawned wide. Panic hit her. She tried to get away, but the crowd pressed her back against one of the policemen. The gurney came closer and, wheeling past her, hit a speed bump. Wedged between the policeman and a barricade, Mina had a clear view.

She shuddered; the sheet covered everything but one red patent leather shoe.

CHAPTER 3

Mina sat in the receptionist's chair just as she had—was it only that afternoon? All was dark and cold outside the big glass windows. Yet, thoughts rushed through her mind like sparks from a fire burst.

Night or day, time didn't matter. Not to her and not to Sarah. Oh, how she wanted to shrink, get smaller and smaller, disappear into that chair. Even her breathing felt shallow. If she kept still and quiet maybe no one would notice her.

She needed time to think, understand, and make sense of this death.

Sarah Fernandez. The girl with the red shoes.

Dio, Dio mio, why? Death had no country, no conscience; it paid no attention to age, race, intelligence, or personality. Death gathers souls indiscriminately, the way bees gather pollen from flowers.

Flowers, yes. She closed her eyes, seeing big, yellow chrysanthemums. *Crisantemi*, flowers of death. In Italy, November second was *Il Giorno dei Morti*, Day of the Dead. To Paola, that was a silly tradition, another senseless Catholic ritual like fish on Friday. But religious or not, every year, Italians kept their date with their dead.

In the cold November morning, after Mass, the townspeople walked the steep road to the cemetery. A row of tall, somber cypresses guarded the way. The bent, old women, black shawls covering their heads, held children's hands. White pebbles skittered under the heavy shoes; weathered fingers rolled rosary beads. Mina remembered passing through the rusty gates, the acrid smell of flowers, the murmur of voices, and the quiet sobbing over the moist dirt of the newest graves.

And *crisantemi* everywhere. Bright yellow, like the California sun, like the police tape— chills ran through her, she wrapped her arms around her body. *Was there a Day of the Dead where Sarah came from?*

Mina opened her eyes. The drab reception area felt downright spooky tonight.

Across from her, Brian sat on the only couch. "Is Sarah related to Rachel Fernandez?"

"Her older sister, I think. It's hard to tell. They have so many relatives working the line and boxing the finished diskettes. Sarah had probably been with the company the longest. To me, all the sisters look so much alike, except for Rachel, and that's because she bleaches her hair. Do you know Rachel?"

Before Brian could answer, Paola came out of Michael's office with Paco Mendez, the girls' supervisor. Paco, in his early fifties, had a bushy head of gray hair and a mustache that threatened to take over his face. Mina didn't know where her sister had found him, but he'd worked at the company from the beginning, moving up from warehouse worker to warehouse supervisor, to plant foreman.

He was also Paola's closest friend.

"Paco found Sarah when he turned on the alarm," Paola said, "but the police think she's been dead for several hours. Poor Sarah."

"What happened?" Mina asked.

"It looks like she fell down the stairs." Paola pointed at the closed door next to Michael's office that led to the loft. "She hit her head on the concrete edge of the last step. If the carpet layers had finished their job in time, this probably wouldn't have happened." Paola paused. "Maybe I should call Adams."

"Afraid of a lawsuit?" Mina asked. Peter Adams was her sister's lawyer and old friend, yet she always referred to him by his last name.

"For what?" Paola hesitated, as if carefully choosing the answer. "She may have forgotten to take her epilepsy medication and had a seizure. It's happened before. Remember? She went into convulsions the day she started working here; caused quite a commotion. I rushed her to the doctor—back then she didn't speak English. I felt so sorry for her, on her own in a new country. I tried to be a big sister to her and the rest of the girls, until..."

Until Rachel entered the scenario, Mina finished her sister's thought.

Paola took a breath before continuing. "Sarah is—I mean, was—careless about her prescription. Anyway, that's what the police suspect."

"How do you know that?" Mina asked.

"I told them about her health problems." Paola passed a hand over her forehead, massaged the space between her eyes. "I don't care if it's late, I'm calling Adams."

She went back into Michael's office and closed the door. Paco collapsed on the couch, next to Brian. The two men greeted each other. Mina wondered if they'd been introduced.

Yawning, Brian stretched his arms over his head. "I could use a ride home. Jet lag is catching up with me, and I'm no help here."

Mina jumped up; she could use a change of scenery herself. "I'd love to take you home, but my sister doesn't let me drive her car."

"Mrs. Davies is a wise lady," Paco said, a gentle gleam in his eyes.

"*Grazie* for that vote of confidence, Paco. Anyway," she flashed Brian a big smile, "if you can talk her into giving you the keys..."

"Sounds good." Brian rubbed his eyes. "Paco, what did you tell the police?"

He swallowed hard. "I noticed the blood first."

"Wait a minute," Mina sat down. "It's not...I don't..."

Paco didn't seem to hear her. "There was a big dark spot under the door to the loft. I thought it was coffee, at first. About a month ago, the girls left the machine on the whole weekend. It exploded, and on Monday I found glass and coffee grounds all over the upstairs room and down the stairs.

"There's a second story to this building?" Brian asked.

"It's just a loft. It used to be for storage, but we needed more space in the warehouse, so Mrs. Davies came up with the idea of turning the loft into an eating area. That freed the dining room, and we were able to expand into it. Most of the remodeling is complete, except for a few finishing touches, like carpet and a new railing." Paco shook his head. "I don't understand what Sarah was doing up there, or how she got in. I'm sure I locked the access door when I left Friday night."

Paco probably had keys to the building that Paola didn't even let Michael have, Mina thought.

"She was wearing her work smock," Paco continued, "but she didn't punch in her time card. I was doing inventory most of the day, but I never saw her. Not until..."

Red patent pumps. Was she the last one to see Sarah alive?

"How did it happen?" Brian asked.

Mina wished he would shut up.

"She must have passed out at the top of the stairs. The police found one of her red shoes up there." Paco's voice wavered. "It looked like she fell face-first. I don't know when it happened. I don't know if I could have helped her. When I found her, her hair—*Madre de Dios*." He made a quick sign of the cross. "The blood had dried and her hair was stuck over her face. I wouldn't have recognized her except for the name on her smock."

The three of them sat, the clock's buzzing the only sound in the gloomy room. Mina felt sick inside. Should she tell the cops about the red shoes? It would help establish that Sarah was still alive around one o'clock when... The memory of a speeding Thunderbird roared in her head. Maybe she should wait, talk it over with her sister. Nothing could bring Sarah back now.

Si, she would talk to Paola first.

Paco said something to Brian, got up and went through the door to the warehouse. As the door closed behind him, Paola came out of the office.

"Done. Where is Paco?" she asked.

"Locking up the back and leaving," Brian said. "He's going to check on the Fernandezes on his way home. They don't have a telephone."

Michael Davies picked that moment to walk in, looking as if he had just returned from a coffee break—no overcoat, no briefcase, hands in his pockets. He used to be a handsome man, but the years and the extra weight had greatly changed his appearance. The full, sensuous lips of his youth now sagged into his fleshy jaws. It was hard to remember the attractive man Paola had brought to Italy to meet their parents. Only his eyes held a glimmer of the charm and sensitivity that had made him so appealing.

Met by a trio of stares, Michael stopped. "What's this, West Coast Software welcome wagon?" He turned to Brian. "Who the hell are you?"

Paola replied quickly. "Mina's new friend."

Mina's first impulse was to choke her sister; instead, she smiled.

"Sorry I'm late, I missed my plane," Michael said. "What's that police tape doing by the flower bed?" At their silence, his tone grew suspicious. "What the fuck is going on?"

Paola pointed to the loft. "Sarah Fernandez fell down the stairs. I'm afraid she's dead."

Michael's incredulous look struck Mina as genuine. "Honey, if that's meant as a joke, it's a sick one."

Paola tilted her head and peered at him from almost-closed eyelids. She spoke slowly. "I said Sarah, not Rachel, darling."

His face reddened with anger. "Of course. Pushing people down stairs is hardly your style."

"Michael!" Paola lowered her voice. "Let's continue this in your office."

After the door closed, Brian turned toward Mina, "It's hard for me to imagine Paula married to that man."

"He wasn't always like this. When they got married, he was quite handsome. All my girlfriends were smitten with him. They used to call him *L'Americano*." Mina swiveled gently in the receptionist's chair. "They came to Italy for their honeymoon. Our parents were alive then. Everyone could see he was crazy about her."

"When was that?"

"Oh, years ago." Before he met Rachel. For the second time that night, Mina wondered why, if someone had to die, it couldn't have been Rachel.

Better change the subject.

"How about you?" Mina said. "How's your love life?"

The amused look in Brian's eyes was the only sign he had heard her question. "I think I'll hit the rest room." He stood, stretched, and walked up the hall toward the warehouse. "Then we can see about getting you those car keys."

After he left, the intercom buzzed. Mina jumped to her feet. Paola's voice sounded scratchy over the wire. "Mina, can you come in here please?"

She had barely stepped over the threshold when Paola threw her the keys to the Thunderbird.

"Why don't you drive Brian home while Michael and I talk."

A smile spread across Mina's face, "Yes, ma'am, *mille grazie.*"

Michael knelt next to her sister's chair and stroked her arm. So, the snake had some residual charm. Mina was just glad to see that Paola had calmed down.

"I'll be back in a jiffy." She held up one hand. "Wait, don't say it—I'll drive carefully, I promise. *Ciao!*" The keys jingled as she gave a saucy wave and closed the door.

Brian came out of the bathroom. "Hey, snoop, guess what?" Mina called.

His eyes were riveted on something behind her.

Mina turned. A woman in a brown tweed coat stood by the receptionist's desk, her back to them. She stared out into the dark parking lot. Mina recognized her by the coarse bleached hair that hung down her back.

"Rachel," Mina whispered.

The woman didn't move.

A heavy wool coat. Mina's mind leapt. She'd been to Chicago with Michael. How dare she come in here!

Mina strode over and tapped the woman on the shoulder. "Rachel." She said the name quietly between gritted teeth. Better than being overheard by Paola and Michael.

The blonde turned. Mina found herself staring into the eyes of a very alive Sarah Fernandez.

CHAPTER 4

Mina's scream rose from deep inside. It wasn't a screech or a shrill, but a loud cry of astonishment. Loud enough to bring Paola and Michael rushing out of the office.

"What is it?" Paola asked.

In complete state of shock, Mina couldn't find her voice. *Sarah?* How could this be? Silently, she stepped aside and pointed at the blonde.

"*Dio mio*, dear God, it's Sarah. But...who is...*Dio mio*, I'm losing my mind," Paola whispered. "Your hair—Oh, Sarah, haven't you heard?"

Sarah turned to Michael. She seemed confused and probably couldn't understand anything being said.

"Well, Paola, she looks alive and well to me." He laughed—a brief, strident laugh—but his eyes never left his wife's face.

"May I use the telephone in your office?" Brian headed toward the office without waiting for an answer.

Mina felt soooo stupid. Screaming, what a mature reaction. She glimpsed at Sarah. Sarah alive! But then, who was the dead girl?

Now Mina understood Michael's earlier disbelief. He knew the dead woman couldn't be

Sarah because she was with him in Chicago. What a fool she'd been, blaming Rachel, when it was her sister having an affair with Michael. To hell with all the Fernandez sisters.

"Paco thought...he's on his way to tell the family. Shouldn't we send somebody to let him know it wasn't Sarah?" No one paid attention to Mina.

"Sarah, how did you get in here?" Paola asked, her voice back to normal.

A puzzled look was the only reaction she received from the young woman.

"Leave her alone," Michael said, "She drove some relatives to the airport. We ran into each other and she gave me a ride."

Mina waited for Paola's explosion. When it didn't come, she snapped, "Paola, wake up! You don't believe his story, do you?"

"Excuse me." Brian was back on the scene. "I just spoke to a friend on the Santa Ana Police Department—"

"You what?" Michael said. "Who do you think you are?"

"One of the detectives is a friend of mine. So—"

"And you are Mina's friend?" Michael sneered.

"To have friends in the Police Department is a good thing," Brian ignored Michael's sarcasm, "especially in a mess like this. We're to meet Detective De Fiore at the morgue."

"Fuck, just what we need, another goddamn wop," Michael said.

Mina flared." You jerk, any one wop is better than you, you bloated—"

"Mina, *basta*, stop it this instant!" Paola said. "Why don't we all start behaving like adults and go meet Detective De Fiore? Where is this place?"

"Off Santa Ana Boulevard and Fourth Street. I know how to get there," Brian said.

"I'm not going to the morgue," Mina said.

"Don't be difficult, *signorina!*"

"You can shout all you want, Paola. I'm not going." She backed up against the wall.

"Why not?" Brian said.

Her face reddened. "I guess...I don't know. *Si*, I do know. I don't want to look at dead bodies. It's morbid. It's sick."

"Well, since you're not involved with this, you could wait here." Brian said.

"Stay here alone?"

"Sure. Sarah, Paula and Mr. Davies need to be at the morgue, and I promised Dan—Detective De Fiore—that I'd go with them. You stay and guard the fort, okay?"

Mina glanced at the door to the loft. "I'm not staying here by myself."

"Goddamn, Mina, make up your mind." Michael's face flushed with anger. "It'll be time for Sunday brunch by the time we're finished with this shit, and I want to go home and get some sleep." Michael said.

"Okay, I'll go. But I'm waiting in the car."

"Is it settled?" Paola asked.

Mina nodded.

"Then everybody out, I'll turn on the alarm," Paola said. "Let's go."

Everyone piled into Paola's car, Paola and Michael in front, Mina in the back, sandwiched between Brian and Sarah. Michael followed Brian's directions to the morgue. The ride was short. In the misleading shadows of the night, the Santa Ana barrio looked like any other poor neighborhood. The headlights of the speeding Thunderbird probed the stillness of the streets on this late Saturday night, yet, like a magic eraser, blotted out the gangs' graffiti, the barred doors and windows.

Twenty minutes later, they parked in front of a brown brick building trimmed with orange glazed tiles.

Forensic Science Center, the sign said. A modern looking place; not at all the gothic horror Mina imagined. She felt a little foolish about her reluctance, but wasn't about to admit it.

The others went inside. Before he closed the car door, Brian leaned over and mouthed, "Chicken."

Mina pretended she didn't see him. Soon she grew tired of staring at the oversized orange lamp glowing in the window of the reception room. She made sure the car doors were locked and leaned her head against the window. Why would anyone decorate a morgue orange? It took her a moment to make the connection. Orange as in Orange County.

Less than ten years ago, Mina had never heard of the place. She knew Paola lived in California, but to an Italian teenager and her friends, California was San Francisco and the Golden Gate Bridge, Disneyland and Hollywood. She closed her eyes and smiled, remembering the way she used to pronounce Hollywood. Howlyvoood, like the howl of a werewolf in the moonlight.

Mina dozed off. The next thing she heard was a tapping on the window. Nervous, she looked outside. Brian flashed his fluoride smile. She rubbed her eyes, careful not to disturb the mascara, and then rolled the window down a few inches. "I don't have to come in, do I?"

Brian dangled the keys of the Thunderbird in front of her. "Wanna give me a ride home?"

Mina climbed into the front seat while Brian walked around and unlocked the passenger door. He handed her the keys. "Paula says—"

"I know, I know," Mina interrupted him. "Be careful, drive safely: the same old stuff." She started the car, loving the roar of the T-bird's engine. Such a nice change from the Bug. "Well, who is she?"

"Who is who?"

"Come on, Brian. The dead girl."

"It's hasn't been confirmed, although I have a pretty good idea."

"Of course, Mr. Detective," she said.

"I talked to Paco. He got here before we did."

"You and Paco seem pretty chummy. He doesn't usually warm up to people that fast."

"I'm Paula's friend."

"Then why don't you call her by her real name: Paola." Mina yawned and stretched. "Where to, Mr. Detective?"

"How about some all-night place where we can get you some coffee?"

"No way, I won't be able to sleep."

"That's the idea." Again, that smile.

Mina's heart went into overtime. "Um, you said the body hasn't been identified. Who do you think it is?"

"I'll tell you over coffee."

"I don't want any coffee. Besides, I don't want to be seen in public like this. I feel—like I need grooming. "

"It was good enough for Coco's, earlier."

He was looking at her, maybe staring, but she wouldn't look back.

Not with her heart pounding like that. What was the matter with her? She shrugged, trying to seem cool. "It's late and I'm tired."

"We could go to a drive-through," Brian said.

"*Va bene*, let's get the damn coffee and get it over with." Mina slapped the car into gear and backed up.

"You're really cute when you're angry."

"And you talk like the soaps."

Brian stirred and retreated to his side.

A sudden desire to let her fingers do the walking— through his hair and down his back— came over her. "Tell me where to go before I get lost."

"Go east on Santa Ana Boulevard. You'll see a Jack In the Box."

Mina craved silence, time to think about the strange twist of the night's events, time to put this all in perspective, but she couldn't concentrate. She was conscious of Brian's every movement, every glance in her direction. Better talk about something neutral. "So what happened back there, at the uh...morgue?" Mina tripped a little over the word.

To her surprise, Brian reached over and stroked her hair. She flinched, and his hand fell back to his lap. "What was that for?" she asked.

"Oh, for an instant, you looked like a little girl with big spooky eyes. I didn't mean to startle you."

Warmth stirred deep inside her. She saw the drive-through ahead. "Here we are. Jack in the Box." The mixed odor of grease, salt and hamburger greeted them as she pulled into the lot.

"You park while I get the coffee. We can drink it in the car. Unless you've changed your mind about coming inside?" Brian said.

Mina shook her head.

Brian stepped out of the car, closed the door, then opened it again and asked, "How do you like your coffee?"

"Dark, hot and sweet." Mina blushed when she realized how that sounded.

Brian gave her a long glance but, to his credit, didn't say anything. He shut the door, strode into the glaring lights of the fast food restaurant. By the time she parked the car, he was back. The hot coffee steamed the windows, and soon they were isolated from the world outside.

"So, who do you think the dead girl is?" Mina stirred the coffee, sipped it.

"The girls in the assembly line wear blue smocks with their name tags sewn on, right? The smock was Sarah's. However, she shared the locker with three other girls."

"Three other sisters," Mina corrected.

"Right. Paco saw the nametag and the long black hair; I can see how he made the mistake. It could happen to anyone."

"Her hair. That confused me, too. Rachel bleaches hers. Sarah's is usually dark. When did they change her hair color?" Mina asked.

"Do you know about Halloween?"

"How could I forget? It was last Tuesday. That night I joined the ranks of the unemployed. Again."

"You lost your job? Sorry."

"Don't worry, it's routine for me," Mina said. "Now, tell me about the hair color mystery."

Taking a sip of coffee, Brian leaned his head against the back of the seat. "I guess there's a resemblance between the sisters. That's what gave Rachel and Sarah the idea. Sarah bleached her hair blonde, and Rachel dyed hers black. They wore each other's clothing and make-up, and fooled a lot of people at a Halloween party."

"How do you know all that?" Mina asked.

"Paco and Sarah told me while Paula—Paola—was in with Dan."

"What's going to happen—*cosa?*" she stammered, "Are you saying that the girl at the morgue is..."

"Rachel Fernandez. It's just a tentative identification based on Sarah's statement. But my gut feeling tells me that's her."

"That's not possible. I mean, Paola said the dead girl had an epileptic seizure that's how she fell down the stairs. Rachel isn't epileptic. You've got to be wrong."

Brian stared at her. "Calm down. Maybe she lost her balance on those spike heels."

"No, no, it just can't be," she moaned.

"Don't get so upset," Brian said.

"Damn it, you don't understand. When I found out Sarah died, I wished it were Rachel instead. Now you're telling me it happened." Mina covered her head with her arms and rested her forehead on the steering wheel.

"Mina, the girl was dead before you made your wish. You had nothing to do with it. You shouldn't feel guilty."

She shook her head. "I'm going to burn in hell for this," she said, and burst into tears.

"Are you Catholic?"

She had been baptized and taken first communion but had stopped going to mass. "Sort of."

"That explains it." Brian propped his coffee against the windshield, reached over and gathered her to him. She turned her face into his shoulder.

"Mina, maybe it's not Rachel. Please don't cry. It wasn't your fault, believe me."

She straightened and wiped her eyes. "I need a tissue." Mina found a box of tissues under the seat, and blew her nose. She'd managed to embarrass herself in front of him twice in one night. "What did the police want from Paola?"

"There were lots of unanswered questions," Brian said. "Since they can't write it off to Sarah's epilepsy, the whole scenario has changed."

Mina froze. Oh God, if it was Rachel, the police might suspect Paola. "What do you mean?"

"I don't know, Mina. There are more questions than answers. Why don't you drive me home? It's only a couple of miles from here. Things'll look better in the morning." He checked his watch. "Or rather, the afternoon. Are you okay?"

"Yes, yes, yes." She started the car and pulled out onto Santa Ana Boulevard.

"You sure?"

"Honestly Brian, you're worse than Paola."

He directed her to his house. It was in an older neighborhood. She pulled in front of his address. "I like it here. The houses have a character of their own."

"I like it too. We've lived here for a long time."

"We?" *Did her voice sound shaky?*

"My mother and I." He yawned. "Jet lag. I can sure use some sleep. Can you find your way home from here?"

Mina nodded.

"I'm glad I met you." His blue eyes, undimmed by fatigue, looked into hers. "The neighborhood is much more interesting in the daylight. Maybe you could come over later today. I'll give you a deluxe tour."

She shook her head. "I'm too tired to think now. *Ciao*, blue eyes."

Driving off, she remembered Patrick and suddenly felt guilty. She had dated other guys off and on during Patrick's long absences—not that she planned on dating Brian. Why did she feel guilty about having a cup of coffee with him?

At the end of the deserted street, the freeway lights beckoned.

She pressed the gas pedal to the floor. The Thunderbird leapt forward, the box of tissues slid to the far end of the dashboard.

"Damn," Mina reached out, it slid away. She stopped the car, grabbed the box and tried to force it under the seat, where she had found it. Something blocked her effort. A hard, sharp object. Cold sweat shot down her spine. A red patent pump, *from under Paola's seat?* "No!" She felt soiled, damaged. Still holding the shoe scorching her soul. Get rid of it. How? The shadowy anonymity of the freeway called to her. No, she couldn't. The muffled thump of the red pump landing in the back seat rekindled more fear, more doubts. *Oh, Paola, why?* Again, Mina floored the gas pedal, the Thunderbird roared into the night. Soon she left Santa Ana behind, but stowed away in her mind, the demons went with her. *You can run, but you can't hide.*

CHAPTER 5

Slices of sun filtered through the mini-blinds, rested on Mina's bed. The blanket lay in a lump on the floor, and a corner of the bottom sheet had popped off the mattress, ensnaring her toes. The bed felt like a prison, a lonely place where nocturnal terrors seemed to multiply. Every time she closed her eyes, nightmarish visions of red spiked heels hammered on her head with haunting precision.

Red shoes and the Fernandez sisters, red shoes and her own sister. *Maledizione*. Red shoes from hell. *Basta*, stop. Her sister didn't own red shoes yet something told her there had to be a connection. Time to talk to big sister. *Si,* as soon as Paola got out of bed, they were going to have a nice, long chat. Well, maybe not nice. Thinking about it made Mina even more nervous.

How about some warm milk? Anything was better than lying here, thinking, worrying.

Mina scooted off the bed and scrounged around for something to wear. Days ago, she'd started to sort her laundry, but never finished it. Small mounds of clothes littered the floor.

An oversized sweatshirt with a Guns N' Roses logo perched on the closest pile. She slipped it on and went downstairs. She put a mug of low-fat milk in the microwave and watched it go round and round until the timer buzzed.

"Is that you, Mina?" Paola's voice called from someplace near.

She hadn't expected her sister to be up or she would have picked a different top. "I'll be right there."

"Up already?" Paola sat in the living room, staring at the wall. "I couldn't sleep either."

Mina tried to read her sister's expression, her thoughts. She looked... somber. Mina gulped down some milk. "Ouch, I burned my tongue."

"Good thing your Frenchman is out of town."

"Paola, I can't believe you said that." She studied her sister's face. There was no reaction, didn't even mentioned the offensive sweatshirt. Suddenly, talking about the red shoes didn't seem so urgent. "I'm lucky I got fired." Mina said. "Otherwise, right now I'd be serving eggs sunny-side-up to the after-church crowd, and they're lousy tippers."

Paola smiled, but her eyes kept the blank look. "You know how to find the silver lining in your cloud, every time. I wish I could."

"Cheer up. Things may get better now that Rachel— *maledizione*, here I go again."

"What? Now that Rachel's dead?" Paola shook her head. "Poor Rachel. Everyone thought she was in Chicago with my husband, having a blast."

"How's he taking it?"

"Michael? He's sleeping peacefully, as if he hardly knew her. Just some Central American refugee who fell down West Coast Software's stairs. Plenty more where that one came from."

"Yeah and from the same family. This time Sarah was the one that went to Chicago with him."

"Mina, no one went to Chicago with Michael. Believe me, I know."

Thanks to Brian Starrs, the would-be detective. She took another sip of milk, wondering how *he* slept.

Paola glanced up the stairs toward her bedroom. "Why don't we go sit on the terrace? The sun's warm and we won't be disturbed by Michael's snoring."

Mina didn't hear any snoring, but she grabbed her mug and followed her sister outside.

Yellow and brown leaves floated on the pool. While pleasing to the eyes, these witnesses of summer's end saddened her soul.

She eased into one of the white pool chairs. "What happened at the morgue? Did they make you sign a deposition or whatever?" Mina asked.

"No. As far as we know, Rachel is the victim of accidental death. An autopsy is being performed right now."

"Are you worried about it?"

"Why should I be? I didn't know she was at West Coast Software. I was here or with you all day, remember? Besides, Detective De Fiore says an autopsy is routine in a case like this." Paola closed her eyes, letting the sun bathe her face, which was beautiful even with no sleep and no makeup. "What's cooking in your wild little head, Mina?"

Mina watched the water's reflection play over her sister's neck and shoulders. *Why would Paola lie?* She hadn't been home when Mina came back with the papers.

"When we thought the victim was Sarah, you had this theory about an epileptic seizure," Mina said. "But Rachel isn't epileptic. What made her fall?"

"I don't know—maybe too much to drink." Paola's detached tone troubled Mina.

"Last night must have been terrible for Sarah. Was she the one who identified the body?" What Mina really wanted to ask, was how the red shoe ended up under the car's seat.

"Both Sarah and Paco. Thank God he offered to take her home and help contact her family. Dear Paco, he's always there when we need him." Her sister's voice warmed the minute she spoke of her old friend.

"He's very fond of you, too."

Paola lifted her head. Her gaze took in the lawn, the trees, and the flowerbeds. "This yard used to be a showcase when he did the work."

"You know, I completely forgot Paco was your gardener. That was before Michael, right? When you were married to that other guy—" Mina waited for Paola to supply the name, but her sister remained silent. "What ever happened to your ex?"

"My former spouse is still defending the rich and famous in court. He isn't someone I like to talk about, Mina. Count your blessings you never met him." Paola glanced around again. "I never regretted giving Paco a job at West Coast Software. Best decision I ever made."

"Why did you hire Brian Starrs?" *Red shoe, Mina, ask about the red shoe.*

Paola pushed her chair back into a reclining position. Mina couldn't see her expression. "I told you, Adams recommended him."

You also told me you were here all day. "That doesn't answer my question. You said it had nothing to do with infidelity, but you had Brian follow Michael to Chicago."

"*Cara*, you know the old saying—if it isn't sex..."

"It's money. Stop playing games. Talk to me."

"I am."

"Whose money, *quanto*, how much? Are we talking thousands, millions or what?"

"Mina, please. Trust me. I'll tell you when the time comes."

Trust me. Two dead leaves, stirred by a breeze, drifted down and shivered on the water. Ripples spread across the pool. Beneath the surface, more leaves, brown and heavy with water, lurked in the depths. Was she like the leaves, waiting for something unknown to suck her down?

"Do you trust Brian?" Mina asked.

"Of course I do." Paola shaded her eyes. "I thought you liked him."

"He's not my type."

"Because he doesn't have a French accent, or because he—"

"Oh, *taci*, shut up." She'd been tired last night and Brian caught her off guard, that's all. He was okay at first, but she didn't really like him. Not the way she liked Patrick.

Patrick was shadowy rooms and silk sheets, imported wine and custom shirts—and that she understood.

Brian was vintage California—open smiles, open skies, and Levi's 501. Too good to be true?

"It's November, and here I am, sitting outside in only a nightgown," Paola said.

"Yeah, *Mamma* would have a fit."

"She'd have more of a fit because it's Sunday morning and we aren't in church. Times changed, but *Mamma* sure didn't. Was she still going to church every single morning?"

"No, only on Sunday, but on Saturday we always went to the cemetery. I hated that. There was a thick, sweet, sickening smell around the graves." Mina wrinkled her nose. "I told *Mamma* dead people smelled funny. It was years, before I realized the smell was from the flowers decaying in their fancy vases. Now every time someone talks about death, I smell it again." She glanced at her sister. "That's why I didn't want to go to the morgue last night. Pretty sick, huh?"

"There's nothing sick about you, Mina. Don't ever change. And don't let anyone change you, either. I love you just the way you are." Paola yawned and got up from the chair. "I think I can sleep now. You'd better try to get some rest too." She kissed the top of Mina's head. "*Sogni d'oro, cara.*"

Sogni d'oro? How can Paola think about sleeping and dreaming? Mina had all those questions, all those doubts clogging her mind. *Sogni d'oro*? Nah. Red nightmare was more likely. She finished her milk and went back to her room.

* * * * *

"Oh, it's you!" Margo Swift, West Coast Software's receptionist, seemed awfully cheerful for a Monday. Her hair was a different color today, Mina noticed. A purplish, reddish kind of plum described it better than anything else.

Well into her forties, Margo fought the aging process with an arsenal of foundation and blush, eye shadow and lipstick that left Mina stunned.

Margo pulled out a bottle of nail polish. "Did you hear about Rachel? There was a reporter from the Orange County Register asking questions, and I didn't have a thing to tell him." She dipped a brush into the metallic gold polish and touched up her acrylic claws. "Why do I always miss all the fun?"

"You're sick, Margo." Mina headed toward Michael's office.

"Wait a minute, there isn't anyone in there. Paula's in Production, talking to Paco."

Mina walked back to the desk. "I guess I'll wait for her here."

"Good, then can you catch the phones for me while I run to the john? I'll only be a minute." Margo blew on her nails to dry the polish.

"The last time I fell for that line, you were gone forty-five minutes. You came back with a different hairdo," Mina said.

"No more than five minutes, I swear. I'll freshen my makeup, just in case that reporter comes back.

He wasn't wearing a wedding ring." She winked at Mina, her jumbo earrings jingling like tambourines.

"Okay, Margo, five minutes. If you're not back, I'm leaving. Don't blame me if you get in trouble."

Margo put the nail polish back in the drawer, grabbed her studded handbag and sashayed into the ladies' room.

Setting her purse behind the desk, Mina settled into the receptionist's chair. Was it really only forty-eight hours ago that she'd come searching for Paola's papers? Poor Rachel.

"Mina." Paola stood in the hall leading to the warehouse. "I didn't know you were here. Where's Margo?" She walked to the desk. "Let me guess — powdering her nose for the hundredth time this morning. That woman. She sees a pair of men's trousers coming her way and immediately piles more makeup on her face. Disgusting."

"No need to ask you how your morning's going."

Paola shrugged. "None of the Fernandez girls showed up for work. I understand, but it meant we had to reshuffle the assembly line. Rachel didn't have many friends among the girls; still, everybody's kind of edgy about her death. Why aren't you in school?"

"Paola, look at your watch. My class is over. I came to see if you wanted to grab something to eat at Columbo's."

"I can't leave now. Paco had to make a delivery, so I'm on my own here."

"Where's Michael?

"With a client. Listen, if you go to Columbo's, bring me back one of their banana muffins, would you?"

"Well, *va bene*. I'll get my food to go and eat here with you." Mina glanced at her watch, hopped from her seat. "The five minutes are up. I warned Margo. I'm going."

"Margo," Paola called in the direction of the ladies' room. Then, in a lower voice, "You'd think by the time a woman wrestles hot flashes, she'd stop acting like a teenager overrun by puberty."

"One banana muffin, coming up. *Ciao*."

What would "muffin" translate to in Italian, Mina wondered on the way to the restaurant-bakery. *Ciambella, pagnotella*? No, of course not. Muffin, sounded like a pet name. Oh, well, another unsolved mystery, like doughnut and shake. Such tasty mysteries!

In spite of the mild weather, the gas log in Columbo's' fireplace flickered non-stop from opening to closing time. A large sign by the entrance listed the day's special. Paisley furniture and pastel- colored silk flowers gave the place a homey feeling. While waiting for her take-out order, Mina checked the bakery display. Everything looked delicious. She was seriously contemplating some giant chocolate cookies when someone behind her said, "Tempting, aren't they?"

Mina recognized Brian's voice. "What are you doing here?" she asked.

"I was about to ask you the same thing."

"I always eat here."

"That's good to know," he said, squeezing her upper arm. He let his fingers slide down her bare skin until they reached her hand, and twined his fingers through hers.

Mina snatched her hand back. "Meaning what?"

"What's the matter? Why are you so defensive?"

"Never mind, Mister Detective," she said.

Mina could tell he was puzzled, but she was in no mood to explain, not with the whole restaurant looking on.

"Let me introduce you to a real detective." Brian pointed to a booth in the non-smoking section. "Dan is just finishing his coffee."

"Who's Dan?"

"Detective De Fiore. You didn't get a chance to meet him last night."

Ah, the detective in charge of Rachel's case. "Does he speak Italian?"

"What?" Brian laughed.

"Just forget it," Mina turned her back on him. "I've got to get back to West Coast Software anyway."

"I'm sorry. Don't be angry." He gently turned her to face him. "Once you meet Dan, you'll understand why I'm laughing."

Columbo's green calico cafe curtains deflected the worst of the sun from the diners. Office workers from the surrounding buildings converged on this place about a quarter after twelve, but for now, the atmosphere was still quiet and relaxed. Mina let Brian guide her to a booth in the back of the room.

"Dan, may I introduce my friend, Mina Davies."

"My last name isn't—" Mina began.

Detective De Fiore looked up from the papers spread on the table and extended his right hand. He was probably between thirty and thirty-five. Straight black hair, black eyes and, despite the Italian surname, definitely Asian.

"You must be Mrs. Davies' younger sister. Would you like to sit down?" He gestured to the booth.

"I...uh." She sat. "I'm her only sister, half-sister to be exact." *How she hated that word—half-sister, like she wasn't really whole.*

Brian nudged her over and slipped in next to her. "She thought you were Italian," he said. "I guess she feels sort of silly..."

"Brian, you set me up." Mina punched his arm, harder than she meant to. He winced.

The detective grinned. "I have that effect on a lot of people. De Fiore is my stepfather's last name. Sorry to disappoint you."

"I wasn't disappointed, just misled." She glanced at Brian, who rubbed his arm dramatically. "I bet you don't get all the stupid *paisan* jokes like I do."

"Only on the phone." De Fiore said. "We thought we'd grab a bite before we headed over to West Coast Software."

Mina sat forward. "Why? Did you find out something about Rachel?"

"You don't know?" De Fiore gathered his papers. "The autopsy on the Fernandez girl determined that her death was caused by circulatory collapse."

"You mean collapse, as in falling?"

"Circulatory collapse is a medical term for heart attack, Mina," Brian said.

"*Grazie, Dottore,*" she said.

De Fiore laughed. Mina noticed the whiteness of his shirt, the silk tie with gray and silver swirls. Nice.

"So she fell down the stairs and had a heart attack," she said.

"She fell down the stairs *because* of the heart attack," Brian said.

"Isn't she kind of young for heart problems? I didn't even know she was ill."

"She wasn't," said De Fiore, "not according to her relatives. They said she was never sick."

"Oh, yeah? Go ask Paco; he'll tell you about all the times she called in sick. Of course, they mostly coincided with Michael's business trips."

De Fiore studied her face. "Are you implying that your brother-in-law was having an affair with Rachel Fernandez?"

Her and her big mouth. Why did she always make such a mess of things?

"Mina's just repeating gossip," Brian said. "I've been following him, Dan. I've never seen him with Rachel."

"You only followed him to Chicago, Brian." De Fiore shook his head. "Rachel was just a kid. What did your sister have to say about it, Miss Davies?"

The waitresses came by and dropped their check on the table. "Your order is ready up front," she said to Mina.

"Let me out," Mina said to Brian. "My lunch is getting cold, so if you two will excuse me." She scooted out of the booth. *"Ciao."*

"Wait, I'll go with you," Brian stood, took her elbow.

Mina tried to pull away, but he held on tight. "I'm on foot, get yourself another ride."

"That's okay, I'll walk with you." He turned to De Fiore. "Take your time, Dan. I'll see you at West Coast Software."

She walked fast, but Brian kept the pace.

"Mina, don't beat yourself up for telling De Fiore about Michael and Rachel. He would have found out eventually. According to Paco, everybody who works at West Coast Software talked about it, even Elena."

Mina stopped. *Elena wouldn't have said anything about the red shoes and the chocolate, would she?* "When did you talk to Elena?"

"A couple of days ago. What is it? You're so edgy."

"I'd better go home and take a nap. If I talk in my sleep, it won't matter."

They walked on in silence. Fear for Paola sickened her. "De Fiore never told me what he's doing here." Maybe Brian wouldn't notice the tremor in her voice. "And why are you with him?"

"He gave me a ride to pick up my car." Brian paused. "Do you want to know what De Fiore said or not?"

Mina shrugged. "If you want to tell me, go ahead."

"Fine. In a young woman with no health problems, circulatory collapse won't wash as an accidental death. The forensic people are running some chemical tests. Normally, Dan wouldn't be involved at this point. He's with Homicide and there's no murder case yet. But he likes to stay in touch with things, just in case."

"In case someone pushed her down the stairs?" Mina insisted.

She heard the exasperation in his voice. "Mina, she died of a heart attack. Now, it's possible Rachel was born with a defective heart, but she didn't fit the profile. That's why they're running more tests."

"A chemical test shows that?"

"No, those tests are to rule out drugs."

Mina shifted the weight of the sack in her arms. "I don't think Rachel used drugs. Everyone who knew about her affair with Michael would have known that too."

Brian nodded. "Not bad. When you're not biting my head off, you think pretty well."

Mina flushed.

"But," Brian continued, "even people who don't do drugs can die of an overdose."

"You mean suicide?"

"Look, this is all premature. In a few days we'll have more answers."

Answers? She couldn't even get a handle on the questions.

They came around to the front of the building and started up the walk.

"There's Dan," Brian said.

A sedan, painted a sickening shade of green, pulled up to the entrance. De Fiore got out and waited for them before entering the front office. The door whooshed shut behind them.

"Shhh." Margo held a bright gold fingernail to her lips and pointed to Michael's door.

"I don't give a fuck what Takawa said." Michael's angry voice blasted through the office. "None of his inventory is missing. That goddamn Jap must be on drugs."

"I had Paco verify it—" Paola began.

"You did what? So that's what you do when I'm out of town, conspire against me with your beaner friend? I'm going to fire his ass right now."

"Michael, don't be ridiculous." Her voice sounded sweet, honey to trap a fly. "All I did was ask Paco to check the inventory. How are you involved?"

Everyone but Margo seemed fascinated by the exchange. Mina noticed her studying De Fiore's left hand. The woman had no shame. At least he was older than Brian. Still, Mina bet he was at least ten years younger than Margo.

"I'm not going to stay here and take your bullshit," Michael yelled. "You can go to hell, along with your faithful hound Paco and that coke-head Takawa." Storming out of the office, Michael slammed the door behind him.

Seeing who was in the reception room, he came to a dead halt.

"Hey, Detective—De Fiore, is it?" Michael managed a lukewarm smile. "How are you? Closing the Fernandez case, I suppose." He reminded Mina of a crab as he edged sideways toward the front door. "Sorry I can't stay and chat with you. I'm late for an appointment with a client."

"That's all right, Mr. Davies. I'm sure I'll catch up with you later."

Michael paled. Mumbling, "Great, great," he bolted out the door.

Margo sat back in her chair with a sigh. "Mina, darling, how about introducing me to your friends?" she said.

Paco came down the hall from the warehouse. "Detective, Brian," he said, "how are you gentlemen today?"

Margo thrust out her lower lip. "Am I the only one who hasn't been introduced?" She extended her hand. "I'm Margo Swift, the receptionist here." She giggled. "Of course, you knew that right off, didn't you, Detective? Well, I'm sure glad to meet you."

Mina expected her to break into a Southern drawl any minute. Opening the top drawer of her desk, Margo held out a box of candy. "Could I interest you gentlemen in a chocolate-covered cherry?"

Before they could reply, Paco hit the box, sending the candies flying.

"Where did you get these chocolates?" He was breathless, as if he'd been running a race.

"Are you crazy?" Margo said. "I bought them. Why?"

Paco sagged. "I'm sorry, Margo." He bent down and began picking up the chocolates. "I thought you were eating Mrs. Davies' candies."

Mina blinked. Was that relief in Paco's voice? She glanced at De Fiore.

The detective watched Paco pick up the chocolates, his black eyes glittered like a cat that had just spotted the mouse's tail disappearing around the corner.

CHAPTER 6

The phone kept ringing. Mina didn't answer. Who would call before ten a.m.? Barbarians. Well, she didn't know any of those, and even if she did, she was in no mood to talk now.

The annoying sound came from a pile of clothes next to the bed. "*Oh, basta,* Shut up!" On cue, the ringing stopped.

With a sigh, she pulled the covers over her head, hoping to recapture the dream brought to a premature end by the telephone.

She'd been lying on the beach. Sand clung to her dewy skin, speckling her tanned, nude body. A shadow descended over her, like a veil over a bashful bride, and peering from under half-closed eyelids, she glimpsed Patrick's silhouette against the blazing sky.

Patrick, his predatory eyes staring with such intensity, it could sear the skin off her quivering body. He lay down next to her, his tongue teasing her earlobe, his fingers playing with the specks of sand around her navel. *"Elle m'aime, elle ne m'aime pas,"* he whispered. "She loves me, she loves me not," removing the grains of sand, one by one, without haste. When no more sand remained, Patrick drew circles on her tummy. His hands moved slowly, the hands of a consummated artist, she thought, as the imaginary loops ran over her whole body. Her breathing quickened, she wound her fingers through his thick, curly hair, pulled his face down to quiet the moan seeping from her lips. Her eyes locked into his. Patrick's blue eyes, so passionate, so...

Blue eyes?

Mina swung the covers away from her and sat up, sweating. Blue eyes, *maledizione*. Patrick's eyes were dark brown and thousands of miles away. Sighing, Mina got out of bed and headed for the shower. After turning off the water, she slid the glass door back, the bare silver bar reminded her that all her towels were on the bedroom floor, waiting to be laundered.

Goosebumps dotted her flesh as she streaked into the bedroom, her wet feet leaving soggy footprints on the thick pile carpeting. She grabbed a towel from one of the mounds and wrapped it around her before she realized it was a beach towel filled with sand from her last outing.

She was afraid to open her underwear drawer knowing the solitary pair of panties lying there had no elastic. Always forgetting to get rid of those. The wastebasket was already heaped, but this time, the panties got stuffed in anyway. Mina found the oversized sweatshirt she'd worn on Sunday, put it on, and started sorting her laundry. Better do whites first, then at least she'd have underwear to put on.

While the washing machine churned, Mina sat at the kitchen table, glancing at the newspaper and eating cereal, another tasty American discovery. The phone rang again. This time, she picked it up.

"Mina, where have you been? I've been trying to get you since nine-thirty." It was Margo.

"So you're the barbarian."

"I'm who? Are you hung over?"

"No, are you?" Mina spoke with her mouth full of crunchy cereal, a habit that drove Paola crazy.

"You've got to drive up here right now. Hurry."

"Margo, I'm doing laundry and eating breakfast. West Coast Software's not high on my list of priorities."

"The cops are here again. Paula wants you to come over as soon as possible."

Mina dropped her spoon. "Is something wrong?"

"Of course something's wrong, you fool." Margo lowered her voice. "It's about the Fernandez—wait a second." It sounded like Margo dropped the phone, then Mina heard her say, "Oh, yes, Mr. Davies. Yes, I'm done." After a long pause, Margo came back in a whisper: "I can't talk anymore. Get over here; your sister's frantic."

Mina replaced the receiver, picked up the spoon and went back to the cereal. Margo always exaggerated. It was hard to imagine Paola frantic. Her sister was like the Statue of Liberty.

Better go, just in case. She threw the rest of her breakfast in the garbage disposal and, with pictures of starving kids in China flashing through her mind, went upstairs to get dressed.

What was she going to wear? The panties without elastic slouched over the side of the wastebasket. She could go without; she'd done it before. But the cops were at West Coast Software. What if they arrested her? She did have all those overdue parking tickets.

Okay, so she would wear underwear. She'd have to borrow Paola's. Her sister would have a fit if she found out, she was so narrow minded about that sort of thing. But if she wore it there and back, washed it, and put it back in the drawer, Paola would never know, right?

As she opened Paola's lingerie drawer, the scent of lavender wafted up. Tied with a white ribbon, the stems of the dried, blue flowers formed a divider between the panties and the matching bras.

Lavanda. Their mother used to keep the same kinds of dry bouquets in her linen drawers. Every spring, she would purchase fresh ones from the mountain people and put the old ones in the folds of the wool blankets being stored until next winter. Mina wondered where Paola's lavender flowers came from.

Her hand was a little shaky as she rummaged through the drawer, looking for the smallest pair of panties. Beneath the underwear, Mina found a white folder with bold blue letters, the same folder she'd gone to fetch for Paola last Saturday when Rachel died. Why were her sister's business papers in with her underwear? Consumed with curiosity, she opened the folder.

Inside were two white envelopes, larger than legal size. One was sealed; the other had been opened, and the edges looked yellowish and worn.

It was addressed to Paola, in their mother's slanted handwriting.

Mina sat on the bed, holding the letter in her trembling fingers. *Mamma* had been dead for almost six years now. The postmark over the Italian stamps read twenty-five Agosto. Two days after her own fifteenth birthday.

She lifted the flap of the unsealed envelope. It contained about a dozen photographs. Old photographs. Mina smiled. There were pictures of her, some with her mother, some with both her parents, but most of her alone. She was just a child, almost a baby.

She checked the envelope again to make sure nothing more was in it, but there were no letters, not even a note. Just a bunch of old family pictures.

Something was wrong, but she couldn't pin point what it was. She turned the pictures over. Some were dated. Others were blank.

Holding those photos full of memories, she lost track of time. Then it hit her, the oddity, and the missing piece. Paola wasn't in any of the pictures.

The ringing telephone jolted her. Damn it. She'd forgotten about Margo and the cops.

Mina returned the pictures to the envelope, placed both envelopes in the folder, and laid it on the bottom of the drawer.

Going back, she grabbed the first pair of jeans that caught her eye. The Guns N' Roses sweatshirt would have to do. To hell with the underwear.

The phone was still ringing when she locked the door behind her and got into her Bug.

West Coast Software's parking lot was full, so Mina parked on a side street and walked over. She didn't see any police cars. Maybe they had left.

Margo, wearing a neon yellow jacket over an orange shell, greeted her as she entered the office. "What took you so long?"

"Margo, *mamma mia*. You're going to blind somebody with that outfit."

"You noticed, huh?"

"Noticed? I'll bet it glows in the dark. Where's Paola?"

Margo jumped up, leaned over the desk and whispered, "You'll never guess what I found out."

"You made me rush over here with some story about the cops and my sister losing her cool. Save your gossip. Where's my sister?"

"Shhh—she's in there, she's going to flip when she sees your shirt." Margo motioned over Mina's shoulder, toward Michael's office, "She is with them."

"Them who?"

"You know, that oriental hunk, Detective De Fiore. They wanted to talk to you. Paula told me to call right away, and that was hours ago."

"You said `they'."

"De Fiore and the other fellow."

Mina's heart beat a little harder. "Brian Starrs?"

"No, some other policeman, I didn't get his name. He isn't my type."

Mina thought that unlikely. All men were Margo's type. This one must be married.

"It's about Rachel." Margo said.

"What about her? Did they found out what was wrong with her heart?"

"I don't know, but mine is going crazy. Sexy De Fiore complimented me on my dress and asked for one of my chocolates. He likes them so much, he wanted to know where I bought them. He is sooo sexy."

"Margo, I don't care about cutie-face. What about Rachel?"

"He told me she OD'd."

Maledizione, Brian was right. It was drugs. "On what?"

"I don't know, but listen. You'll never guess, not in a million years—"

"Margo!"

"Okay, okay! Rachel Fernandez was pregnant."

CHAPTER 7

"I thought I heard your voice." Paola spoke from the doorway of her office. Beyond her, Mina saw Michael sitting at his desk, and De Fiore in front of him. "Do me a favor and go get Paco. Detective De Fiore needs to speak to both of you."

Mina tried to read Paola's thoughts. *Did she know*? Rachel pregnant! How was she supposed to nod and act as if nothing happened, nothing was wrong? *Povera Paola*, she must have heard about Rachel. No wonder she wanted Mina to rush over. She seemed different though—not frantic, but not calm either.

Mina's heart went out to her sister. Michael, *bastardo*, how could he?

"*Signorina*, unless you're telepathic, you're not going to find Paco while standing there." Paola's eyes were locked on hers, as if trying to convey a silent message. But what? "Come on, De Fiore's been waiting for you all morning."

"Right," Mina said. "Just as soon as I'm done talking to Margo."

Paola put a hand on her hip and tilted her head.

Mina got the message. *"Va bene, va bene*, I'm going." After her sister shut the door, Mina whispered, "Margo, how did you find out about Rachel?"

The receptionist smiled sweetly. "You don't have time for gossip, remember? You heard your sister. Scoot."

Since West Coast Software's operations were divided between two buildings, the quickest way to the production building was through the warehouse. The back building housed the expensive disk duplication equipment. There the programmed discs were boxed and shipped by a flock of unskilled workers.

Mina wasn't knowledgeable about all that technical stuff however she did understand that it had to do with programs and information created by others. Paola liked to say that her company was the safe keeper of intellectual secrets.

Leaving the warehouse, Mina came face to face with a noisy yellow forklift, its prongs loaded with huge boxes. She couldn't see the operator. Assuming it was Paco, she walked up to the open side. An olive-skinned stranger sat in the driver's seat. Short crooked teeth shone white under his thin mustache. He smiled at her, but his eyes—mere slits—remained unreadable

Without logic or warning, chills ran down her spine. She stepped back and the stranger maneuvered the machine away.

"Hi, Mina." Paco's voice behind her was a relief.

"Thank God, Paco. Paola sent me to get you." Mina slipped a hand through the crook in his arm, steered him toward the open bay door. "Who is that guy?"

The forklift operator jerked his head around and looked at her. Surely he couldn't hear her over the racket.

"Ishmael Fernandez," Paco replied.

"Fernandez? Another one?"

"Their brother."

"What do you know—the old man had some male chromosomes after all."

"Well, some man did."

She laughed, the fear gone. They crossed the warehouse.

"Paco, how come all the Fernandezes have Jewish names?"

"Not Jewish—biblical. Old lady Fernandez was probably trying to make up for past sins. Lot of good it did her. I've never seen a more ungodly bunch, except maybe for Sarah, and she is the only one I have hopes for." As they headed into the reception room, he asked, "How about your name. Where does 'Mina' come from?"

"Oh, it's the name of a famous singer. Mina is Italy's version of Barbara Streisand. A great voice. I bet Mina was the first singer to go by a first name only. Way before Madonna." She paused and then added, "but she doesn't go out in public anymore. At least not while I was living there. She had a really sad life. And when she was young and at the peak of her career, she gave birth to a love child. We are talking a long time ago here. And all that in our old fashioned, narrow minded, Catholic Italy. You've got to admire the lady. Anyhow, she became a recluse in her big villa by the Swiss border, and then she got big. I mean, fat. So, now she records in her own studio and never, never sings in public. Poor lady."

"That's a very sad story. I guess what they say about money not buying happiness applies to all countries." Paco said. "Mina, where are we going?"

"Michael's office. De Fiore wants to talk to us.

When they entered the office. De Fiore rose and shook Paco's hand. His smile was polite, but not friendly. He grabbed two chairs and motioned them to sit. Michael remained seated behind his desk, Paola to his right. A Dunkin' Donuts box rested in the center of a round table in the corner. *Cops and doughnuts—try to explain that to an Italian*. Still, Mina hoped they'd left her a chocolate-covered one.

"Now that we have established the time and cause of death in the Fernandez case," De Fiore began, "I would like—"

"Excuse me." Mina raised her hand like a schoolgirl.

"Yes Miss Calvi, what is it?" De Fiore asked.

"Oh, you do know my last name. Did Paola tell—" His scowl stopped her. Not in the mood for chitchat. Better get to the point. "Before you give us the third degree, what about Rachel? You never gave us the whole story."

"The whole story? An interesting choice of words." De Fiore tented his forefingers. "Rachel Fernandez ingested approximately one gram of cocaine—"

"Ingested?" Mina interrupted. "You mean she ate it? I thought you were supposed to sniff it or smoke it or something."

"Miss Calvi." De Fiore's voice was ice water.

Mina shut up.

"The liquefied cocaine was injected into a chocolate cherry cordial," he continued. "Fifteen to twenty minutes after eating it, Rachel would have gone into convulsions. We know this from stomach contents and rate of digestion. She was probably trying to get help when she fell down the stairs."

Paco looked confused. "She died of an overdose? I thought it was a heart attack."

"Taken internally, cocaine causes a heart attack."

A chocolate cherry cordial, red patent pumps, a speeding Thunderbird and Paola's empty bedroom. Mina felt like a huge twister grabbed her and spin her around and around until the truth and the lies all blended together.

"Mina, are you all right?" Paola's voice brought her back to reality. "You look like you're about to faint."

Were her doubts written on her face? She jumped up, grabbed a doughnut from the box and stuffed it in her mouth. "Hungry," Mina said, puffing out a cloud of powdered sugar. "Starving to death, sorry." She took another big bite, avoiding De Fiore's speculative stare.

"Time of death, approximately two p.m.," he said. "Mina, do you have something you want to tell me?"

"I was home by then," Mina said. *Dio mio, the spiral of deceit was sucking her in.*

Paola's tone was calm and sweet. "Detective De Fiore wants to know if you saw Rachel that Saturday. He's asking everybody who was in the building."

"Elena was here; I spoke to her." There, that was a non-answer. After all, she wasn't positive it was Rachel in the red shoes. Paola smiled at her. "Excuse me, but what exactly are you investigating?" This time, Mina met his gaze.

"We're investigating the murder of Rachel Fernandez."

Paola smoothed imaginary wrinkles from her suede skirt. "Maybe it would be helpful, Detective, if you ran down the particulars of the case. Perhaps that way, we'll be better able to help you."

Mina sensed the game of give and take her sister and De Fiore played—who would tell, and how much?

De Fiore ran a finger between his shirt collar and his neck. A move to buy time while considering the answer?

"On Saturday, November fourth," he said. "Rachel left home while the rest of her family slept. We don't know when she arrived at West Coast Software. She may have already been wearing Sarah's smock or she may have put it on here." His tone reminded Mina of the old *Parroco,* the parish priest, and his Sunday's sermon. "At some point, she ate a chocolate covered cherry cordial, went upstairs to the loft and died. We are interviewing all the people who were on the premises last Saturday."

"What people?" Michael said.

The detective ticked them off on his fingers. "Two workers in the back. Mr. Mendez, here, traveled between the two buildings, doing inventory and keeping an eye on the duplication room. Elena, who I understand cleans the offices but not the loft. And of course, Miss Calvi," he bent his head in Mina's direction, "came to get some papers for her sister, who was at home. You, Mr. Davies, called from Chicago, thinking your wife would be here catching up on paperwork, and instead spoke to your sister-in-law." He let his hand drop to his lap. "That was between eleven-thirty and twelve, our time, which covers Elena's approximate time of arrival. All these people here and still, no one saw Rachel."

"I wonder how Rachel got here," Paco said. "Maybe someone saw her on the bus."

"We're checking that out," the detective said.

Mina cleared her throat, and De Fiore glanced at her. "Maybe Rachel got the poisoned candy on Halloween night," she said.

"These chocolate cherry cordials are very popular around here, aren't they?" When no one replied, he continued, "Elena mentioned that Mina was searching around for some chocolate that Saturday and was disturbed when she couldn't find any."

Mina choked.

"Something wrong, Miss Calvi?"

"No, no. Elena hallucinates, you know. All that cleaning fluid." Wait till she caught up with Miss No Comprendo.

"Your receptionist keeps a supply of them in her desk," De Fiore said, "and yet everyone refers to them as `Mrs. Davies' chocolates'. I understand that you, Mr. Davies, put one of these candies in your wife's in-box every time you leave on a trip. Sort of a love ritual, I gather?"

Michael looked at Paola with the same twinkle in his eyes Mina had seen when they came to her hometown in Italy for their honeymoon. No doubt about it; it was a look of love. But if Michael still loved his wife, then why Rachel? Or Sarah? And the fights or, worse yet, the silences.

"These are not exotic bon-bons," De Fiore said. "They can be bought in most supermarkets. You, Mr. Davies, get yours from the Hallmark store. Lately the owner remembers you buying romantic cards in Spanish. You told her your wife was Italian, but you thought Spanish would be close enough."

Mina's brother-in-law had turned cardinal-red and was doodling ferociously. Paola sat like a wax Madonna, except for a tiny muscle twitching at the corner of her red lips.

But the detective wasn't finished yet. "The owner of the Hallmark Store didn't work last Saturday, but the salesgirl distinctly recalls a lady who bought a box of chocolate cherry cordials. It was around twelve-thirty and she appeared to be in a great hurry. She made quite an impression on the young clerk, who described the shopper as 'a striking brunette with wild hair and wearing a fabulous violet silk blouse, the same color as her eyes'."

The pen slipped from Michael's grasp, slowly rolled to the edge of the table, and dropped to the floor.

Her chin quivering and her eyes filled with tears, Mina looked at Paola. "My sister was home in bed all day long," she said.

"Mrs. Davies," De Fiore said, "perhaps we should discuss this in private?"

"Perhaps," Paola answered. She lifted her hand in a gesture of dismissal. "How about you people getting back to work while detective De Fiore and I chat a while?" she said.

"But, Paola—"

"You too, Mina. The detective is not a big, bad wolf. Trust me." Her smile seemed sincere enough but only lips deep.

Dismissed. Why was Paola always treating her like a child?

Mina walked to the front room in time to see Michael closing the warehouse door behind him.

"In a big hurry to disappear, isn't he?" she said to Margo. But when the receptionist's chair spun around, Mina found herself facing Brian Starrs. "What are you doing here?"

"Answering the telephone." The smile started in his eyes, spread to his lips.

"Where's Margo? Wait, don't tell me." Mina knew she sounded brittle and catty, but she didn't care. "She urgently had to go to the ladies' room. What'll it be this time, I wonder; a permanent, a pedicure or a simple nose job?"

"What happened in there? Nothing good from the look on your face."

"Ask your buddy, Mr. Detective. He seems to have all the answers. I'm leaving."

"Can I give you a ride?"

"No." She had to get outside before the tears started again. Heading out the door, she closed it after her. Brian pushed it open and grabbed her arm before she made it to the parking lot.

"What is it with you? You're always acting as if the whole world is out to get you. Were you born this way, or do you put on a performance around me because you think it's cute?"

She pulled away, "You're hurting me."

"I'm not." He loosened his grip but didn't let go completely. "Why are you so mad at Dan? What happened in there?"

"As if you didn't know."

"Mina, I swear, I didn't even know he was here. I stopped by to say hello. Margo told me about the meeting, so I decided to wait—that's when I got roped into answering the phones."

"He accused my sister of poisoning Rachel."

"What?"

"Well, maybe accused isn't the right word, but still."

"Let's go somewhere and talk about it." He let her arm go, but stayed close. "We can take my car."

"No. I need some air; I need to move. This is crazy. I should do something. Adams should be here. That's what I'll do, I'll call Adams." She walked fast, almost running. Brian strode along.

"Adams is in court," he said.

They crossed Columbo's parking lot. Brian grabbed her arm, slowed her pace. "Buy you a cup of coffee—" he volunteered.

Mina followed him inside and they sat in the same "non-smoking" booth they had the day before. "You worry too much, I'm sure there is a very simple explanation to—Mina, are you listening?"

She nodded, but kept her eyes on the silverware.

A waitress brought two glasses of water, and took Brian's order. Mina asked for coffee. They sat in silence. A dreadful kind of silence, the silence of the guilty, the dejected, the hopeless. *Get over it, Mina*.

Brian's order arrived, and her coffee too. She sipped it slowly, anything to keep from looking at Brian. The coffee tasted like it was poisoned with strychnine, she thought. Of course she had no idea what strychnine tasted like. Better stop the nonsense. "You said Adams is in court?"

"That looks good. May I join you?" said a familiar voice.

Mina looked up from her cup. "Not you again."

Detective De Fiore ignored her remark and sat next to her.

"Hi, Dan. What's up?" Brian said.

"I want to talk to Mina."

"What are you, off duty? No more 'Miss Calvi'? How did you know we were here?" Mina asked.

"I'm a detective, remember?" De Fiore now seemed relaxed, friendly.

That didn't mean she could trust him. "Well then, Mr. Detective, have you solved the Fernandez puzzle yet?"

"No, and that's why I'm here. I need your help. Nice shirt by the way."

"Sorry, I'm not a detective, and I left my crystal ball at home." She wasn't going to discuss her choice of clothing.

De Fiore leaned forward, elbows on the table. He wore a navy blue tie with tiny stars that looked more like polka dots. "I want you to think about Saturday morning, when you came to West Coast Software to get your sister's papers."

"I found them where she said they'd be, went home and gave them to her. What about it?"

"Mina," he wagged his finger as if to warn her, "Paola and I had a good straight talk, so you can drop that story." He pronounced Paola the correct way. She was impressed.

"What story?" Brian asked.

"Paola said you told her that Elena ate her chocolate. But then you added something that confused her: You said that you *unwrapped* it but Elena *ate* it."

Mina fidgeted with her napkin. Did Paola really want her to tell everything? She wiped her mouth, and then told them what had happened, including the part about the red patent pumps.

When she finished, it was as if a heavy burden left her. Her coffee tasted like coffee now. Under the table, Brian took her hand, squeezed it. She met his eyes and smiled back.

"Mina," De Fiore said, "what did you do with the wrapper?"

"The wrapper?"

"The gold paper from the chocolate cordial."

"I don't know. I guess I threw it away," she said.

"Did you throw it away before or after Elena emptied the wastebasket?"

"Before...wait." She'd spilled the trash and left it for Elena to clean up, but the wrapper—"I don't remember."

"Think, Mina, think."

"Why is it so important? Are you looking for fingerprints? I'm the one who unwrapped the chocolate— you think I killed Rachel?"

"Did you?" De Fiore asked, his black eyes looking straight into hers.

"*Oh si, come no?* I always put cocaine in my chocolate cherries, it makes them taste better," she said lightly. "Hey, I put it in my pocket!"

"What?" Brian said.

"I crumpled the wrapper and put it in my jeans pocket," she said.

"Bingo," De Fiore said. "Are those the same jeans you're wearing now?"

She blushed remembering the absence of underwear, "No, not these. The ones I wore on Saturday."

"Where are they now?" For the first time since she'd met him, De Fiore sounded excited.

A picture of her bedroom, with clothes in heaps on the floor, flashed through Mina's mind. She took a deep breath. "Somewhere in my bedroom. The wrapper's still in the pocket. I haven't washed the colored clothes yet."

De Fiore stood. "Let's go."

Over her dead body, they were going to set foot into her bedroom. "I'll go get it for you, Detective. It'll only take an hour or so, and I'll bring it directly to the station. I've always wanted to see what a real police station looks like."

He grinned. "I will personally give you a guided tour after we drop off the wrapper at the lab."

"I'd rather go myself," Mina said.

"I'll get a search warrant if I have to." De Fiore was no longer smiling.

Brian's look said: do what he wants. But Mina couldn't give in so easily. "Why is that wrapper so important?"

De Fiore's eyes narrowed. "It could be evidence."

"What if I ride with Mina?" Brian asked De Fiore before she could object. "I'll drive back with you."

De Fiore hesitated. "I guess that would be all right."

Brian got up, took her hand and led her out of the restaurant, leaving De Fiore to stare at the bill, for the second time in two days.

CHAPTER 8

"Let's stop by the office," Mina told Brian. "I need to let Paola know that I'm going home." Together, they walked into West Coast Software's reception room. There was Margo, near the closed door of Michael's office, her back to them. She didn't bother to turn when they entered. No need to guess what she was doing, Paola's angry voice resounded through the closed office's door.

"How dare you hire another Fernandez? We can't make payroll for our good workers and you bring in another parasite."

"Paola," Michael began.

"You hired him; you fire him. Now! I don't want to see his face. I don't want to see any Fernandez face around the warehouse. Understand?"

Without a word, Mina went back out the front door, pulling Brian along. She didn't want him to hear her sister like this. This wasn't Paola, not her Paola. When they got to the car, Brian waited on the passenger side probably waiting for her to unlock the door.

"It's open," she said, getting in.

"You don't lock your car?" The old VW squeaked as he pulled on his seatbelt.

Mina looked at the car's shabby interior. "The way I see it, anyone who steals this piece of junk must need it more than I do. So let them have it."

"It's a classic. It could be restored."

She could feel his puzzlement but before she answered De Fiore pulled up behind them. He waved at Mina as she started her engine.

For a while, they drove in silence. Mina dreaded getting there. In general, she didn't care about her messy bedroom. But somehow she felt different about Brian's opinion. Conflicting thoughts whirled in her mind, and she wondered what Brian's bedroom looked like. Spotless probably. Maybe she'll get lucky, and he would wait in the living room. If she were like Paola, there'd be no trace of that wrapper by now.

If she were like Paola... From kindergarten to teens, every time she looked in the mirror she'd thought that same thing.

As far back as she could remember Mina wanted to go to America, join her big sister in the new world. She'd soaked up her new country through every pore, but in the end it didn't matter. New country, new people, same story. Even when no one reminded her, she couldn't forget it.

If she were like Paola, she'd be so much better.

"Mina." Brian's voice startled her. "About the chocolate wrapper—"

She took a deep breath. "Yes?"

"The person who put the cocaine in the candy probably used a syringe to inject it into the cherry liquor. Dan will want to give the wrapper to the lab experts, hoping they'll find the perforation left by the needle. That would establish Paola's chocolate as the poisoned candy."

Some idiot up ahead was going too slowly in the fast lane. Mina pulled over and punched the gas, making the little Bug shudder. Finally, she passed the other car and cut back into the lane. "You mean Michael poisoned Paola's candy and left it in her mail tray?" She wasn't Michael's biggest fan, but she couldn't believe he'd do that kind of stuff.

"Just about anyone could have injected the cocaine. Even before the box was sold."

"*Oh, Dio mio.* I almost ate that candy."

"But you didn't. Calm down Mina. You're doing seventy, with De Fiore right behind you."

"I could be dead. I accused Elena of taking it, but if she had, she'd be dead. Poor Rachel!" Those red patent pumps under the desk seemed so pathetic now.

Then something occurred to Mina. "Rachel wasn't the intended victim, was she?"

"At this point, without sufficient evidence, that can't be established. That's why the wrapper's so important to Dan," he said.

Mina glanced over at Brian. "How come you know so much about police work?"

"I've taken classes in Criminology and Police Science, and I attend workshops for police officers. At one point, I considered joining the force."

"But...?"

"My mother. I mean, the effect it would have had on her life."

"You two are very close, uh?"

He nodded.

Lately, she had felt closer to Paola than ever before. "Sometimes, you take families for granted."

Brian reached over and brushed her hair back from her forehead. "Precisely," he said.

Mina parked in the Davies' driveway, with De Fiore right behind her. The mailman was closing the box, and he waved at her, smiling. "Good day for correspondence, Mina."

"What does that mean?" Brian asked.

Mina shrugged. She knew what the postman meant: there was a lavender letter in the stack of mail.

"You can get the mail later." De Fiore appeared by her side, his walk almost a jog.

"Neither wind nor snow, Detective." Turning her back on him, she went to the mailbox and retrieved the letters. After fumbling with the keys for a minute, the big double doors swung open.

"Wow." De Fiore glanced around the impressing foyer. The entrance, with its *Gone with the Wind* staircase and imported Venetian chandelier, often affected first time visitors that way.

Brian whistled. "Your sister sure knows how to decorate a house."

"Paola bought the house with her first husband," she explained. "He was a famous lawyer and they did a lot of entertaining." She stopped babbling. Why should she make excuses for her sister's dramatic flair?

"Oh yes, I remember," said Brian.

Mina stared at him. *He remembered what?*

"The wrapper, Mina," De Fiore said. "Where's

your bedroom?"

"Okay, okay. I'll be right back." She climbed the stairs, hoping the men wouldn't follow her, but they did. By her bedroom, she paused, took a deep breath and opened the door wide.

De Fiore stepped past her, stopped. "Can you point me in the right direction or do I have to dig through all this?"

The clutter seemed even worse, if that were possible. Coming in behind the detective, Brian made no comment.

Mina strode to her bed and sat on it, dropping the mail next to her. "You're a detective, you figure it out." Why was she being such a bitch? Misplaced anger? Possibly. Well, she only had herself to blame. De Fiore walked around, carefully lifting and dropping clothes.

"I don't have a contagious disease," she said. "Besides, aren't you supposed to wear gloves or something so you don't destroy evidence?"

"You watch too much TV. What kind of evidence could possibly survive this?"

She flipped on the radio on the night table, turned the volume up high, and sorted through the mail. Something inside her was seething. It wasn't only anger, but a sort of sadness, and intense discomfort. *Was Brian judging her?* Brian came over to the bed, knelt beside her. "Mina, where are the jeans with the wrapper?"

"I don't know."

Brian's hand covered hers. He turned off the radio. "Yes you do."

Mina sighed, jerked her hand away, and jumped

off the bed. She moved to a pile of dirty clothes by the closet door and, with a theatrical gesture, picked up a pair of jeans and handed them to De Fiore.

"Here."

He patted the pocket's lining and a big smile lit up his face. With the white linen handkerchief from his breast pocket wrapped around his hand, he pulled out a crumpled gold wrapper stuck to a shred of pink tissue.

She could swear his fingers trembled with excitement when he took a plastic sandwich-size bag from his pocket, dropped the wrapper inside, and sealed it. An expression of triumph filled his dark eyes as the bag disappeared into his coat pocket.

"Let's go, Starrs," he said.

Mina, who had gone back to her bed, saw Brian glance at her, but she refused to look back. She lay stretched out, staring at the ceiling, her arms folded behind her head, feeling like a complete jerk.

"I'll call you," Brian said, and followed De Fiore out the door. Mina heard their footsteps on the stairs.

"Don't bother," she yelled back. *Go ahead, be a bitch to the end.*

A minute later, the front door closed and the house was quiet again. She picked up Patrick's letter and tore open the envelope.

CHAPTER 9

The class was ending, the aerobics instructor slowly raised her arms over her head; a graceful gesture, like a swan. "One more time: breathe in, hold it, hold it. Now slowly exhale. Thank you very much. You were a wonderful class. Have a good evening." She clapped her hands, signaling the end. The class applauded and began to disperse.

In a state of euphoria, Mina picked up her towel and headed for the lockers. Taking the class had been a good idea; she felt so much better, relaxed. Now she could go home and break the news to Paola in a semi normal way, not like a wind-up talking toy.

"Hey, Mina. Wanna go for a drink?" a friend called out.

"Not tonight. I'm going straight home."

As she hurried past the gym's front desk, the girl behind the counter said, "What's with you tonight? You look like you swallowed a light bulb."

Without stopping, Mina gave her a big grin. She hopped down the front steps and ran to her car, humming *La Vie en Rose*, an old French song that was her sister's favorite.

Paola must be home by now. She couldn't wait to tell her the news. Thanksgiving weekend in New

York with Patrick. Whoa! The ticket was taken care of, he had written, and all she had to do was pack.

Like a sapphire, the early evening was clear, cold, and precious.

Viva l'America. Life is good!

The lights of the Davies' front yard were lit, but that didn't mean much since they were on a timer. The house itself was dark. Maybe Paola was in her room, which looked out the back of the house.

Mina entered through the kitchen door and dropped the gym bag to the floor. The clock on the microwave, the only source of light in the room, read six-thirty p.m. Stepping into the dark foyer, she called out; "Paola."

No answer. She was alone. Her black leotard, still damp with perspiration, clinging to her skin, she went back into the kitchen. First things first: a drink, and then a shower.

As she turned to get a glass, she noticed the door to the garage was ajar.

Michael, the jerk *must* have come home and left again. Mina pushed the door open with her elbow, and stopped. Paola's red T-Bird was in the garage. So her sister was home; or at least her car was. Michael's black Corvette wasn't there, but Mina couldn't believe they'd gone out together. Not with everything that had been happening lately. She opened the door to the garage wider. A faint smell of exhaust reached her.

Mina put down the glass and went upstairs.

Paola's double bedroom doors were open, but the bedroom was dark. "Paola, are you home?" she said, then walked into the room and stumbled.

Patting the ground at her feet, she recognized the shape of a high-heeled sandal. Fear crawled up her spine. *Was it red?*

Enough of this nonsense. She turned on the light and heard a feeble cry from near the window. "Please don't."

Paola sat in the chair by the dark window, staring into the night. A mystical Gauguin's rendition, her ebony hair hanging limp around her pale face. Black rings, like smudged mascara, circled her eyes. This was such a bizarre scene. What was going on?

"Paola, what are you doing here in the dark? Didn't you hear me?"

"Off," her sister said.

"Are you okay?" Paola didn't answer. Mina switched off the light, took a step and promptly tripped over the other sandal. Once her eyes adjusted to the dark, she moved toward her sister.

Outside the window, the wind ruffled tree branches, and their shadows played over Paola's features. In a state of absolute puzzlement, Mina knelt by her sister, stroked her cold hand.

"Paola?"

The violet eyes looked empty.

"Paola, *cos'e?* Talk to me."

Paola let out a sob and put her hand on Mina's head. "I never wanted this to happen," she whispered. "Never. It's all over. We're finished. It's the end of West Coast Software, and the end of us, too."

"What are you talking about? Rachel's murder?"

The hand withdrew. Paola tilted her head, looked straight into her sister's eyes. "Murder?" she shook her head. "It's money."

Mina sighed. "Here we go again, money problems."

"Takawa's inventory is missing along with the copyright content he entrusted us with. And a hundred thousand dollars' worth of disks are also gone."

"What does that have to do with you?"

"We've always offered free disk storage for our large accounts. A stroke of marketing genius, as Michael put it. Takawa is our largest. He's been with our company from the beginning. Even if we could replace the disks, I have no way of knowing in whose hands the original copyrighted programs ended up." Paola's voice was almost inaudible.

Mina felt uncomfortable. She didn't like to talk about money, and she didn't like to see her sister this way. Maybe she was the burden, and Paola was telling her in a creative way. She searched for something appropriate to say but her mind was on pause. "Paola, you have plenty of disks in the warehouse. Can't you replace Takawa's stock with West Coast Software?"

"You don't understand." A sob wracked through Paola. "Once word gets out we misplaced patented info we'll be done, and Takawa will sue us." Even though Mina's leotard had dried, chills ran through her. Robbers, murder what next? "Did you call the cops?"

Paola sat up, wiped her face. "No, no cops. It's not that simple. People in this line of business can't afford that kind of publicity. Besides, it didn't happen overnight."

"What do you mean?"

"Paco suspected something. Several times he had a feeling that someone was playing games with our disks. He told me, but we were always so busy, I didn't pay much attention. Then Takawa dropped the bomb. When he came to pick up inventory, some of his boxes were empty. And it wasn't the first time. He insisted he'd spoken to Michael about it, but of course, Michael denied it.

"When he went to Chicago, I had Paco check. The only disks left in any of the boxes were defective. And the originals are missing from our locked files." Paola closed her eyes.

Mina searched for something that would erase the hopelessness from her sister's face. "Tell Takawa the duplicating machines aren't working. Make him wait a few weeks, that will give you time to locate the original copyrighted content. We can scrounge up the cash to buy new disks. Come on, Paola, it's just money. We can make this work." *We?*

"It's never just money, never. We've already exhausted our credit line. Add the Fernandez's mess to it; the whole situation is hopeless."

"Don't say that. How about the money from your divorce settlement? Let your old ex-moneybags pay to kick-start the business."

"What do you think Michael and I used to get the company going?"

Mina sank back on her heels. "Your money? All of it?"

"We formed a partnership; my money and Michael's knowledge. An invincible combination, he used to say."

"Where is the bastard?"

"Michael? Let's see, it's after six o'clock." Her sister's light tone bordered on hysteria. "He could be at Silky Sullivan—happy hour, you know. Or he may be in one of the second floor rooms at La Quinta. He likes high places for his fucks." She laughed.

Mina never heard her sister use that language about anybody. "Why haven't you divorced him?"

"Money, darling. Just money, like you said. He's the one with the knowledge and the reputation. He brings the clients through West Coast Software's front door. Of course, I take it from there, but the outsiders don't know that. They all think Michael runs the show." Another laugh.

"Is he having an affair with Sarah Fernandez?"

"Sarah, Ruth, Martha, Rachel...who cares? They're only names, young bodies earning money on their backs. Or on his back—whatever it takes to keep him signing the checks."

"Paola, *cosa ti succede,* what's happened to you? You sound so hard. Is it because of the baby?"

Paola grabbed Mina's shoulders, shook her. "What baby?"

"Margo told me that Rachel was pregnant." She pushed her sister back into her chair.

"Oh, that." Paola turned, a cold smile on her lips. "Oh, you think that Michael...? No, Michael can't."

"Michael—Are you sure?"

"Yes, we were tested. Did you think I was the one? Well, you thought wrong. Don't worry about Michael making babies." The way Paola said `babies' was chilling. Beneath the calm, Mina sensed a quiet, primeval rage.

"What can I do, Paola?" Seeing her sister this way tore at her.

"Grazie cara, but there's nothing you—or I, for that matter—can do right now." Paola sounded almost normal. Or maybe it was good acting. "Are you hungry? All of a sudden I'm famished. We could order a pizza." She cupped Mina's face in her hand. Her violet eyes, gazing into Mina's, were once again the eyes of her dear sister.

"I need to take a shower first." One of Mina's legs had gone to sleep, and she stood slowly. "But yeah, I'm starving."

"Okay. Take your time and don't worry—I know exactly what you want on it."

Mina limped to the doorway on tingling limbs. Paola's voice stopped her.

*"*I don't know what I'd do if you weren't here."

Mina smiled. "That's what sisters are for."

In her room, she stripped and got in the shower. As she lathered the soap, she thought about what Paola had said: she knew what Mina wanted on her pizza. She had no idea what Paola liked on hers. In fact, her sister knew a lot about her—but what did she know about Paola?

The photographs in her sister's drawer leafed through her memory. Her with mom, with dad, by herself, even with their pet dog. But what about Paola? Why couldn't she remember her sister during their childhood?

She stopped, soap bubbles slipping over her hands. There'd been letters from the States to their mother, postcards to Mina, and Paola and Michael's honeymoon trip. But what about before that?

Their parents had always been reluctant to talk about Paola, yet they'd let Mina bring her colorful postcards to school for show-and-tell. Pictures of America, all addressed to Miss Mina Calvi.

"Miss"—Mina smiled. It had made her feel so grown up. Her teacher collected foreign stamps, and Mina had given her every one, carefully prying each from the precious postcard. All those years, all those letters, she dreamed of living with her sister in America.

The warm jets of water soothed her face. Paola and Michael, so happy and now so miserable. It would never be that way for her and Patrick.

Patrick! In all the commotion, she'd forgotten to tell Paola about his letter. Mina turned off the water and jumped out of the shower, grabbing the same unwashed towel she'd used the day before.

Thanksgiving was only a couple of weeks away. She laughed. Brian who? Now she'd see Patrick, and realize that Brian was just a fluke.

She dressed in a hurry; she liked her pizza hot.

CHAPTER 10

"So you're going to New York to meet your Frenchie." Margo swiveled back and forth in the Naugahyde chair. The color of the day was purple—purple suit, purple scarf, purple nails.

Mina nodded. "Thanksgiving weekend. Who told you?"

"And he's paying for your trip?" Margo opened her desk drawer and pulled out a lipstick. Corkscrewing the tube, she applied thick purple bows to the top of her lips.

"He sent me the plane ticket," Mina said.

"Where will you stay?" She puckered and stretched her lips, reapplied purple lipstick.

"I don't know. It's a surprise. Patrick's flying in from London. We'll get to Kennedy airport about the same time, and he'll take it from there."

"How romantic," Margo said. "Almost like a honeymoon."

"What honeymoon?" Paola asked.

Mina hadn't heard her coming. Her sister looked much better than last night with color in her face and her hair perfectly coifed. Mina hoped the improvement went deeper than that.

"American Alarm sent the information by messenger." Margo slipped the lipstick back in the drawer and handed Paola a manila envelope.

"Why didn't you buzz me like I asked you?" Paola demanded.

"I was about to—it just arrived." She winked at Mina.

Paola tore open the envelope, pulled out the contents and stared at the papers without unfolding them. Mina watched without really comprehending the meaning of it all. And then Paola sighed and said, "Mina, how about something to eat? My treat."

They were barely out the door when Margo came rushing after them. "Paula, your lawyer is on the phone!"

Paola hesitated, glanced at her sister, who shrugged.

"Sorry, I'd better take the call, I'll only be a minute. I'll get it in Michael's office." She went in and closed the door.

Mina flopped down on the couch, and picked up a magazine. While leafing through it, she noticed that Margo hadn't hung up the telephone yet.

"Hey, Margo, what are you doing?"

The receptionist motioned her to hush. Mina got up and walked toward the desk. "Margo..."

Margo carefully replaced the receiver. "Party pooper," she said.

"So that's how you knew about my trip to New York," Mina said. "You listened in when I called. You should be ashamed of yourself."

"Somebody's got to mind the store." She dug out her box of chocolates and offered one to Mina.

"No thanks. Until they find out who killed

Rachel, I'm not touching those things. You shouldn't either."

"Nonsense." Margo helped herself to a chocolate, put the box back on the desk, then pulled out a thick book and began to read.

Mina tried to get a look at the spine, but Margo set it down on the desk. "What are you reading?" she asked.

"I'm studying Spanish."

"Spanish? No kidding. Let's see, Antonio Banderas is already taken, Julio Iglesias is single." She paused to study Margo's expression, "Too old?"

"Puh-leese. I want to learn basic Spanish so I can communicate with the workers who don't understand English."

"*Mamma mia*, this sounds serious. Career advancement?"

Before Margo could answer, Paola opened the office door. "All done," she said. *"Andiamo*, let's go." Then to Margo, "We won't be long."

* * * * *

In the nearly empty restaurant, the sisters settled at a table with a view of the parking lot and ordered their food.

"I'm sorry about last night," Paola said. "I didn't mean to let things get so out of hand. Anyway, I decided to take your advice and buy more disks and talk frankly to Takawa. We're back in business." She smiled.

"That was quick. I thought you didn't have any money left."

"True. However, I have equity. That's what

Adams' call was about. He's setting up a deal that will let me borrow against the value of the house."

"How much do you think it's worth?"

"We'll soon find out. An appraiser is supposed to come by tomorrow. Can you arrange to be there? I'd rather not to be away from West Coast Software right now."

"What does Michael think about this?"

After taking a sip of water, Paola replaced the glass precisely over the water ring. "I didn't discuss it with him. For one thing, it's my house."

"Si, but this is California, everything is fifty-fifty."

"Not this house. I owned it before our marriage, and we have a pre-nuptial contract. It's all mine after the divorce is settled, and I intend to file as soon as this mess with Takawa is taken care of."

"Does Michael know? About the divorce, I mean." Here they were, discussing divorce over lunch. *Unreal*. Divorce destroys families, breaks hearts, changes lives forever.

"What are you thinking?" Paola cocked her head, her eyes burned with an unsettling spark.

"Seems like there are lots of things you two haven't discussed."

Paola shrugged and unfolded the papers from the alarm company. The waitress brought their food.

As Mina munched on her turkey sandwich, Paola examined the report, ignoring her green salad with dressing on the side. Her expression became more and more tense.

"Bad news?"

No answer. She laid the papers next to the salad plate and began to rifle through her handbag. She pulled out her appointment book, fingered through the pages. Finally, she put everything down on the table and stared into the empty parking lot. Mina ate on, trying to chew quietly while her sister thought.

"I guess this leaves Michael out." Paola said, attempting a smile. "I mean the report from the alarm company seems to clear him."

"Clear him of what?"

"Mina," she moved her dishes off to the side and set both elbows on the table, "do you remember that Sunday a couple of months ago when I sent you to West Coast Software to get me a phone number and you—"

"And I screwed up the alarm and almost got arrested by the K9 squad? How could I forget? I thought we had a deal not to talk about that."

The smile on Paola's face was genuine this time. "I just wanted to remind you how it works. After unlocking the door, you punch in the code numbers and then call the alarm company to give them your access code."

"That's what I forgot to do."

"Right. Well, it seems that someone has been visiting West Coast Software at night—without forgetting. The access code used was always either mine or Michael's."

Mina threw her hands up in mock horror. "I swear to you Paola that I don't even remember your code."

Paola leaned forward. "This is where it gets interesting. Michael's number was used the Friday night he was in Chicago. I know he was there — Brian saw him." She sat back in the booth. "How about that?"

"You mean you suspected your own husband of stealing the disks? *Cara Paola,* you're full of surprises." Mina stared deep into her sister's eyes. Would she ever know this woman completely? "Tell me, why would Michael steal from his own company?"

"It's my company."

"Yeah, we know that, but legally—"

"It's my company," Paola repeated. "We have a written agreement, sealed and notarized. In case of divorce, I become the sole owner. He gets nothing. I have the option of keeping him on. That's all."

Mina stared at her, impeccable Paola. Slowly she lifted her glass of water in a toast. "Here's to love—and trust."

Paola gave her a withering look and began collecting her things.

"Hey, wait a minute," Mina said. "I get dessert with my lunch. And you didn't even touch your salad. Paola!"

"You're welcome to it." Without another word, Paola got up and moved toward the cashier.

* * * * *

They stepped into the West Coast Software lobby just as Margo hung up the telephone. Detective De Fiore, she mouthed, pointing to Michael's office. Paola walked toward the open office door with Mina in her wake. De Fiore was bending over one of Michael's desk drawers, his back to the door.

"Have you lost something, Detective De Fiore?"

Paola's icy voice made him jump. He spun around. In his hands was an open box of chocolate-covered cherry cordials.

Paola stepped back, and Mina craned her neck to look inside the box.

The rows of gold-wrapped candies looked like jewels.

Only one thing marred the gleaming display: one of the chocolates was missing.

Mina watched Paola's gauzy blouse stretch over her heaving breasts. Something about her sister's outrage triggered a childhood memory of herself at Easter time. She saw herself sitting on the cool hearth of the fireplace, coloring Easter eggs while her mother and the Parroco stood by the window, whispering. The parish priest, who wore a white stole over his black robe, had come to bless the house, as he did every spring.

Mina had looked up and met the priest's eyes; she was surprised by the intense curiosity she read there. He had turned away quickly, and Mina went back to coloring the eggs. Her mother's voice rose, then fell back to a murmur. Mina heard her sister's name mentioned, and the phrase "so implacably righteous."

It was the voice of this implacably righteous Paola she heard now, saying, "I demand an explanation."

De Fiore stretched his lips into a smile.

Without letting him reply, Paola went on, "How dare you barge in here and go through my desk? I've tried to be understanding. I've tried to accommodate your investigation. But unless you have a warrant, this is trespassing and I will no longer allow it."

De Fiore ignored her tirade. "Your desk?" he said, still smiling. "Then these must be your chocolates?" He pulled a folded paper from his pocket and handed it to Paola. "Search warrant, all in order." His eyes didn't leave her face. "Check it, please."

"Fuck you." Paola let the document drop to the floor, turned and walked out of the office.

De Fiore laughed so hard Mina could see tears glittering on his cheeks. "Has everybody gone mad?" she said.

His tie-of-the-day was a rusty abstract on a black background. "Sorry." He wiped his eyes. "Your sister's reaction caught me by surprise. That doesn't happen much in my line of work. And it's hardly what I expected from her."

"No kidding."

He picked up the search warrant and walked out to the front office. Mina hurried past him.

"Where did Mrs. Davies go?" he asked.

"Warehouse." Margo pointed up the hall. "No need to run, your colleague is right behind her."

"Colleague?" Mina whispered to Margo. "You mean Brian?"

"Starrs is not my colleague." De Fiore moved toward the warehouse.

"I know that." Mina glared after him. Turning to Margo, she mumbled, "The less that monster has to do with Brian, the better."

"What does Brian have to do with you?" Margo

said. "Aren't you flying to New York to meet the love of your life?"

"Yeah, look who's talking: Margo of a thousand men."

"Hey, watch your tongue. First your sister says the F word to the cop..."

"Really Margo, why don't you become a detective? Then you could get paid for eavesdropping."

"Who needed to eavesdrop?" she huffed. "You were all shouting with the door wide open."

"Forget it. So who came with De Fiore?"

"Couple of cops, including that one who was with him the first time. You remember—tall, doesn't talk much."

"Oh, right. So where was he while we were in the office with De Fiore?"

"Up in the loft. One of them was standing outside the front door when you came in. Didn't you notice him?"

"I don't have your sensitivity to anything in pants, Margo."

The receptionist bent down and pulled out her Spanish text, cracked the binding back before setting it on the desk. "Go away, Mina. I have better things to do than be insulted by you."

Mina rubbed her hands over her face. "Sorry I'm being bitchy. So, who's giving you Spanish lessons?" she asked.

"What do you mean, who?"

"Are you taking night classes?"

"Night classes," Margo's eyes glinted. "Yeah."

Mina knew that look. "Okay, Margo, who is he?

De Fiore doesn't speak Spanish, so it must be one of his men. Tall, dark, and silent, maybe?"

"It's not what you think."

Someone cleared his throat. Both women turned toward the sound.

A short, dark-skinned man in a Hawaiian shirt stood by the open warehouse door. He looked edgy. Mina recognized the thin moustache; Ishmael Fernandez, who'd almost skewered her with the forklift.

Margo pulled down her short skirt, attempting to cover her knees. *Latent modesty?*

"Buenas dias, Ishmael," she said.

His eyes flickered from Mina to Margo, back to Mina. "Buenos," he mumbled. He turned and went back into the warehouse.

"What did he want? I thought he'd been fired," Mina said.

Without a word, Margo went back to her Spanish book.

"Margo, have you got something going with pencil-moustache Fernandez?"

"Shut up," she said, her brown eyes as cold as a cobra's.

Mina looked at Margo in disbelief. "What's gotten into everybody? My sister uses words I wasn't even aware she knew. De Fiore goes into hysterics on the job. And now, you bite my head off over a Fernandez?"

"Mina," Margo's eyes remained on her book, but her fake eyelashes quivered like palm fronds. "everyone's going to be weird until Rachel's murder is solved."

"You're right. I'm sorry. I, of all people, shouldn't criticize anyone in the love department." They were both silent for a moment. "Margo, why did De Fiore bring those other cops with him?"

"He had a search warrant. I suppose it's routine. One to watch doors and two—"

"To keep people from leaving while they search the place?"

"Look, why don't you call up Brian and ask him? You two seem pretty chummy."

Mina turned red. "What are they looking for?"

"Chocolate."

"Aren't we all?"

"No, I mean the cops are taking away everyone's chocolate-covered cordials."

"Why do they need the candies? I already gave the wrapper to De Fiore."

"What wrapper?" Margo's bovine eyes came to life.

"The one from Paola's chocolate—you know, the candy Michael left in her mail tray. De Fiore wanted the forensic lab to check the wrapper."

"Fingerprints?"

"No, a needle mark."

"That's ridiculous!" Margo slammed the book shut without marking the page.

"De Fiore thought it was from the candy that poisoned Rachel."

"Who gave it to her? You or your sister?"

"Hey, no one gave her anything. She snuck in here and took it. If it wasn't for her, Paola would have eaten it."

Margo glanced at her in a strange way, and then

shrugged and said, "I'm glad I don't work weekends. Anyhow, De Fiore already confiscated my box of chocolates; he promised me a new one."

"He took Paola's too."

"I thought those were Michael's." That strange look was back again.

"Maybe they were; what difference does it make? Do you think my sister is stupid enough to use her own candies to poison her husband's mistress? Get real. I'm so sick of this place. I can't wait to get to New York and forget about this whole mess."

The telephone rang, and Margo answered it on the first ring. Mina got up and stretched. Where could Paola be?

The warehouse door whooshed open and in came De Fiore, looking like a hunting dog that just got a whiff of something good. Paola and Paco were behind, sandwiched between two uniformed cops.

"Well, Detective," Paola was saying, "Do I get handcuffed now or in the car?"

"Are you looking for sympathy or just trying my patience?" De Fiore stopped, turned to look at her.

She returned his stare, a muscle twitching at the corner of her lips.

"Mrs. Davies, it's going to be okay, really." Paco sounded like a father reassuring his child.

"Ladies," Paola announced to Mina and Margo, "The detective insists that Paco and I join him for a ride to the station. We are not, I repeat, not under arrest—we are guests of the police department."

Mina opened her mouth but nothing came out. Arrest her sister? A minute ago she had declared

Paola's innocence to Margo, and now she was speechless.

By the entrance, De Fiore leaned against the open door, watching Paola's performance. The other two cops kept their eyes down. Were they embarrassed or just well-trained guard dogs?

Paco walked outside first. Paola hesitated, then straightened her shoulders and moved to the door. De Fiore gestured her through with a small bow, a Renaissance man doing the minuet.

She turned back to Mina. Her twitch had increased almost to a spasm, and there was fear in her eyes. "Adams," she said, then walked out the door and got into the black and white.

CHAPTER 11

"Yes Mr. Takawa, I understand." Margo spoke into the phone. "No, he hasn't called. Mrs. Davies is also out of the office right now. I'll give her the message. Thank you, sir. Good bye." She slammed down the receiver and scribbled on the note pad.

"Third time this hour," she said to Mina.

"I know, Margo; I've been standing right here."

"Where the hell is your brother-in-law? He was supposed to meet Takawa for lunch at one-thirty. Never showed up, didn't phone. I've been calling his cellular, all I'm getting is: 'The mobile customer you are trying to reach is not available or is out of the area.' He probably turned off the phone. He's so irresponsible."

"Are all the Fernandez girls accounted for?"

"Accounting is not my job." Margo took a mirror out of the top drawer and fluffed her hair. "I need to go to the bathroom. Sit here, will you? I'll be right back."

Even knowing what Margo's 'right back' meant, Mina was too depressed by the latest events to argue about it. More than an hour had gone by since she'd phoned Paola's lawyer. Adams said he would meet Paola at the police station and bring her back to West Coast Software as soon as the police were through. He bluntly ordered Mina not to make any visits to the Santa Ana Police Department.

All the gaps in Paola's story made Mina crazy. Why did Paola buy a box of candy the day of Rachel's death? Why did Paola come to West Coast Software when she supposedly had a bad back? And above all, why did she lie to her?

Her brother-in-law didn't even know the police had taken Paola in for questioning. When Margo finished in the bathroom, Mina would get in her car and start making the rounds of Michael's favorite spots. Adams didn't say she couldn't do that.

The front door opened and Brian walked in, grinning. He startled her out of her reverie.

"What are you doing here?" she asked. *Why did he have to smile like that?* Just remember—Patrick and Thanksgiving.

"Is that any way to greet a friend?" He gestured at the desk. "Trapped again, huh? Where's Margo?"

"Did I hear my name mentioned?" Margo appeared outside the ladies room, pert and flirtatious.

Brian ignored her. "I was sitting in Adams' office when you called," he said to Mina. "I thought you could use some company."

"Would you look at him?" Margo said. "He's all dressed up."

Only then did Mina notice the dark gray pleated trousers and navy cashmere sweater he wore over a blue shirt. The same blue as his damned blue eyes that made her insides—

"I've got to go. I'm going to look for Michael. Ciao."

Mina grabbed her bag and headed for the front door. Brian beat her to it and held open the thick glass door.

"Mind if I tag along?" he said. His cologne smelled fresh, clean.

"I don't know." She fidgeted with the zipper on her bag, aware of Margo's attentive silence.

As if sensing what bothered her, Brian said, "Maybe I should walk you to your car."

She flashed him a smile of gratitude. His blue eyes, so close, surprised her, as did the rush of blood, heat, and desire darting throughout her body. She wanted them to be alone. She wanted him to kiss her. She wanted...

Stepping back, Mina said, "Yeah, maybe you should." Her car was parked in the far corner of the lot, under shade trees. The cool air outside let her breathe. "What do the police want from Paola?" she asked.

"Well, I'm not sure, but I can guess." Fallen leaves surrounded her car. He scuffed at some of them with his foot. Mina shivered. "Are you cold?"

"I guess I am." He put an arm around her shoulders, pulled her close, but she shrugged him off. That was all she needed. Old binocular-vision Margo would never let her hear the end of it.

Brian looked puzzled. "Why don't we get in the car?"

"Good idea." She searched for her car keys, hands shaking.

Brian took the keys from her but stopped just short of the keyhole. "I forgot that you don't lock your car." He opened the door for her, went around and got in the passenger side.

Mina put her hands under her legs. "So what's your guess?"

"About Paola? Well, the wrapper you gave De Fiore didn't pan out—no needle marks."

"So? Someone could have put the cocaine in the chocolate after I unwrapped it."

"C'mon, Mina." Brian shook his head. "The cherry was in Paola's in-basket. You had the wrapper, but no candy. Rachel ate a chocolate, but no wrapper was found in the loft. De Fiore thought he had the real thing, only the evidence didn't back him up, so now he has to try again."

"What does that have to do with my sister?"

"Paola is West Coast Software's number one chocoholic," he said.

"That's not a crime."

"No, but combined with the fact that Rachel was her husband's lover."

"That's not Paola's fault," she interrupted.

"But now De Fiore is forced to approach the case from a different angle."

Poor Paola, at the mercy of Detective De Fiore. He didn't give a damn about her sister. He just wanted an arrest, probably a promotion. And right now, when Paola needed her the most, Mina was sitting in her car with the California poster boy for dental care, worrying about whether or not he wanted to kiss her.

"You can't go down there," Brian said quietly.

Mina started. Did he read her mind?

"That's why I'm here," he continued. "Adams knows you too well. I'm supposed to keep an eye on you and make sure you don't do anything impetuous." He fiddled with the lever under the car seat until it slid backwards, giving him enough room to stretch his legs. His eyes were steady on hers, full of warmth and understanding.

"Did Adams really send you over?" she asked.

"Yes and no. Actually, I volunteered before he had a chance to ask. Adams cares a lot about Paola and you."

"Because I'm her sister?"

"All I can tell you is that Paola is like a daughter to him. They've known each other a long time."

Mina shrugged. "I guess."

"Don't you know that story?"

Mina shook her head. "Paola won't tell me much about her past. I don't know why. And I don't remember. I was a baby when she left."

"Well, when your sister arrived in the States, she went to Adams' house as an *au pair*. Adams was just starting out, a young lawyer with a wife and a newborn baby. Paola worked for him for years, became like a part of the family. In fact, he introduced her to her first husband."

"Oh, that creep. She won't even mention his name."

"That creep," Brian said, "was incredibly wealthy, even for a lawyer. I wonder why Paola didn't sell the house after their divorce. Considering the circumstances."

"The house is paid for, and it gives her a sense of security. But I know what you mean. That staircase must be a constant reminder. She calls it her million-dollar staircase."

"Well, throwing your wife down the stairs in front of a group of guests can get pretty expensive."

"Fifty-thou a step seems cheap to me," Mina said. And now that money was invested in another bad husband. "Life is so strange."

"If you make it that way, it is. How about I go inside and call Adams? Get us updated about what's going on."

She beamed at him. "Great!"

"Promise to stay put?"

"I'll do better than that." She started the engine. "I'll drive you to a public phone." No eavesdropping for Margo this time.

The telephone booth was a short block away, in a gas station. Mina filled the Bug up with gas while Brian was on the phone. She finished before he did and pulled the car over to the phone booth. It was all she could do to stay in her seat until he was done.

Walking to her side of the car, he motioned her to roll down the window. He leaned down, rested his arms on the door. "I got Adams on his mobile, and he said the best thing you can do for your sister, at this point, is to go straight home."

"Why? Is she there?"

"The connection wasn't very good, it was hard for me to understand him, but that would make sense. You go ahead and take off. I'll walk back to West Coast Software and get my car." He seemed in a big hurry to get rid of her. What was going on?

Before she could ask, Brian reached in, took her hand and kissed it. When she tried to pull away, he turned it over and kissed her palm, the warmth of his breath sending a current of electricity from her fingers to her toes. *"Ciao,"* he said, smiling, and walked away.

"Hey!" The word formed in her brain, never left her lips. Mina stared down at her hand. Brian was lying about the phone call. She sensed it. So now she could either run after him, or go home and find out what was wrong.

The window rolled up, she started the engine. To hell with him, she'd go home. Brian had long since disappeared around the corner, anyway, and she wasn't about to pull back into West Coast Software's lot looking for him.

Fifteen minutes later, barreling down the 405, she could still smell Brian's cologne on her skin. With sudden insight, she realized that Brian must have gone home and changed after he left Adam's office; maybe even showered. Why else would it have taken him over an hour to make a fifteen-minute drive?

His open manner and that smile made Brian seem so simple and straightforward, but actually he was more complex than...

Patrick and Thanksgiving.

She got off the freeway, took side streets the rest of the way home. Life was too complicated for all this. Patrick was more than enough for her. No need to ask for new problems, at least not now.

While stopped at a traffic light, she rubbed the palm of her hand against her jeans. But when the light changed, she smiled, looking at her hand on the steering wheel. She could still feel the tingle of Brian's lips.

CHAPTER 12

Mina parked her bug in front of the house, waiting as the engine gave a couple of dying gasps before shutting off. She wasn't even completely out of the car when she had to jump back in; Michael raced backwards out of the garage in his black Corvette. *Was he trying to hit her?* He swerved the sport car out to the street, all squealing tires and shifting gears, not even bothering to close the garage door.

A man in a hurry? A man mad as hell? Or a man running away from something?

At least he was gone. And that was good. So, when she saw the red Thunderbird her heart sang. Paola was home. Paola wasn't in jail.

Inside, all the lights were on, and a sound of groaning wood came from upstairs. Mina's mind flashed. Would Michael hurt Paola? Then something soft-landed on her face. It was a pair of men's briefs, done in that paisley Mina recognized from Michael's laundry. She threw them away as though they carried the plague.

"Yuck," she said, grimacing.

Paola emptied another drawer over the railing. Dress shirts, the dry cleaning ribbons still intact, cascaded down on her head.

"Hey, watch it," she yelled.

Paola leaned over the railing. "Sorry, I didn't know you were home."

Mina grinned at her sister, so relieved to see her it made her giddy. Stretching out her arms, she said, "Romeo, Romeo, wherefore art thou, Romeo?"

"That's my line," said Paola, attempting a smile. "I'm the one on the balcony."

"Whatever. Isn't it a little early for spring cleaning?"

Her smile gone, Paola shook her dark mane. "This cleaning is way overdue."

"I hate to tell you this, Paola, but usually the disgruntled spouse throws their mate's belongings out the window—ideally on the street side."

"I know, but I didn't want to litter."

Mina laughed and, after a moment, Paola joined her. "I feel silly talking down to you," Paola said.

"Never stopped you before," Mina said.

"*Signorina,*" Oh, the way she said it, with such tenderness—"come on upstairs," she added, making a face at her.

"I'll grab something to eat and be right up."

"Wait, I'll join you in the kitchen. I'm sort of hungry myself."

Paola dashed back to the bedroom, and Mina heard the sound of the drawer being replaced in the dresser. Impeccable Paola. She waited for her sister to come downstairs, and they walked to the kitchen arm in arm.

At the kitchen table, Paola nibbled on cheese, sipped her wine. Mina devoured a peanut butter and jelly sandwich. "I'm dying to hear about the jail.

And Michael," she said.

Paola winced. "Please don't use the word 'jail.' What do you want to know?"

"Michael first—no, wait. Jail, I mean De Fiore, you know. *Si, si,* start with De Fiore." Mina took a big bite of her sandwich, felt the jelly sliding down her chin.

"You're dripping," Paola said.

Mina stopped short of wiping it with the back of her hand. She used a paper napkin, instead. "De Fiore," she said, her mouth full.

"You know," Paola's fingernail traced designs on the table, "in a way, I feel sorry for the man. I understand the kind of pressure he must be under."

"Paola, I don't want to hear excuses. I want the story, all the details. Did he handcuff you? Did they take your fingerprints? A mug shot? Tell me!"

"Don't be ridiculous. I wasn't even arrested. De Fiore asked me questions about the box of chocolates I bought the Saturday that Rachel—" Her sister stopped. Mina looked up and was surprised to see tears in Paola's eyes. She waited.

Finally Paola cleared her throat and continued, "The sales clerk from Hallmark was sitting in the front room of the police station. We had to walk right past her to get to De Fiore's office. What a ringmaster that man is."

"What was the point? You already told him you bought the candies."

"De Fiore thought he could get me to confess."

"To what?" Mina said. "Being a chocoholic?"

Slowly, as if handling a fragile figurine, Paola put down the glass of wine she'd been holding in her cupped hands. "De Fiore is trying to prove that the drugged chocolate came from the box I purchased that day."

Mina stopped in mid-chew. "Did it?"

"Mina!" Paola's violet eyes blazed.

"I'm not suggesting that you murdered her. Someone could have taken one of your candies. Don't look at me that way. I'm just trying to understand what's going on."

Paola closed her eyes and her voice sounded pained. "Someone from the printing shop next to West Coast Software said they saw Paco talking to Rachel by the back door of the warehouse."

"I thought Paco said he hadn't seen...oh." Mina gulped. Maybe peanut butter hadn't been such a good idea. The sandwich lodged in her throat like a lump of glue.

After a long pause, Paola spoke again. "When I left Hallmark, the girl watched me walking back to my car. She saw Paco waiting for me."

"What in hell is going on?" It burst out of Mina's lips before she could stop it. "I thought Paco was at West Coast Software when I left. Is there anything else I don't know about?"

Paola's eyes looked almost liquid, darkened by some fear that Mina couldn't decipher. Mina lowered her voice. "Paola, this is making me crazy. What were you doing in Santa Ana that day? I went to get your papers because you said your back hurt."

Paola picked up her wine again, stared at the garnet liquid in the stem glass for a moment, and then put it back on the table without drinking.

"Once upon a time—" She gave Mina a

tremulous smile, tears quivered in her eyes. "Once upon a time, there was a young Italian girl who came to America to search for..." She shook her head and suddenly she was the same old Paola: in control. "Forget about the young Italian girl. Let's get back to Paco and the mess we're in."

"Good." Mina studied her sister's face. "I don't want fairy tales, Paola. I want the truth."

"Right." Paola pushed her wine glass away. "After you left to run errands that day, Paco called me. As you said, he was taking inventory, and he had just confirmed my suspicion: Takawa's disks and programs were missing."

Paola continued. "I got so angry that I decided to get out of bed and go see for myself. Paco said he was going to grab something to eat at the Mexican restaurant next to Hallmark, and I told him I would meet him there. He wasn't finished when I arrived. I walked over to Hallmark and, on impulse, I bought a box of chocolates. You know how I am when I get depressed. Anyway, when I got out of the store, Paco was standing by the car. We talked about the missing disks and more important, the information. He said that Sarah had stopped by West Coast Software to pick up a smock that needed washing. He didn't believe her story, and neither did I, but we decided the best thing at that point was to finish the inventory before we confronted anyone.

"While we were talking, I opened the box and ate one of the candies. I offered Paco one, but he's not much for chocolate. The way I felt, I knew that if the box stayed with me, I'd end up eating all the chocolates. So I gave it to Paco and asked him to leave it on my desk."

"Both Sarah and Rachel were at West Coast Software that Saturday?"

"No, only Rachel. Paco didn't know about the hair color change at the time. Rachel probably thought it was funny and didn't bother to explain."

"So, the stuff De Fiore has against you and Paco is just circumstantial."

Paola smiled. "You've really got the terminology down. Is it too much television or too much Brian Starrs?" Mina blushed, covered it by taking a swig of milk and choked.

"Anyway," Paola said, "by the time De Fiore dropped all his little bombs, Adams arrived at the police station and I was out of there. Paco too." She lifted her hand to caress Mina's cheek. "If something ever happens to me, or you find yourself in trouble and need someone to trust, Adams is the one. Remember that."

Mina didn't know what to say. She had never seen her sister so solemn.

Paola got up and stretched. The mood was broken. "I think I'll watch the six o'clock news," she said.

"You haven't told me the best part, about throwing Michael out of the house."

"Oh, that. After the news." She turned on the small black and white TV on the kitchen counter. Macy's was advertising their End-of-Month sale.

"That reminds me," Paola said. "We need to go shopping before your trip to New York."

"If you're planning to buy me some fancy

lingerie, you can forget it. I don't care for it, and neither does Patrick. He likes me *au naturel*." She waited for Paola to be shocked, but her sister didn't even flinch.

"Relax. I was thinking more along the lines of a warm coat. It's going to be cold there, believe me. How about one of those fake furs? Would you like that? Consider it an early Christmas present."

Mina started to protest, and then changed her mind. November in New York. "Thanks, Paola. That sounds like a good idea. As long as I don't get red paint thrown at me."

"You won't. Your plane is leaving awfully early in the morning, and the day before Thanksgiving, too. The freeways and the airport are going to be a disaster. It would be smart for you to get there the night before and stay in one of the hotels by the airport. You can park your car there and use their courtesy shuttle the next morning."

Mina watched the television screen. "*Va bene*, okay. I thought you wanted to see the news," she said, stuffing the last of the sandwich in her mouth.

The phone rang. Paola reached it first.

"Good evening, Adams. Fine, thanks to you." Paola put her back to Mina. "You were right, of course. I understand. Yes, I will. Thank you for calling and, Adams, thank you for caring. You too. Good night." After returning the receiver to its cradle, Paola turned around, her eyes weary. She picked up her glass, walked over to the wet bar and uncorked a new bottle.

"Paola."

"Yes?"

"Why did Paco lie about seeing Rachel, I mean Sarah—well, you know what I mean."

"'Lie is not the word I'd choose," Paola said, refilling her wine glass.

"Isn't that what it's called? Paco never mentioned Rachel, and he certainly didn't say a thing about meeting you. That didn't keep De Fiore from finding out."

"Must you remind me of that terrible man?" She took a sip of wine. "I'm going upstairs."

"You promised to tell me about Michael."

"Well, since you're done eating, you can come up to my bedroom. I'll tell you while I get undressed."

"Turn off the kitchen light," Paola ordered from the foyer. One of Michael's ties lay in her path, and Mina saw her kick it aside.

In Paola's room, Mina sat quietly on the plush white carpet, her back against the bed, watching her sister undress. Under her clothes, Paola wore an old-fashioned slip made of soft white silk, with real lace around the edges and almost invisible spaghetti straps. Paola insisted manmade fabrics made her skin itch.

From where Mina sat, her sister's legs looked endless. How did she get stuck with short legs and a small, boyish body?

"Something wrong?" Paola bent over to remove her stockings, which were held up by a silk garter belt. The movement caused her breasts to come together against the lace of the slip, and their dark nipples showed faintly underneath.

"How come we don't look alike?" Mina asked.

The sheer stockings stopped at mid-leg. "Different fathers. Mina, I hope you aren't feeling sorry for yourself. You are a beautiful young lady with a great personality and," Paola's eyes twinkled, "certainly no shortage of suitors." She removed and folded the stockings, putting them in a lace-washing bag. "Well, I want to take a shower, so I'll make the Michael story short. I told you that Adams was arranging for a loan against my house?"

Mina nodded.

"It seems someone beat me to it."

"What?"

"The appraisal company contacted by the bank said that they'd done an appraisal of the house less than six months ago that was still valid, and didn't I receive the copy that had been mailed to me two weeks ago?"

"Do you have the copy?"

"Mina, aren't you listening? I didn't know anything about it."

"Who ordered the appraisal?"

"According to the papers, Michael and Paola Davies. The copy in question was mailed to the West Coast Software address. I wonder if Michael knows I'm going to divorce him, and that's why he's trying to cash in all he can."

"What a weasel!"

"Well, the only thing he's getting out of it is a quicker divorce. Now my conscience is clear." Paola, wearing only her panties, crossed her arms to cover her breasts. "I'm going to take a shower."

"And I'm going to watch *Ally McBeal*." Mina got up from the floor as Paola opened the shower door. "Do you think Michael's going to get any of your money?"

"Over my dead body," Paola said, and turned on the water.

CHAPTER 13

"Here Mina, try this one." Paola entered the fitting room and handed her sister a short, soft black Ultrasuede coat closed by a gold metal zipper "I hate doing things at the last minute," she sighed.

Mina took off what she was trying on and grabbed the coat Paola held. "Oh relax, I'm all packed. As soon as we decide on the coat, I'll get on the freeway."

"We still have to drive back to West Coast Software to get your car," Paola said.

"It's not a big deal." The collar of the coat zipped up to her chin, Mina spun around, mimicking a model on the runway. "Hey, I really like this one, what do you think?"

"Move your arms. How does it feel? Remember, you'll wear it over sweaters and shirts, so you don't want it too tight."

"Sweaters and shirts, huh?" Mina grinned.

The salesgirl peeked inside the fitting room. "How are we doing, ladies? Everything all right?" Her eyes appraised Mina in the Ultrasuede coat. "That looks lovely."

"We're trying to make up our minds," Paola said. When the young woman left, she checked the price tag. "I guess we can swing it."

"Do you want to try Macy's?"

"Mina, if you like the coat, let's buy it. It's getting late and I don't want you on the freeway at rush hour."

Mina unzipped the coat and ran her hands over the soft imitation suede, parading in front of the mirror again. "Yeah, I really like it. I can wear it on the plane with my jeans and black boots."

"And a top, I hope."

A mischievous smile was Mina's only answer.

"Would you like it on the hanger or do you prefer a bag?" The clerk asked.

"No, no, just remove the price tag; I'll wear it," Mina said.

The trees surrounding Nordstrom's parking lot already wore their Christmas tiaras. Come evening, they would blink and shine, the great sparkling divider between ritzy Newport Beach and the Santa Ana barrios.

They walked toward Paola's Thunderbird.

"Look what time it is. I told Margo I'd be back before three o'clock, and I didn't even take my phone." Paola started the engine. "You're going to get caught in the downtown crunch, leaving this late." A few cars away, a pretty blonde in a silver Jag waited for the parking space.

"Have you heard anything from Michael?" Mina asked.

Paola shrugged. "Sarah hasn't shown up for work since he left."

Mina studied her sister's profile, but the beautiful face was inscrutable.

"I wonder if the weather is changing," Paola

said. "My back hurts. I'd better get my prescription refilled, just in case."

"Aren't you angry at him?"

"Not really. In a way, his actions just validate my decision about the divorce. I don't feel so guilty now."

"Guilty? I don't think I ever heard you use that word before."

"Yes, well, you know what they say about Catholics: they raise their children on bread and guilt."

* * * * *

Twenty minutes later, they arrived at West Coast Software, parked in Paola's marked stall and went inside.

"Anything important going on?" Paola's voice clearly startled Margo, who dropped whatever she was reading under the desk.

"How's your Spanish coming along?" Mina said.

Margo was wearing a navy pantsuit; the most subdued outfit Mina had ever seen her in. She gave Mina a drop-dead look, and turned to Paola. "The police were here again. They've arrested Paco."

"What?" Mina gasped.

Paola's face turned pale. "Mina, I'll handle this. You'd better get going."

"But what about Paco?"

"There's nothing you can do for him. I'll call Adams; he'll know exactly what to do." She stared at Mina, her eyes wide. "Now, go." She moved closer and gave her a big hug. "And remember, the room reservation is in my name."

An overwhelming urge to hold onto her sister and forget about New York and Patrick gushed through her soul. "I love you, Paola."

Her sister pushed her away. "*Va, va,* go on, get out of here. And have a good time." She kissed her cheek. "Everything will still be here when you get back, *ciao.*"

* * * * *

Paola was right. It took Mina almost two hours to travel from Santa Ana to Los Angeles. On her way to The Hyatt, the hotel Paola had chosen for her, all she could do was think about Paco. Was De Fiore insane? Paco wouldn't hurt anyone.

It was the lies that got him in trouble. Poor Paco, he should have been raised by a mother like hers. "*Le bugie hanno le gambe corte*, Mina. Lies have short legs, no matter how fast they run, they always get caught."

Score one for Mamma. But why had he lied, anyway? What was the big deal about saying hello to Rachel?

Obviously, Paola hadn't told her everything. Her sister and Paco were keeping something secret. Maybe Paola was lying too.

After checking in, Mina ignored Paola's advice about room service, and ate in the coffee shop. She liked the noise and bustle, the crabby kids and tired travelers. When she was done, she arranged for her wake-up call and transportation to the airport in the morning. Finally, she settled down for the night.

Sleep eluded her. After an hour of tossing and turning, she flipped on the television. She didn't want to watch the news, and one of the independent channels was showing the movie *Airport*. Disgusted, she turned it off.

She toyed with the idea of a shower, but she'd rather have one in the morning. If she didn't get to sleep soon, she'd need it just to wake up.

In desperation, she called Paola. The phone rang three times before her sister answered it.

"Paola, it's me," she said. "I can't sleep. I'm going to look all puffy when I land in New York."

"No you won't. Youth is on your side. Is everything all right? Did you remember to ask for the wake-up call? You don't want to miss your plane."

"Relax Paola, I took care of it. Besides, I can't miss my plane. I wouldn't know how to get in touch with Patrick. Maybe that's why I can't go to sleep."

"You're just excited, as you should be." Paola didn't sound as lighthearted as her words.

"What's going on with Paco?"

"Adams is working on it."

"You mean he's still in jail? What have they charged him with?" She could feel Paola's hesitation.

"Oh Mina, these things can get very complicated. You shouldn't concern yourself with it, at least not tonight. Enjoy your holiday with the Frenchman. Make the most of it."

"I happen to like Paco a lot."

"*Lo so cara*, I know."

Mina checked the luminous dial of the clock on the night table. "Do you realize I have to be up in less than five hours?"

"It would be nice if you called me from New

York," Paola said. "I'm not keeping tabs on you. I'll just feel better knowing that everything is fine. *Cara*, when you come back, we need to talk." She paused. "There's Michael. I just heard his car pull into the garage. I'd better say goodnight. *Ciao, signorina*, take care and remember, I love you." Her voice was almost a whisper. Mina felt an incredible amount of emotion packed into the last few sentences. She tried to speak, but Paola hung up before she could slip in a single word.

Michael, the bastard, had a lot of nerve, coming back home. What were they going to talk about? Mina wondered if he knew about Paco's arrest.

Thinking of Michael made Mina wish she had his throat in her hands, but after a few minutes she started to fade. She was more tired than she thought and slipped into bed with the covers tucked under her chin. Below, Century Boulevard's traffic coursed like Mediterranean waves, and in a few minutes the shadows closed in and she was asleep.

CHAPTER 14

Tired of sitting at the boarding gate, Mina decided to make a final trip to the restroom before getting on the plane. The toilets on the aircraft gave her the creeps; she was sure she'd be sucked out or something.

"Mina Calvi, paging Miss Mina Calvi to the white courtesy telephone." Mina Calvi. Wow, she was being paged.

She got up, and hoisted the carry-on over her shoulder. Wearing the new coat had been a mistake—she should have packed it. Instead, she sweated her way over to the ticket desk. Who could possibly be paging her?

Maybe Patrick had missed his flight.

The airline's customer service rep told her to pick up any of the white phones against the wall.

"One moment, please." The operator said. There was a click and some buzzing.

"Hello? Goddammit, is anyone there?"

"Michael?"

"Mina, is that you? They've been jacking me around for half an hour."

"Sorry, I just heard the page. I got here as fast as I could. What is it?"

"You've got to come home right away."

"Are you nuts? They're gonna call my flight any minute."

"Cancel the damn flight and get your ass home right now."

"What's the matter? Did something happen to Paco?"

"Paco's been released."

"Don't tell me De Fiore arrested Paola. Where is my sister? Put her on the line."

"I won't talk about this on the phone. Just trust me, and get home right away."

"Check my bank account, Michael. I don't have enough money to trust you. Please, put Paola on the phone."

"Goddammit, Mina, your sister is dead." Michael's voice, full of rage and tears, pierced her ear like a hot wire. "Now are you happy? I said it, dead." The line clicked and went blank.

Mina didn't remember hanging up the phone or leaving the airport or driving down Century Boulevard, yet she found herself southbound on the 405 freeway. Her brain went in circles, dizzying her until she wanted to throw up. She tried to concentrate on one thing at a time.

The signal, clicking so slowly she thought it was broken. Merging into traffic. Anything, just so she didn't have to think about what Michael had said.

Could this be his idea of a joke? Could anyone be that sick?

Nothing moved on the freeway, in either direction. Michael had to be lying. Paola was fine; she was at the office, working, fine. Michael hated Patrick. He didn't want her to see him. He wanted to scare her.

Peeking from the pocket of her leather coat was the lavender envelope her plane ticket had come in. She checked her watch; her flight to Kennedy airport left thirty-five minutes ago. Somewhere, high over the Atlantic, another plane was bringing Patrick to their rendezvous, and she wouldn't be there to meet him. All because her brother-in-law, that bastard, played sick games.

Her fingers on the steering wheel looked bloodless.

The car behind her honked and made her jump. Releasing her foot from the brake pedal, she let the Bug inch forward. A siren howled in the northbound lanes while the southbound traffic was at a standstill. A car accident? Could that be what had happened to Paola? She didn't want to think about it. She couldn't think about it. Tears rolled down her cheeks.

Driving in the slow lane was new to her, but then, all the lanes were slow right now. Better play it safe, anyway—she had to get home. Paola might need her.

Behind her, the Toyota was tailgating again. Looking up, she saw a huge billboard on the side of the freeway. It depicted blue skies, turquoise waters, and happy people aboard a sailboat. "The California Promise," the ad said. "Live it in Mission Viejo."

Not my sister, please God, you can't let this happen. She can't be dead, she's too young and she's all I have. Dio, Dio mio. You can't do that, God, not now, oh, please.

The driver behind her rolled down his window

and yelled an obscenity. She turned her head and glared at him, a wall of tears obstructing her vision. *Not Paola, dear God.* Wiping the tears from her eyes, Mina tried to focus on the slow road taking her home.

* * * * *

Clusters of people stood across the street, loitered by the driveway. When Mina opened her car door, they all became still, like a freeze-frame. No one spoke, even though she recognized some of the neighbors.

Avoiding their eyes, she walked toward the open front door.

Hushed voices came from the dining room. When she reached the archway doorway, silence fell.

Where is Paola? The words assembled themselves in her mind, but her lips wouldn't move.

Dr Martin sat next to Michael at the dining table. De Fiore stood next to the tall, silent cop she remembered from Rachel's case. Everyone but Michael seemed surprised to see her. Closing the folder he was holding, De Fiore took a step toward her.

She said it now, "Where is Paola? Michael..."

Michael's bowed head didn't move. He rubbed his hands repeatedly, without looking up.

He was responsible for whatever had happened to Paola; it had to be his fault. Mina walked around the ivory marble table and, before anyone could stop her, she grabbed his shirt collar, forcing his head backward.

"Where is my sister? What have you done to her? Answer me, you bastard," she sobbed.

"Mina, don't. Michael couldn't help it." The hands holding her back with gentle strength were those of Dr. Martin, Paola's doctor and an old friend of the family. He pulled her close, caressing her hair.

Not caring that her tears soaked the lapels of his dark suit, Mina clung to him. A faint smell of mothballs made her sneeze, and he handed her a tissue.

Mina looked at her brother-in-law, his unshaven face, his dazed eyes. "Paula is dead," he said, raising his hollow eyes to her. "She's dead, Mina. What will I do?"

She wanted to hit him, but Dr. Martin kept his arm around her shoulders and walked her to a chair opposite Michael. Sinking into the chair, her strength left her suddenly—as if some secret valve opened and let her life pour out of her body. She put her head down on the cold tabletop and wept.

Doctor Martin's hand was warm and heavy on her shoulder. "Mina, this isn't going to be easy for you to hear." His voice was low, his speech deliberate. "Your sister committed suicide."

"No. That's impossible."

"It's true." His eyes followed her stare across the table. She couldn't stop staring at Michael.

"You've known me for a long time, Mina," the doctor said "You know how much I loved Paula. Why would I lie to you?"

Mina didn't answer. Doctor Martin ran bony fingers through his silver hair. "Detective, may I talk to her alone?"

De Fiore's answer must have been yes, because

she saw Michael get up and walk out of the room with the other two men. Somewhere in the house, the phone rang. Doctor Martin took Michael's seat across from Mina.

"Your sister was under a great deal of stress."

Mina started sobbing. "Michael." It seemed to be all she could say.

"He was part of the problem, I agree. But he never would have harmed your sister — not intentionally. He loved her. Besides, he was unconscious, almost comatose until this morning. He had enough alcohol in him to kill a horse."

He handed Mina the box of tissues, and she blew her nose.

"Where is she? I want to see her."

"There's no need. Michael identified the body. Don't do this to yourself."

"I should have stayed home. How could I be so selfish when she was in so much pain? My own sister. Oh God, how did..." She couldn't say it. "Did she leave a note?" She looked up at him, sensing his hesitation.

"Pills," he said, his voice choked.

"What pills?"

"She called my office for a refill. I should have talked to her myself, but it was late in the afternoon. The prescription was just routine."

"I want to see her. I won't believe it until I see her. Where is she?"

"The morgue. They have to perform an autopsy."

"No, not on Paola," she cried. "I won't let them desecrate her body."

"It's necessary, I'm afraid," he said.

"Why? You said it was the pills. What else do they want? Tell them to leave my sister alone. Michael can stop them; he just won't sign the papers. I'll talk to him." She tried to get up from the chair, but Martin reached across and held her arm. "No one needs Michael's approval; it's standard practice in cases of questionable death."

In case of what? "You're not telling me something."

Dr. Martin shook his head as if debating with himself. "There was a peculiarity. The people from the Coroner's office noticed it, too."

Mina held her breath.

"When Paula called the office, she said she didn't have any more tablets left and her back was causing her great discomfort. The refill calls for a full container."

"So?"

"The Soma Compound was on her night table next to an empty glass. The man gathering the evidence remarked that the container was almost full."

"What are you trying to say? Did Paola take the pills, or didn't she?"

For the first time since she'd arrived, he looked straight into her eyes. "We're asking ourselves the same question."

Silence fell over them. After a while Mina said, "How did you find out?"

"Michael called me, panicked. He'd already called nine one one." Martin paused. "The police arrived first. They wouldn't let me in until I told them I was her doctor. When De Fiore arrived—"

She knew her thinking was fuzzy, because it just occurred to her to wonder why De Fiore was there. "He works for the Santa Ana Police, he has no jurisdiction here."

"It's because of something in the letter that has to do with the Fernandez murder."

"You didn't tell me there was a letter. Where is it? I want to see it."

"I'm afraid I can't help you. The police took everything. Evidence. I'm sorry." De Fiore and Michael entered the dining room together.

"Michael!" She jumped to her feet and ran to him. He backed away, fear in his bloodshot eyes, and she stopped.

"Michael, what did the letter say?"

De Fiore stepped in front of her. "It's being examined and will be returned when the police are done with it."

She pushed him aside, her eyes on Michael. "You read the letter, didn't you? Didn't you?"

They looked at each other. She took another step, but Michael didn't move this time. De Fiore held her arm.

"Yes, I read the letter," Michael said. "Paola confessed to Rachel's murder."

CHAPTER 15

Late afternoon light sifted through the blinds, giving an alien look to her bedroom's most familiar things. Mina's tongue lay thick and coarse in the dryness of her mouth. What had Dr. Martin given her? A tranquilizer? Tranquility hardly justified the way she felt. Sluggish and spent, not tranquil. So sluggish that getting her eyes open seemed a complicated task.

Too bad it didn't affect her emotions. Inside, her mind performed somersaults.

Paola had killed Rachel, and then committed suicide? No way, not her Paola.

When Mina first arrived in the United States, she had hardly known her older sister. Her first impression of Paola was—intimidating. Paola was everything Mina wanted to be: tall, statuesque, and beautiful. Following in her sister's wake, she watched the heads turn as Paola parted the LAX crowd with her feline stride.

On the drive back from the airport, Mina wished she could be sucked into the plush seat of her sister's large American car. Paola tried her best to make conversation, in her Americanized Italian, but it was apparent they had little in common. Glancing sideways at the perfect profile, Mina couldn't help wondering why her sister asked—begged—her to come to America.

During the first few months, Mina often felt Paola's stare. Her mother had stared at her like that. More than once, as she turned to meet her sister's eyes, Paola would smile and say, "I love you." After a while, their relationship got easier. Paola taught her how to drive at sixteen! Back in Italy, her friends had to wait two more years before they could even get a learner's permit. Paola took her to Disneyland, bought Mina her first hamburger and fries at a drive-through. They talked about the Pill, and the same sister who rode the Matterhorn four times running took her to the dreaded gynecologist.

Hardly memories of a killer.

There must be an explanation. When she'd left for the airport, Adams had been busy with Paco's case. She should call him, have him get a copy of the letter from the police. She had to read it—maybe then she'd understand.

The thought hit her. Oh God, had anyone told Adams? And Paco, poor Paco, first jail, now this. She squeezed her eyes shut, the eyelids still puffy and tender from all the crying.

The silence of the big house filled her head with wants. She needed to hear a human voice. She craved words of assurance, words of love. *Paola, Paola, Paola.*

What time would it be in Italy?

Did it matter? There wasn't anyone left there to mourn her sister. Her beloved sister, lying dead in the morgue, where the indifferent hands of a stranger would cut into the softness of her body.

No, no more. She couldn't think about that. She had to stop the hurt.

Patrick was in New York, waiting for her. The realization hit her so hard that for a moment she couldn't breathe. Where was he? He should have called by now to ask what had gone wrong, why she didn't make the flight.

Moaning, she craned her neck to see the digital clock on her nightstand. Four-thirty p.m. Seven-thirty in New York. Stretching to reach the lamp, she heard engine noise on the street outside and stopped cold. Paola's Thunderbird. Breathless, she waited. The car hummed past the house and silence reigned again.

The emptiness inside her became unbearable. How long would every car sound like Paola's, every step in the hall be her sister's step?

With shaking hands, she turned on the light. She needed Patrick. The company he worked for had an office in New York. They should know how to reach him.

Damn. Her address book was in the car. That meant going down to get it, walking past Paola's empty room. She didn't think she could, not now, not yet.

Information, maybe. If she could remember the name of the company— *Gourmand*? No. *Gourmandises*, that was it; *Gourmandises Internationalles.*

Lifting the receiver, she waited for the dial tone. Nothing. She pounded the small bar. Click, click, silence. One of the other phones must be off the hook. When had that happened?

What if Patrick had tried to call her?

Mina couldn't remember how she got into bed—Dr. Martin, probably—but she was wearing her faithful oversized sweatshirt. It didn't really matter, not now.

Barefoot, she opened the bedroom door and tripped over her luggage. Someone had brought her belongings in from the car, including her new coat. She edged her way around it and went down the stairs without looking at Paola's door.

In the foyer, shadows crept from every corner. Mina walked across the cold marble, into the kitchen.

Flipping on the light, she hoped to see the receiver lying on the kitchen counter.

No such luck.

The only other phone in the house was in Paola's bedroom.

She climbed the stairs, her legs quivering. What if the pills were still lying by the bed? The police would have cleaned that up, wouldn't they? She stopped outside the big double door, her hand trembling on the knob.

Control yourself; you can do this. Mina turned the knob, pushed the door back.

The sun's last hurrah filtered through the open blinds, drawing long, trembling stripes across the bed. She couldn't get herself over the threshold, and grasped the doorframe as nausea threatened to overwhelm her.

The white princess phone beckoned from the night table, the receiver lying on its back like an upended turtle. She stepped into the room. Was that

Bucheron, Paola's perfume, floating in the air?

Tears started in her eyes. Wobbling over to the phone, Mina picked up the receiver and placed it on its cradle.

Someone had removed the linens from Paola's bed. In evening's half-light, two down pillows seemed to float like useless life buoys on the blue damask that covered the mattress. Mina turned, stumbling, and fled.

Before she reached her room, the phone began ringing. She sobbed in relief. Patrick. He must be so worried.

Grabbing the telephone, she fell onto the bed. "Patrick?"

"Miss Davies? I heard about your sister. I'm so sorry," said a woman's voice.

"Who is this?"

"Oh, sorry, my name is Betty. I live two houses down from you. I am—was—a good friend of your sister's."

Mina closed her eyes. Betty. Blonde, petite, a back-fence snooper. Paola couldn't stand her.

"Thank you for your sympathy, Betty. I'd love to talk to you, but I need to keep the line free."

"I understand, of course. I'll just be a minute. You know, your sister and I used to do things together, like shopping. I was with her when she bought that great car of hers—you know, the Thunderbird? She practically stole that automobile from the dealer. We got a real good price."

"Betty, what do you want?"

"Well, I was wondering what your brother-in-law is planning to do with the car? I'm in the market for transportation and I..."

Mina slammed the receiver down. Now she understood why the phone had been left off the hook. She retrieved her suitcase and pulled the address book from her carry-on.

The number in New York was a recording. "You have reached the Gourmandises Internationalles automated attendant. All our offices will be closed until Monday morning in celebration of Thanksgiving. Thank you for calling Gour..." Mina hung up.

How could she find Patrick? He probably thought she stood him up. Why did it have to be Thanksgiving weekend, with everything closed for four long days? *Stupid pilgrims.*

Wait—Thanksgiving was strictly an American holiday, not celebrated in Europe. She could call the company's central offices in France. Except she didn't know which city they were headquartered in. What kind of blind fool was she? First Paola and now Patrick. How could she be so uninformed about the people closest to her?

She tried Paris first. All the international circuits were busy. Sitting on her bed, her toes tapping the floor, she played a waiting game, staring at the phone in her hand. It took her three calls to get through.

The operator spoke very little English, and must have eaten a stale croissant for breakfast, judging by her tone. "Non, *Mademoiselle, Gourmandises Internationalles* is not listed in Paris, so sorry." She pronounced 'sorry' the way the French say *cheri* — heavy on the R. She disconnected before Mina could ask for another city.

Mina rocked back on the bed and closed her eyes, trying to recall anything that would give her a clue.

She remembered one afternoon on the beach, lying languid, Patrick by her side. Her mind had drifted, content, until her peace was interrupted by a growl. She jumped; her eyes flung open, and met her lover's teasing glare. "Have I frightened you?" he asked.

She nodded. He laughed, pushed her back onto the towel, and began to cover her bare skin with love bites, all the while pretending to growl.

"Patrick, Patrick," she giggled, "You sound like a lion."

"*Un lion, oui,* my little lamb. I was born a lion in a city of lions." He roared and she let out a squeal.

Later—much later—he had explained his riddle. Born under the sign of Leo, in the city of..."

She dialed the phone. Paola would flip when the phone bill arrived.

Oh God. Mina put the receiver down. Paola would never get upset with her again, about phones or anything else. Tears welled in her eyes. She let the wave of grief pass before picking up the phone and redialing.

A different operator this time. Within thirty seconds, Mina had the number of the headquarters in Lyon.

A woman's voice, pleasant and melodious, answered on the third ring. *"Les Gourmandises Internationalles, Bonjour."*

"Hello, my name is Mina—"

"L'Amerique? Attendez, s'il vous plait."

Mina waited. After two clicks, a man came on the line. Very British. "How may I help you?"

"I'm a friend of Patrick's. Patrick Dubois. We were to meet in New York, but I missed my flight. Can you tell me how to contact him?"

Pause. "A friend?"

"Yes." Mina sensed a sudden coldness on the other end of the line. "Can you give me the name of the hotel he's staying at in New York?"

"Madame," he said, "There must be a misunderstanding. Monsieur Dubois is in London. Are you a business associate?" Heavy on the sarcasm.

Mina's impatience grew. "I'm a friend, I told you. I need to get in touch with him. He was expecting me in New York."

"Give me your number and I will have Madame Dubois contact you. Collect."

Patrick's mother? Maybe that's why he was in London. Mina gave him the number and hung up the phone.

After twenty minutes of waiting, the call finally came. She picked it up on the first ring. "Yes? Hello?"

The call wasn't collect, but the caller was French. She spoke with a heavy accent—like Patrick's, but more of a roll on the R's.

"Excusez moi, you are Patrick's, um, *amie? Oui? Je comprend pas* New York, *mon mari* is in London."

Mina's heart stopped. *Mon mari?* "Madame

Dubois?"

"Oui?"

"Excuse me, but are you Patrick's mother?" She waited; dogs were barking in the background. A short laugh came from the receiver she was holding.

"Mother? Oh non, non. *Je suis sa femme.* His, um, *qu'est que vous dites,* wife."

CHAPTER 16

Not a ripple disturbed the dark water. Mina let her bare toe brush the surface then watched the circles spread, multiply, and chase themselves, only to die one by one to the outmost border of the concrete. A chill gripped her and she quickly backed away from the edge of the pool without letting go of the tall glass just re-filled with brandy. "Never, never, bring glass into the pool area." Paola's words played in her mind.

In spite of the alcohol burning inside, her small body shivered in the oversized sweatshirt, *Paola*. Could she simply slide into the water, close her eyes, and go to sleep? Oh, if only it could be that simple.

Clouds in the night sky parted to reveal a faint moon ray. It played on the few ripples still looping in the pool. The water cast its spell and Mina had no will to fight it. This was worse than when her parents had died. She remembered her awakening in the hospital room, surrounded by familiar faces. People she had known from childhood. People she loved, and who loved her. They held her in their arms and told her about the car accident, her parent's death, and the miracle of her survival. Maybe because she was numbed by painkillers, or because she was only sixteen, back then Mina had known she would make it through.

And of course, then there was Paola waiting for her in a new country—America. A country Mina knew only from postcards and movies. A country for the hope-fueled, the dream-chaser. Her kind of country. That was yesterday. All was different now. No friendly faces, no loving arms. Paola was dead, and Patrick—waves of nausea twisted her stomach.

If she closed her eyes, would it stop? Her eyelids felt so heavy; Mina let them drift down. She swayed, her head spinning, falling, falling. Instinct steered her hands, outstretched, searching for something to grab, to break her fall. And her hand met the warmth of a human touch. She cried, to the hand touching her, to the indifference of the silent sky. She cried to the dreams and the hopes that spread, multiplied and died, one by one, in this orphaned house, in this perfect country. The brandy glass shattered on the pool deck.

She wanted to run, she wanted to fight, but before she could do anything at all, two arms encircled her and Brian lifted her up, whispered in her ear, "It's all right. It's me."

"No, no, put me down."

"You'll cut your feet. Let me carry you inside."

"Lasciami, put me down. I mean it. Brian, I'm going to be sick."

He let her down by the patio door and held her forehead while she vomited violently. He was talking to her, but she couldn't understand, couldn't think. Stench of regurgitated brandy permeated the air.

She didn't want to open her eyes, ever again. Gasping for breath, she fought away Brian's helping hands. Just that much movement gave her another attack of nausea, forcing her to her knees, landing on her own vomit.

Without warning, the automatically timed floodlights went on and lit the place bright as daytime. No shadows to hide her shame. Only the distant buzzing of the freeway disturbed the silence. Mina buried her face in her hands, but Brian picked her up and carried her upstairs. She gave up resisting and closed her eyes. Now she only wanted to go to sleep and never wake up.

Maybe this was how Paola felt—alone, helpless, desperate. She didn't even argue when Brian removed her sweatshirt. Water from the showerhead warmed and soothed her skin. Brian gently sponged her off, washed her hair.

He wore a light blue shirt, the sleeves rolled up past his elbows. As he leaned in to rinse her hair, drops spattered his shirt, formed growing spots until she could see his tanned skin through the wet fabric. Her head rested on his shoulder as he turned the shower off and began toweling her dry.

She must have drifted off, because the next thing she knew, she was in bed. Heaves wracked her body. "Brian," she choked.

"It's okay, I'm here."

Beads of cold sweat covered her forehead, and her wet hair dampened the pillow. Brian put his hand over her brow. "I know it's horrible, but they're just dry heaves," he said. "There's nothing more in your stomach to come up. I'm going to get you some orange juice."

"No. I can't drink it."

He smoothed a wet strand of hair from her forehead. "Just wait. It'll taste better than you think." Leaning over, he kissed her forehead and, without listening to her protests, went downstairs.

The taste of bile lingered in her mouth. If only she could brush her teeth, maybe she'd feel better. She lifted her head, but the spinning increased, and so did the nausea. *No way.*

Thank God Brian had turned off the lamp. The only light came from the open door. When he reappeared in the doorway with the orange juice, his body cast a shadow, *a reassuring shadow.*

"Take small sips." Cradling her head, he brought the drink to her dry lips. To her surprise, it did taste good.

After taking a couple of sips, Mina lay back down, "What are you doing here?" she asked.

"Shhh, get some sleep, and then we'll talk. I'll sit right over there," he said, pointing to a chair by the window. He cupped her face in his hand, kissed her forehead again. "Don't worry, I won't leave. Get some rest now."

She felt so tired, but every time she closed her eyes the spinning started. Hot tears formed under her eyelids, and she opened them to find Brian watching her. "I can't sleep, I'm too sick."

He came and knelt by her side. "Here, try holding my hand," he said

She grasped his hand with both of hers, closed her eyes again. It wasn't good, but it was better than before. His fingers lightly stroked her temples.

Resting her cheek on his hand, she finally fell asleep.

Voices woke her, angry voices from Paola's room. Mina listened fearfully; the thumping of her heart constricted her throat. She recognized Brian's, and then Michael's voice.

"It isn't only wrong, it's illegal," Brian said.

"Why don't you go back to what you were doing," Michael said.

"And what would that be?"

"Fucking my wife's sister."

Mina heard something—or someone—crash to the floor. She jumped out of bed, but had to grab the bedpost to steady herself. The spinning was still there, but not quite as strong. It took her another second to realize she was naked.

The floor of her room was bare and the only article of clothing in sight was Brian's sport coat, so she put it on and walked to the door, one hand against the wall to help herself, each step an exertion.

The two men struggled on the floor of Paola's bedroom, their arms flailing. Mina got a look at Michael's crimson face when his back slammed against the side of the bed.

Brian drew his fist back for another blow.

"Stop it!" she cried, then put a hand to her forehead to stop the reverberation through her head that threatened to make her sick again.

As if she had pushed a pause button, they froze, both of them breathing heavily. Michael glared at her, his eyes traveling from her painted toes to the tweed coat that rode about halfway up her thighs. A smirk appeared on his face. "What's the matter, couldn't find your panties in a hurry?"

Brian's fist landed on his lips.

"Are you two crazy? What is your problem?"

"I caught him stealing." Brian got up, took a step back.

"This is my house, you son of a bitch." Michael wiped a streak of blood from his lips.

Brian took a step toward him. "Shut up, Davies."

Afraid he'd hit Michael again, Mina grabbed his arm. Her coat fell open. She let go of him and pulled the lapels together, blood rushing to her cheeks. "Stop this nonsense, both of you."

Getting up, Michael ran shaky fingers through his sparse hair.

"What are you doing here?" Mina asked.

"He was taking your sister's jewelry."

Michael laughed, his lips distorted by the swelling. "May I remind you that her sister happened to be my wife? That jewelry is mine now—I paid for most of it, anyway. And if you're a fortune hunter, you're wasting your time." He hooked his thumb at Mina. "She's not getting a penny."

Next to Brian, Mina felt tension roll off him in a palpable wave. Once again, carefully this time, she took his arm. "Don't."

"Miguel?" a woman's voice called from downstairs.

The anger rising in Mina, cleared the nausea, the spinning, everything. "You bastard! How dare you, in my sister's house?" Moving so quickly Michael didn't even have time to duck, she slapped his face.

She ran out onto the landing and leaned over the banister. Before looking, she knew who stood below.

Sarah Fernandez. Their eyes met and Sarah bowed her head, hiding under her mass of cotton-candy hair. "Get out of my sister's house," Mina said.

Michael passed Mina on his way down, moving briskly, without looking back. At the last step, he stopped and said to Mina: "This is my house now. I want you out by Monday." Grabbing Sarah by the arm, he pulled her toward the garage. At the doorway to the kitchen he turned, and said, "By the way, Happy Thanksgiving."

Mina heard the door slam behind them, felt Brian's arm come around her shoulders. They stood for a moment, looking down on the imposing entry hall and the magnificent chandelier. Tears rolled from her eyes.

Without a word, Brian turned her towards him and hugged her tightly.

"Thanksgiving," she mumbled against his shirt. "What should I give thanks for? Being the surviving family member, again?" She stepped back, wiped her eyes. "Listen to me, now I'm blaming God. Where was I when my sister needed me? Poor Paola. She used to tell me: `Have a child, plant a tree, write a book, and you will live forever.' Well, she never had a child, someone else planted her trees, and she didn't write a book."

Brian tried to hold her again, but she pushed him back. His gaze on her face was troubled. "Why don't you get some clothes on and we'll drive to my house for dinner," he said.

"Thanks, its sweet of you to offer, but no."

"Mina, you can't stay here by yourself. And you should eat something."

"What time is it?"

He checked his watch. "Five minutes to eleven."

For the first time, the sun shining through the beveled windows made an impression. "In the morning? I must have slept a long time," she said.

"Not really, it was almost dawn when you fell asleep."

She rubbed her face. God, he had seen her naked, and without her mascara. "How long have you been here?"

"Why don't you get dressed, and we'll sit down and decide what we're going to do. Unless you'd rather wear my coat." His hand stroked the collar and he smiled.

Blushing, she moved away. "I'll be right back."

"Take your time, I'll be downstairs."

"Wait! Where are my clothes?"

"Oh, I forgot. They're in the dryer. But I unpacked your suitcase and hung the stuff up in the closet."

"Great." The closet—no wonder she couldn't find them. Returning to her bedroom, she found the jeans and black top she'd worn to the airport the day before draped over a chair, neatly folded. How'd she miss them? She flung Brian's jacket on the bed, put them on and went downstairs.

Brian sat quietly on the bottom stair. She sat next to him, drawing her knees to her chest, her elbow brushing against his.

"Adams asked me to check on you last night," he said. "Your phone was out of order so he became concerned. I knocked, then tried the doors. They were locked, but the side gate to the backyard wasn't. That's where I found you, in the dark." He stared straight ahead, and Mina took a long look at his profile. He was so—nice. She didn't usually look for that in a man. Resting her head on his shoulder, she felt the warmth of his body, the almost imperceptible movement of every breath. She closed her eyes.

"Mina?"

"Hmmm?" So tired. She could fall asleep, just like this.

"About last night. I wasn't sure—I'm sorry that I, I—I hope you don't think that—"

Mina's eyes were open now.

"Anyway," he continued, "I'm really sorry that I, uh..."

"Brian, look. It's embarrassing for both of us. I got sick all over myself, and you cleaned up the whole mess. You were great, really great. I'm the one who's sorry. Although," she grinned, glad he couldn't see her face, "you did see me naked."

She felt his shoulder shake with laughter. "Vomit versus nudity? I think I got the raw end of that deal."

Sitting up straight, she raised her fist to punch him. "I hope that was a pun."

He didn't draw back like she expected him to. Near him like this, his blue eyes gave a feeling of space—like the ocean, like the sky—waiting for her. For a split second her heart froze, and then began to pound.

He leaned forward. The slower he moved, the faster her heart beat. "There's no Margo this time," he whispered, and kissed her.

It wasn't like a first kiss. His lips lingered over hers, slow, as if he'd kissed her a thousand times.

Sliding one hand up her back, he entwined his fingers in her hair.

Mina wanted his touch anywhere, everywhere. When they finally broke the kiss, she rested her head on his chest, her ear snug against the beat of his heart. "I shouldn't feel like this."

Leaning back against the wall, he pulled her closer. "Don't feel guilty, not about this. Paola wouldn't have minded."

Not minded? Paola would have been ecstatic. She never could stand Patrick. In fact, if she'd known the truth, Paola would have killed him.

That's why her suicide made no sense. It made Mina furious when Paola glossed over or even hid things from her, all in the name of protection. So why would Paola kill herself, something she could never shield Mina from?

"How long will the police hold Paola's..." she couldn't say suicide "letter?"

Brian stiffened. "Oh no. You're going to kill me."

Mina pushed herself up to look at him. "Why?"

"The letter your sister left. Adams gave me a copy to bring you."

"You've had it since last night, and you never said anything? Where is it? Give it to me!"

"Calm down. I'll get it. You know, Adams has some connections at the Police Department."

"Brian, the letter."

"In my jacket."

Mina bounded up the stairs two at a time, Brian behind her. His jacket had slipped to the floor, and she tore at it, searching for the letter. "It's not here. You've lost it."

"Give it to me." He pulled a folded sheet of paper from the inside pocket. Mina shook as she opened the letter.

"I cannot watch people suffer for what I did."

The typed words blurred as her eyes filled with tears. Knuckling them away with one fist, Mina tried again:

"I cannot watch people suffer for what I did. I killed Rachel Fernandez. I lured her into the loft, telling her I needed her help to move some furniture. I offered her the poisoned chocolate. When she began to feel ill I left. I locked the door behind me so that she couldn't get help. Then I went to meet Paco and bought a new box of candies to replace the one I had used.

You know the rest. Paco is innocent.

Michael, I love you. I couldn't stand to lose you. Please watch over my little sister.

Forgive me,
Paola

Mina threw the letter down. "No way, I don't believe this."

"You aren't the only one who feels that way."

She turned to look at Brian, wishing she were as calm as he was.

"Why would she confess to save Paco?" he said, "He was already a free man."

"They let Paco go?" Mina heard the tremor in her voice and wrapped her arms around herself so she'd stop shaking. "Because of Paola's letter?"

"No, they let him go because he told them how Rachel got the chocolate. There was no reason to hold him."

"Then Paola committed suicide for nothing?" The expression in his blue eyes needed no explanation. "You don't believe she killed herself."

"No," he said, "and certainly not over Michael."

"And the police? What do they think?"

He shrugged. "I doubt Dan's buying the suicide either."

"Then what are they going to do?"

"Look, can we sit down?"

Mina led the way downstairs to the living room, curled her feet under her on the couch. Brian sat down next to her, but not too close. She didn't want to admit how much that bothered her.

"It seems Paco felt funny about Michael's habit of leaving little love bon-bons for Paola," Brian began. "He overheard someone in the front office comment on how easy it would be to slip some poison into a chocolate-cherry cordial."

"Yes, it was one of the suppliers"

"Paco said he was joking around with Margo. But it made him think. So, every time Michael left a candy, Paco replaced it with one from a box he bought. Nobody, including Paola, seems to have caught on."

"Did he have Michael's chocolates tested?"

"His suspicions didn't really go that far. He was just being cautious. Usually, he threw them away in the bin behind the warehouse. Except for this last one. He put the candy in the front pocket of his lab coat, then got busy with inventory and forgot about it. Later, he ran into Rachel, coming in through the back. She saw the chocolate in his coat pocket, and teased him about stealing Halloween candy from some poor kid. She took the chocolate before he could stop her."

"Why did he let her have it?"

"He didn't know the candy was poisoned. What was he supposed to do, make a scene? Rachel told him she was there to pick up some smocks that needed washing. One of the workers came out and asked him a question about then, and Rachel disappeared into the warehouse. Paco had no idea she went into the loft. By the time he found her, she was dead."

The phone rang. Mina had about a hundred questions to ask, but she got up and walked to the kitchen. "Hello."

"Mina, my love."

Patrick's voice came through loud and clear. She leaned against the kitchen counter, closed her eyes. "Hi, Patrick."

"My darling," he said, "I waited for you. What happened?"

Brian came into the kitchen and sat down at the table. Mina turned toward the counter, her back towards him. "What's the name of your dog?" she managed to ask in a low tone.

"Le nom de mon chien?" Silence lingered, then

he spoke cautiously. "I don't remember us talking about my dog."

"No, I don't think you mentioned it. I heard it barking when I talked to your wife."

"What?"

Anger gushed through her when she heard the outrage in his voice. This was the man she wanted to turn to when Paola... "You heard me."

"You spoke to my wife!"

"You're being incredibly slow. She called me this morning."

"Ma femme ?Ce n'est pas possible. You are lying to me."

Her lying to him? Mina couldn't help but laugh.

"Do you find this funny?" he demanded.

"I don't. Does your wife?" She slammed the phone on the receiver.

Brian seemed engrossed by the back of the orange juice carton. Standing by the counter, she wondered what she could say to him. He wasn't an idiot; he knew something was going on. Just as she opened her mouth, the phone rang again.

Maledizione, damn. Why hadn't she taken it off the hook? Exasperated, she picked it up. "*Va all'inferno,* go to hell, Patrick," she yelled into the mouthpiece.

Without looking at her, Brian got up, and disappeared into the foyer. *She really knew how to crash land a relationship, didn't she?* Moving over to the table, she slumped down in a chair. "What do you want Patrick?"

"Mina? Mina?" She sat up. Oh God, it was Adams. "Are you there?"

Her voice came out as a squeak. "Yes, I'm here. I'm sorry—I thought—I didn't know it was you."

"Don't apologize, dear. I know what you're going through. How are you doing?"

"I'm fine, thank you." She hated that response, but it came out automatically. "No, that's a lie. I'm not fine, but I'm okay."

"I understand exactly what you mean." There was a long pause, and then a cough. "Excuse me, Mina. Is Brian there with you?"

"He's in the house. Would you like to speak to him?"

"No, not right now."

Neither spoke for a moment. The big house was so quiet. She kept expecting Paola to burst in any minute, full of joy or anger or fear. How could that life be gone? "I wanted to thank you for my sister's letter. It meant a lot to me."

He didn't seem to hear her. "Mina, I need to see you immediately. I know it's soon, and a holiday at that, but some things won't wait." His tone had changed, suddenly business-like.

Until that moment, Mina hadn't even thought about the practical ramifications of Paola's death. "You mean about the funeral? Adams, I'll need your help. I don't even know where to start."

"No, I've already taken care of that. Due to recent events, I'm afraid I must —" There was a pause, and he coughed again. "As I was saying, I wanted to give you time to get over the shock of your, of Paola's death. I have a letter in my possession that could help the police in their investigation. I feel compelled to release it.

However, I want you to see it first."

"Didn't you hear me, Adams? I've already read Paola's letter. Brian brought it over, remember?" She heard that light coughing—or was it weeping?

"It's a different letter, Mina. I couldn't give it to Brian. Would you like me to come to Mission Viejo? We're going to sit down to dinner in about a half hour, but I could be there around two."

"No, it's all right. I'll come to you." She heard the hall bathroom door unlock. A second later, Brian appeared in the kitchen doorway. "Is there room for one more at dinner? If I promise you'll feed him, maybe Brian will drive me."

"We'll set two places. I'm sure you haven't eaten either. Get here as soon as you can."

"Okay. Thanks, Adams. Bye."

Without a word, Brian took the phone from Mina's hand, punched in a number. "Hi Mom, it's me. Look, don't count on me for dinner." He grinned up at Mina. "I got a better offer—The one I told you about last night—Yeah, I think she'll pull through—I love you, too. Happy Thanksgiving. Bye." He hit the off button and set the receiver down. "Are you ready to go?"

"Let me grab my bag." Mina raced to her room, found her handbag. She was halfway down when she remembered her coat. They would probably be back before dark, but better to be safe.

The Ultrasuede coat hung in the closet. Fingering one sleeve, tears rose in her eyes. Her last gift from Paola. Taking it down from the hanger, she draped it lovingly over one arm and went downstairs.

Brian opened the door, held it, waiting for her to pass through. She stopped in front of him, reached up to pull his face down to hers, and kissed him.

He put his arms around her waist. "Your neighbors are going to have something to talk about now."

"They're all stuffing their faces with turkey. Come on. The traffic will probably be horrible."

He opened the car door for her. "That's okay. It'll give you time to tell me about Patrick."

CHAPTER 17

The old Santa Ana residential district—turned professional—looked like a ghost town, deserted for Thanksgiving. Because of the proximity to the Courthouse, the whole block was dotted with lawyers' offices. Without major changes to the architecture, the old little houses had been 'groomed' so that they now looked like very polished old little houses. During the summer months, colorful Jacaranda trees gave a coquettish look to the otherwise dull streets. But the Santana winds had dispersed the last lavender blossoms a long time ago.

Brian parked his Mustang in the lot behind Adams' office. The white cottage, once home to families with noisy children, appeared sad, shadowed by an old bare tree. "I guess I'll go back to Adams' house for pie and coffee while you two conduct business. Unless you want me to stay."

Mina gave him a weak smile. "No. He wants to speak to me alone."

Brian nodded out the window at the car next to them. "He must know a short cut, he beat us here." Reaching across the seat, he took her hand. "Did you have enough to eat?"

"Yes, thank you. Mrs. Adams is a great cook,"

Mina said, "I'd better go. Adams is waiting."

Squeezing her hand, he released it. "Call me when you're done. I'll be waiting."

The metal sign on the front door read Knock Please. In spite of the vicinity to the Courthouse and the plentitude of lawyers, this wasn't the safest of neighborhoods and Adams kept the door locked most of the time.

At Mina's knock, the door opened immediately and Adams invited her in. She turned to wave at Brian, but he had already left. Adams pushed back a lock of silvery hair. Again, she noticed how thin he was. Tall and thin. He couldn't have grown, and she knew she hadn't shrunk. He must have lost weight. Yes, that would explain why he seemed taller than she remembered him. His pale blue eyes were kindly. In spite of the circumstances—or maybe because of them—his face maintained a look of serenity.

When he closed the door behind her, she inhaled a light aroma of roast turkey from his clothes. The smell made her slightly nauseous. She hadn't eaten anything at his house, luckily, no one had noticed. Through the entire meal she thought about her first Thanksgiving, her amazement at the sight of corn, *chicken feed to an Italian,* and sweet potatoes topped with marshmallows. As it turned out, sweet potatoes are known to Italians as *patate Americane,* American potatoes, and the marshmallows, well, neither Mina nor Paola could come up with a translation for the simple reason that marshmallows are totally alien to Italy's supermarkets. Michael tried to convince Mina they grew on bushes and that she should export the seeds. That was a really fun Thanksgiving and Paola's cooking was the best.

"Come, dear," Adam said.

She sighed, followed him into the office. The familiar stained wooden shutters were now closed, the dark room illuminated only by the lamp on his desk. Adams sat in his large, leather chair, Mina across the desk from him. His hands fidgeted with a stack of papers, and he seemed to be avoiding her eyes. After a long sigh, he said, "I thought I'd begin by bringing you up to date. First, I have a piece of good news. Both Paco and Elena are spending Thanksgiving at home with their families. They've been cleared and released."

"That's nice," Mina heard herself saying. *I didn't even know Elena was in jail. How can I be so out of touch?*

"The police have established that Rachel ate the poisoned chocolate outside Michael's office, just before she went up into the loft."

"How can they be so sure?" she asked.

"Apparently Rachel dropped the paper outside his office door. The police think it happened while you were under the desk. The approximate time of death fits." Pausing, he waited for her reaction. When none came, he asked, "Did you see anything?"

Mina found herself fascinated by the cleanliness of Adams' fingernails.

"Mina?"

"Sorry. You were saying?"

Adams raised his eyebrows, but didn't push the point. "Rachel got the candy from Paco—did you know that?"

"Brian told me," Mina said. "But what happened to the candy I unwrapped? The one in Paol..." her voice broke. "My sister's in-box."

"Elena ate it. De Fiore told me she was lying about something, and he was right. She also hadn't told them that, while she was cleaning, she found the wrapper Rachel dropped. Elena assumed it was from the chocolate she ate, and so didn't tell the police."

So many little secrets. "Is there anything else?"

Again, that sense of avoidance, she could sense it, feel it. *Why?* What was Adam hiding? He took an envelope from the top of the stack, hesitated, and then handed it to her. Paola's handwriting—royal blue ink on pale gray paper—spelled out her name. The envelope looked so flat and felt so light that she gave Adams a questioning look.

Avoiding her eyes, he got up from his chair. "I'll be in the next room if you need me."

Slowly, she opened the envelope and stared at the date. Six years ago. *Dio mio,* the year her parents died. Her whole body quivered, was it anticipation or was it fear?

My Darling Mina,

Today I watched you getting off the plane and entering my life. How you have grown. How I have missed you. I wanted to hug you and cradle you in my arms. Above all, I wanted to tell you why—but I can't. So I'm writing this letter to you. As my pen draws letters forming words, I fantasize that my pen is my finger and the paper your face and every stroke becomes a caress from my heart to yours.

Oh, how I love you, soul of my soul, breath of my breath. Why have I had to pay for someone else's sin? And why, why, have you had to be the pawn?

As you read this, I'm no longer with you, and so now my story can be told. Seventeen years ago, when I was a frightened young girl, barely fourteen, I gave birth to you. It's true, my darling, I am your mother. The truth was so inconceivable, I couldn't tell you. Even my mother did not believe me, thought I was insane.

Immediately after your birth, I was sent out of the country, without you. My mother claimed you as her own. I didn't see your first smile, didn't hear your first word. Those years are just a dark, painful memory, buried deep inside me. But time is the great healer.

I ended up as an au pair in the Adams' household. They helped me find my path to acceptance.

When I married my first husband, I began to dream about getting you back. He was rich and powerful, a famous lawyer. I saw him as my knight in shining armor who would fight for us and put you back into my arms forever.

You know how that fairytale ended. But in a twist of fate, mother and her husband died in a car accident that spared your precious life. Before I realized what was happening, here you were stepping out of that silver plane in your best Sunday clothes.

"Paola," you said, timidly smiling at Michael and me.

I wanted to cry out. "Mother, call me mother." But I kept my mask on, simply saying, "Welcome to California, sister dear."

Please, don't judge me harshly. In spite of what the world may think, all I ever wanted was for you to know and accept me as I really am,

Your loving mother

Mina didn't know how long she sat there, lost, confused, and fearful. The touch of Adams' hand startled her.

"Are you okay?"

She stared at the gray paper, her body shaking. "Adams..." Her voice was just a murmur. She had trouble focusing. *Paola was her mother*? Her first reaction had been surprise, and skepticism. Now she felt hurt. Somewhere between her belly and her throat, where her heart must be. A hurt so deep, it took her breath away.

Adams gently squeezed her shoulder, walked around the desk and sat in his chair, waiting.

"Adams?"

"Yes?" He leaned across the desk in an effort to hear her.

"Do you know?" she waved the letter.

He nodded.

"Ma perche? Why..." Swallowing her tears, she tried again. "Why didn't Paola, why didn't she tell me before?" She couldn't say "mother".

"Circumstances, dear. When you first arrived, you two were strangers to each other. One can't tell a young girl who just lost her parents and is arriving in an unknown country, 'Hello darling, forget your parents because I'm your real mother.' It simply wasn't a sensible thing to do."

"Adams, it's been over five years."

"True, and I did encourage her to tell you, but you know Paola, she wanted everything perfect. At first she thought you should have time to get to know her. I understood that. In the meantime, problems began to surface in her marriage and in the business. Soon they grew so great that her sense of priority seemed to be lost. That's when she decided that Michael had to go. She promised me she would 'clean house'. That included telling you the truth."

"I could have helped her."

"You did. You gave her the strength to face what was happening instead of looking the other way." He paused. "I wanted to wait for a better time to give you her letter, but after seeing a copy of the alleged suicide note, I knew I had to act fast. We must tell the police. This letter proves her death wasn't suicide. She couldn't possibly have called you "my little sister" in her suicide note. In the meantime, your brother-in-law is, no doubt, grabbing everything he can get his hands on."

"Does he know? About me, I mean." She pointed to the letter.

"No, she never told him."

"Will it make any difference?"

"Yes, Mina, it drastically changes your legal

rights to Paola's estate. As you know, I'm the executor of her estate. I can't discuss her will until everyone is present. That includes Michael, of course." The last statement was said with some contempt. "Just a few weeks ago, we received the last documents necessary to make your status legal."

Adams lifted the white folder Mina had picked up at West Coast Software the Saturday Rachel died. The sight sent chills up her spine. *Had Paola hoped she would look inside?*

"Do you know who my father is?" The words were out before she realized what she was going to say.

Adams looked astonished at her question. His lips moved, but she heard no sound.

"Well, do you?" she repeated.

"Mina? Adams, are you done yet? Your wife says the pie is waiting at home. With freshly whipped cream." Brian's cheerful voice came from the entrance. Adams got up from his chair and, without looking at her, went to open the door.

CHAPTER 18

Mina drifted in and out of sleep.

Paola, oh Paola, I miss you. Sister or mother, I don't care, I miss you. Why didn't you tell me? Why, why? Everything could have been different; maybe you'd be here with me right now. Oh, Paola, why?

She stirred, searching for a cool spot in the bed.

Where was Michael? She hadn't seen him since the morning's confrontation. What would happen when he found out? If Paola was her mother, then her "mother" would have been her grandmother and her "father" was her—step-grandfather?

Mio Dio, such confusion. Who was her biological father? Adams had maneuvered himself out of answering that question. She kicked off the covers, and sat up, her body wet with perspiration. What time was it? A car drove by, salsa music blaring. Michael? No, he wouldn't dare, would he? Tense, Mina listened as the vehicle drove past the house and away.

She rubbed her eyes with her fists. Emotions and feelings she ignored during the day all came at her in huge waves. No use denying, she felt overwhelmed, too much to sort out, and no one to sort out with. Sleeping had been easier last night with Brian sitting by her side. Sweet Brian, when she'd told him about Paola's secret, he hadn't seemed surprised.

"I've always felt a special bond between the two of you," he said. "Remember what you said before? That someone else planted Paola's trees and she didn't write a book. But she did have a child, and you are that child."

She'd been too immersed in her own mixed emotions to even thank him. All those new feelings. So different from the way she would have normally reacted.

Before he'd left this evening, Brian insisted on going through every room in the house, just in case. He latched and secured every window, locked all the doors. He hinted around, but stopped short of offering to stay. Oh, the temptation of saying yes! But her feelings were raw and fragile; she didn't want to make any more mistakes.

The clock on her night table said one-thirty. She had to get some sleep.

Lying still, she searched for thoughts to quiet her mind, dull her soul.

The phone rang. Once, twice. Mina watched it ring. "Don't," said her brain. Her outstretched hand, picked it up, brought it to her ear. She heard a crackle—music—a voice, a man's voice, singing, "...*Put on* your red shoes..." And a laugh, soft, like a whisper, long, like eternity.

The phone dropped from her fingers, hit the side of the bed. She recoiled from it, her throat choked with fear. Cold sweat trickled down her spine.

She felt helpless, vulnerable and incapable of

even the simplest thought.

Dio mio. She lay still, paralyzed, hoping to decipher the darkness, understand the silence.

"If you need to make a call..." The mechanical voice from the phone jerked Mina back to reality. She switched on the lamp and inhaled deeply. It had to be a coincidence. A wrong number. Someone calling from a bar, that would explain the background music.

Put on your red shoes...

Something familiar about it. No, familiar wasn't the right word. Mina was sure she had heard the song before. *Where? When? Wouldn't this night ever be over?* The days ahead would all seem long, without Paola there. She might as well get used to it.

Closing her eyes, she whispered, "Please, let the morning come soon."

* * * * *

Mina walked into West Coast Software Friday morning not knowing what to expect. She wanted to be sure that Paco knew about the meeting at Adams', but she dreaded running into Michael.

Margo put down her rainbow coffee mug and ran to hug her. "I'm so sorry about your sister." Her eyes were red and puffy. Mina wasn't sure what to make of that. Bloodshot eyes weren't that unusual for Margo after a holiday.

She wanted to tell Margo that Paola was her mother, not her sister, but Adams had been specific; no one was to be told until the meeting at his office, scheduled for this afternoon.

Adams hadn't said if Paco knew about her and

Paola. Maybe she shouldn't have told Brian yesterday, but she had to tell someone, and he hadn't seemed to fit into Adams' warning. Distractedly, she returned Margo's embrace.

With one final squeeze, Margo released her. "Coffee?" she said, her tone back to normal. Margo's emotions never lingered.

"No, thank you," she said. "Is Michael in?"

"I haven't seen him — Paco opened up this morning. Speak of the devil." She winked at Paco as he came in from the warehouse.

Pinned on the sleeve of his freshly laundered lab coat, Paco wore a black armband. The sight brought tears to Mina's eyes. Coming to her side, he put an arm around her shoulder.

"Isn't that a pretty picture?" Michael's voice made them both turn around.

He stood by the entrance, wearing a herringbone suit Mina had never seen before. His sparse hair was combed back, gleaming with grease. At his side was Sarah, whose wiry hair had been re-dyed to its original black. Its glossiness made her look Oriental, rather than Hispanic. Though she wore no lipstick, her eyelids were loaded with bright blue shadow, and she wore a form-fitting gold lame dress.

In the morning? And was that one of Paola's gold chains around her ankle? With a cry, Mina lunged at her.

"Mina!" Paco stopped her, tightening his hold around her shoulders.

Michael jumped back and Mina saw fear flicker in his eyes, but Sarah stood her ground, her colorless lips parted in a defiant smile, her cold black eyes locked on Mina's.

"Goddamn it, what are you doing here?" Michael had regained his composure—and his manners.

Before Mina could answer, his eyes traveled to Paco, and he noticed the armband. "What the hell? You old fool, take off that stupid rag. Better yet, take off the lab coat too and turn it in. You're fired."

Paco silently shook his head, sadness in his eyes. Walking away, he lowered his eyelids as if fighting back tears.

In a manner so calm that it surprised even her, Mina said, "Yes Paco, why don't you change and take the day off. With pay, of course. You could use a break." She punched each word of the sentence, staccato, her eyes on Michael's face. "And I'll see you later this afternoon, Paco. In Adams' office."

Everyone in the room stared at her, stunned. She felt Paola's presence, her approval.

"Let's go into my office," Michael said to Mina. He took Sarah's arm, but she shook him off and stood looking at Mina with those cold, black eyes.

Eyes like the dead.

The phrase came into Mina's mind unbidden, and she suppressed a shiver. "Sorry, Michael," she said, not about to back down now. "Whatever it is will have to wait until after the meeting."

His face turned purple. Mina had never thought about it before, but Michael was probably a prime heart attack candidate. She waited for him to clutch at his chest. Instead, he stormed into his office alone and slammed the door.

The look of astonishment on Paco's face made her smile. "Don't worry about Michael," Mina winked at him. "After the meeting, you'll understand."

"I would like to talk to you," Paco said and motioned toward the office.

She understood and followed him.

"What is it, Paco?" She asked.

"It's about Takawa's disks. Well, more about the copyrights information he entrusted us with. This may be nothing, but I just need to talk to someone about it," Paco said.

Mina wasn't sure what he meant; she knew nothing about it. She let Paco talk. "I told you I had high hopes regarding Sarah, treated her like family, I may have been too trusting, I may…"

"You may what?" Mina grew impatient.

"Well, I sort of talked to her about some of the confidential info we gather from clients. Clients like Takawa. Information that could be worth a lot to competitors."

"*Mio Dio*. You think Sarah is behind all this?"

"I never would have thought she could, until now, seeing her with Michael…I don't know. I hope I'm wrong. I could never forgive myself."

"Paco, let's not go there yet. Nothing matters more than our meeting with Adams. Clear your mind."

His eyes warmed. "Until this afternoon, then." Turning, he left through the warehouse.

As Mina walked to the door, she passed Sarah, who still stood where Michael had left her. Her foot with Paola's jeweled anklet tapped furiously. "Enjoy it while it lasts," Mina said.

Sarah's spiteful gaze flickered past Mina and her expression changed; she seemed to glow.

Turning, Mina saw Ishmael Fernandez. He had entered the office and was standing behind Margo's chair. His fingers circled slowly, massaging the receptionist's neck. Margo's head was bent back, eyes closed, the picture of sensual bliss. But Ishmael was staring over her, gazing at his sister with such intensity that Mina felt she was witnessing something unnatural, something sinful.

The telephone rang, and Margo opened her eyes. "Are you still here?" she said to Mina, then answered the phone.

Ishmael's dark fingers lingered on Margo's shoulders, but the disturbing gleam in his eyes was still focused on Sarah.

Feeling an urgent need for fresh air, Mina stepped outside. Things would change, once her situation was out in the open. Starting with the Fernandez clan.

She checked her watch. Not quite noon. The meeting was scheduled for three o'clock. Now that she knew for sure Paco would be there, she didn't feel like waiting around.

Getting into her car, she drove to the freeway. Traffic was light because of the four-day holiday, and she reached Mission Viejo in record time. She parked her car in the usual place, in front of the house. Entering by the front door, she had to fight back the impulse to call out, "I'm home!"

As usual, she was hungry. She dropped her

purse in the foyer and went into the kitchen, her mind set on the contents of the refrigerator. Getting the milk out, she took a swig from the carton. *She was the only one drinking it*. When she lowered her head, she noticed that the door leading to the garage was ajar, the garage light on.

She pushed the door wide and gasped. Paola's red Thunderbird was gone.

CHAPTER 19

Mina pulled into the small parking lot in front of Adams' office. She noticed Michael's black Corvette first. Paco's truck wasn't there, but an old beat-up green sedan looked familiar. *De Fiore?* One last time she checked her hair in the rearview mirror, smoothed her skirt and got out of the car.

Coming around the corner, she saw Michael by the front door, talking to a man. Oh, yes, Detective De Fiore! The proud owner of the green monster in the parking lot. Should she talk to him about Paola's missing car, or ask Michael first?

"Just don't leave town," De Fiore finished saying as she walked up to them. *Interesting.* The detective wheeled about, bumping into her. Mina smiled, but De Fiore barely nodded. Brushing past her, he strode toward the parking lot.

"What was that all about?" Mina asked Michael.

Ignoring her, he knocked on the door.

The attractive young woman who let them in wasn't Adams' secretary. She must have read Mina's quizzical expression. "I'm Gloria, a temp," she offered. "Cindy is on vacation." She pointed to the waiting area, "If you'll sit down, please. Mr. Adams will be here momentarily."

Michael sat on a blue velvet chair by the

window, grabbed a month-old magazine and tried to act absorbed.

"Michael," Mina began.

"Yeah."

"I need to talk to you about Paola's Thunderbird."

"What about it?" He spoke without lifting his head.

"It's gone."

"Oh?"

"Is that all you can say? `Oh'?" She mimicked him, but her voice wasn't playful.

"What do you want me to say?" He finally looked up.

"Aren't you worried about it? What if it's been stolen?"

"I don't see how that is of any concern to you." He paused, then added. "It's being repainted."

"Why? It's practically new. There isn't a scratch on it." *The red shoe in the car, my God!*

"It's none of your goddamn business, Mina. It's my car now and I can dispose of it as I please. Understood?"

"What's that supposed to mean?" Mina noticed Gloria peeking at them, trying to act nonchalant.

Someone knocked at the door. The temp got up and let Paco in.

"Hello, Mr. Davies," Paco said.

He smiled at Mina and sat next to her on the couch. Michael settled back into his seat, a smug smile on his face.

Mina was damned if he was going to get off that easy. She tried to control the trembling of her hands as she spoke. "Michael. About the Thunderbird."

"Fuck!" He slammed the magazine shut and thrust his face inches away from hers. "Sarah doesn't like red," he said, then sat back in the chair, a smirk curving the corners of his mouth.

Before she could reply, Adams opened the door to his inner office. "Please, come in. I'm sorry to be late. Gloria, can you bring one more chair?"

Paco wouldn't let Gloria carry the chair in by herself and, smiling, she let him help her. When they were settled, Adams said, "Before we get started, would anyone like coffee?"

Michael spoke. "Let's get this over with. I've got things to do, decisions to make."

"Very well. Hold my calls, please," Adams said to Gloria.

She nodded, hand on the doorknob. "Let me know if you need anything, sir."

After Gloria closed the door, Adams cleared his throat. It sounded like thunder in the small quiet room. Mina stared at the different diplomas hanging on his wall. If only Michael wasn't here. He was like an overfed scavenger, greedy to pick over the remains of Paola's estate.

Paco betrayed his nervousness by picking imaginary specks of lint from his spotless trousers.

She glanced at Michael. His forehead looked shiny, although the room was cool. "So, what are we here for?" he asked.

Adams finished realigning his papers and set them on the table with a slap. "You already know that I'm the executor of Paola's estate." His eyes went from face to face. A smile for Mina, a nod to

Paco, and finally, a look of concentration at Michael.

"Normally," he went on, "I wait until after the funeral to read the will; however, in this case, it has become necessary to do it now."

"Oh, yeah? What's so special about her will? We already know the conditions." Michael's apparent casualness wasn't convincing. "I get everything. Our pre-nuptial agreement doesn't count since we didn't get divorced. So, maybe she wanted to leave some jewelry to her sister and some personal belongings to the old man," he said, pointing at Paco. "I can understand that. And I'm sure there's something there for your trouble." He looked at Adams with contempt. "Have I forgotten anyone?"

"You are correct, the pre-nuptial contract is void because there was no divorce. However, the main clause made you sole heir only if Paola died childless."

Michael tried to interrupt, but Adams stopped him with a motion of his hand. He pulled out a document of an odd size, wider and longer than most legal papers Mina had seen. As he handed it over to Michael, Mina recognized the Official Seal of the Italian Government.

"And here is the English translation, notarized and properly signed," the lawyer pushed another paper toward Michael.

No mistake, Adams was enjoying the moment. He turned to Paco and said, "That's Mina's birth certificate. Paola was her natural mother." An amused glint appeared in the lawyer's pale blue eyes as he watched Paco's mouth open and close again.

Michael threw the papers on the desk, slammed his fist on top of them.

"Bullshit!" he yelled into Mina's face. "If you think I'm falling for this crap, you're all nuts. He put you up to this to get your sister's money."

The pulse in his neck throbbed. Mina watched the purple flush creep through his skin, just as it had that morning at West Coast Software. "You'd better watch yourself or you'll burst a blood vessel, Michael. I had nothing to do with this. I only found out yesterday, myself. That's the truth," she said.

But Michael didn't let her finish. He kicked back his chair and walked to the door. On the threshold, he spun around, his eyes glossy, predatory. "You don't know who you are dealing with, you old fool," he said to Adams. "You'll hear from my lawyer. In the meantime, I don't want to see any of your faces." His arm swept to include everyone present. "Stay away from my house and my business or I'll blow you all away." He slammed the door behind him. Another loud bang told them that the front door had received the same treatment.

"Adams." Her internal tremor came through in her voice, "Can he do that?"

"You mean keep you out of West Coast Software and the house? My dear, I'm one step ahead of him. That's why I was a bit late. I was in court." He picked up a thin stack of papers, showed them his name on the top left and numbers running the length of it, "Restraining orders," he said.

"In plain English?" she asked.

"Michael can't come near you. While we're here talking, Brian Starrs is at the house in Mission Viejo having all the locks changed. When Mr. Davies wants to collect his belongings, he'll have to do it with one of us there, and in the presence of a deputy." Adams beamed, absolutely pleased with himself.

Mina didn't know how to react. She felt lightheaded; part of her wanted to thank Adams, yet another part felt almost sorry for Michael. Paola was dead. *Did he ever even knew what he had, what he'd lost?* The door-slamming act was probably a way of denying his fear and longing. She glanced at Paco.

He patted her hand and said, "Mr. Davies has brought this upon himself."

"What about the company, what's going to happen now?" She pulled a tissue from the box on the desk and blew her nose.

"I'm so glad you asked." The smile on Adams' face was almost impish now. "Here," he said, handing her a page from a yellow notebook. Her name and Paco's appeared next to some numbers.

"What's this?" Mina asked.

He rummaged in a drawer, pulled out some keys that looked brand new. "Those are your codes for the alarm system, and these" he dangled the keys in front of her "are for West Coast Software."

"Let me guess," she said. "You had them installed while we were in your waiting room."

"Very good, my dear." He looked at his watch, "One of you will have to go back there today, to close up. And remember, no one else has clearance with the alarm company. Only you and Mr. Mendez."

She stared at the yellow paper. The numbers seemed to have a life of their own, moving around as she tried to read them.

"I'm not good at this." Her voice was low.

"You'll learn. You're a smart kid. You're Paola's daughter," The fire in Adams' eyes surprised her. " You've got the best genes—"

"Excuse me..." Paco said.

"Of course, I almost forgot. With Michael leaving in such a huff, we never got to the will."

Mina fidgeted in her chair. The grin on Adams' face made her squeamish.

"We can skip the usual legalese for now, I suppose. Here we are, my dear, the part regarding the business: I leave the software company called West Coast Software, Inc. to my daughter Mina Calvi, as her sole and separate property, with all of its right, title and interest, provided she agrees to keep Paco Mendez as Vice President of Operations for the duration of five years minimum with optional rights of partnership. Should one of the two become incapacitated by—"

"When did Mrs. Davies do all this?" Paco asked, his voice shaking. "She never said a thing to me."

"Why are you so upset?" Mina asked him.

"Mina, I loved Paola like my own daughter. You know that." He was almost in tears, and obviously embarrassed by his show of emotion. "She should have prepared me for the responsibility. I don't understand. A legal paper, it seems so impersonal. I don't understand."

Mina got up from her chair and hugged him.

Adams, his voice serious again, said, "Mr. Mendez, Paola left a letter for you. I'm sure you'll find your answers there. By the way, Mina, I may be over-cautious, but I would like you to park your car in the garage from now on. Brian said you usually park on the street. He has had the opener reprogrammed, and gotten you a new remote."

Oh no, she had forgotten Paola's Thunderbird.

"Adams, Michael is giving Paola's car to Sarah Fernandez. He told me it's being repainted because Sarah doesn't like red. He's already taken some of Paola's jewelry. I saw one of Paola's anklets on Sarah this morning. What can we do to stop him?"

"Let me worry about that. Go back to West Coast Software; you and Mr. Mendez need to get accustomed to running the business. I'll talk to De Fiore about Michael."

"He was just here."

"Who?"

"De Fiore. He was talking to Michael outside your office when I drove in."

"He probably warned him not to leave town."

"How do you know that?"

"Well, logically Michael must be one of the prime suspects in their murder investigation."

"Did you say murder?" Paco whispered.

"Yes, Mr. Mendez, the results of the autopsy are in. There's no doubt—Paola was murdered."

CHAPTER 20

Thank God it was over.

Still wearing the black dress borrowed for Paola's funeral, Mina glanced at the people gathered in her living room. When would they leave? She felt emotionally spent. Ready to snap.

Paco, Brian and Adams had accompanied her home from the funeral. The at-home was supposed to be for relatives and close friends only, but—to her surprise—De Fiore followed them. As far as she was concerned, he didn't fit either category. Being a cop undoubtedly cleared his way into many situations.

Michael wasn't here. He'd left the funeral alone, and probably didn't have the nerve to show up. But she wouldn't put it past him. What puzzled Mina was that Margo hadn't attended. Or called. She was so ghoulish about things like this—a true voyeur. Not that Margo didn't care about Paola, but a funeral was really up her alley.

Adams had left early, whether from tact or impending business, Mina didn't know. Now the rest of them sat in the living room, listening to De Fiore. Mina sipped espresso, Paco drank beer—only Brian was empty-handed. Any minute her duty as hostess would require her to ask if anyone wanted anything, when really she wanted to tell them all to leave. Nothing at all like an Italian funeral where everybody gets together the night before for *la vigilia,* the wake. Neighbors and friends got together, if the dear departed was in the house, some of the neighbors brought their own chair to lean on. And everyone prayed, chanted and recited the rosary. Of course, in Italy and especially in her rural village, Catholicism was the only game in town. Next day, the funeral procession would parade through the narrow streets, from the church to the cemetery, businesses would close their shutters and doors to show respect and onlookers would make the sign of the cross as the funeral went by. After the cemetery, everyone went home. She tried to remember her parents' funeral; it seemed so long ago. She craved solitude, silence. Silence... that reminded her of those phone calls.

Put on your red shoes...

Every night, at one thirty a.m. And the laugh, whispery, long, couldn't tell if it was from a man or a woman. She kept assuring herself she wasn't going to pick up the phone, no, not tonight. It was like an addiction, the anticipation, and the cold sweat of fear.

The song's beat played and replayed on her head, continuously, even now, sort of *Name That Tune* of terror...If she could be alone, maybe she would recognize the title of the song and—if De Fiore didn't shut up, she was going to gag him. Why was the detective so talkative, anyway? Was he giving information or cleverly getting it?

She put her demitasse on the coffee table and sat

back in her chair, studying the men.

The Tiffany lamp cast a rosy shadow on the group. Paola always said that pink lighting was the most flattering, if you were over twenty-five. The others all were past that landmark, but Mina didn't feel younger by comparison. She didn't know how or what she felt. She seemed to be watching her own life from a great distance, as if it belonged to someone else.

Brian caught her attention when he mentioned her name. Was it just she or could the others see the glow in his eyes when he spoke about her?

"Mina came to see me with Paola when I got back from Chicago," he said. "That was the first time I'd met her. She acted like a brat most of the evening."

She'd almost forgotten that meeting. "Why had you gone to Chicago? Paola was very vague about the whole thing." Was that really her, asking the question? Her voice sounded so far away.

"That whole trip was a nightmare." Brian looked at Paco, as if asking permission to tell her. Paco nodded. "Paola sent me to follow Michael. She thought we were going to catch him with his hand in the cookie jar, so to speak. We'll never know for sure, I guess."

"Know what?" she asked.

Brian sat forward. "When Michael made several trips to the Chicago area without bringing back any orders, your sis—sorry, I can't get used to this—your mother became suspicious.

"Up to that time, Paola didn't believe Michael was involved with the missing disks. But what if he was making these trips to sell disks that weren't his in the first place? So, on that trip to Chicago, I followed him. Everything seemed on the up-and-up—until we got to the airport."

"Was he alone the whole time?" Mina asked.

"Well, he had lunch with the purchasing agent of one of the businesses he visited. But no female company, if that's what you mean."

Paco twirled his Corona and sighed. "Some mess those missing disks got us into. Almost put Mrs. Davies out of business. I just knew there was something wrong. I would walk through that warehouse and—even though everything looked the same—I knew someone had been there. Weird, I tell you. I kept telling Mrs. Davies we ought to do inventory and we ought to be more careful. But she trusted that two-timing husband of hers."

De Fiore spoke into the silence. "Maybe you should have done something about it, taken charge maybe."

"Well," Paco grinned up from his beer, "I did."

It seemed like an invisible hand suddenly turned up the thermostat in the room. All the men sat forward, their attention riveted on Paco.

"What did you do?" De Fiore asked.

Paco swigged the last of his beer, shrugged and put down the empty bottle. "It's quite simple. Every time we received a new shipment of disks, I marked them."

De Fiore slumped. "The boxes?"

"No, too easy to get rid of those. I marked the disks."

"All of them?" Brian asked.

"Every one."

"That must have taken you forever." Mina said.

"Not really. After I opened the boxes with a razor blade, I slashed a precise line on the edge of the disks. Always the same way, in the same spot." Paco's eyes twinkled. "One long swipe and all the disks had an identical, almost invisible notch. To anyone else, it would look as if it had happened when the box was opened."

"Doesn't that ruin the disks?" Mina asked.

"Oh, no. I didn't cut deep enough to do damage. Just enough for identification."

Mina didn't get it. She looked over at the other two. Brian shrugged.

Only De Fiore seems to understand. "Clever, Paco. Very clever. Any luck so far?"

"No, but I haven't given up. I still make my rounds."

The detective fished a card from his wallet. "This isn't really my department; however, there may be a connection. If you think you're getting close to something, call me on this direct line." He handed the card to Paco. "Don't try to play the hero."

"Excuse me for being stupid," Mina said, "but what exactly is Paco doing with the slashed disks?"

"After I'm done, I reseal the boxes," Paco said. "They usually disappear within a couple of days. On my days off, I drive with a friend to Computer Swap Meets—both here and in LA—and I shop around. I'm hoping someone will offer me the notched disks—at a greatly discounted price, of course."

"Because they're stolen," De Fiore added.

"That was a great idea, Paco. I hope something comes of it." Brian got up and stretched, then sat down next to her on the couch. Mina knew he hoped the other two would leave.

"Care for another beer?" she asked Paco.

"No thanks, Mina. I should get going. Detective Fiore..." He hesitated. "I don't mean to intrude, but what's going on with Mrs. Davies' investigation? I mean, do you think there's a connection with the other? You know. Rachel."

"Hard to say, hard to say. Paola Davies' murder doesn't make too much sense," De Fiore said. "There wasn't any forced entry. The entire world could have walked in. Michael Davies left the garage door wide open all night. The drunken fool was passed out cold in his parked car."

The anger in his voice brought fresh tears to Mina's eyes. "I didn't know that," she said. Brian touched her hand with the tips of his fingers.

De Fiore continued. "Some neighbors noticed the lighted garage on their way back from a party. They stopped to check, saw Michael in the car. Realizing he was drunk, they weren't sure what to do, but he seemed all right. Just sleeping it off. They went home, forgetting Michael until they heard about Paola." He paused. "She was probably already dead when they came by, but we'll never know for sure. Such a waste."

Mina sobbed softly. Brian slipped his arm around her, caressed her hair.

"I'm sorry, Mina," De Fiore said, his voice more human than she had ever heard it. "I shouldn't bring this up right now. Being a policeman makes you socially inept."

"No, go on," she managed to say, "I want to know what else you found out—please."

"There isn't much more to tell. The paperboy came by in the morning, saw a man passed-out in a black Corvette, and called the police. I wish we had something to pin on Davies, but we don't."

"It would comfort me to know that she didn't suffer," Mina said.

De Fiore got up, began pacing. Couldn't he see the pleading in her eyes?

"She went to sleep, Mina, that's all. That's why we thought suicide."

"In other words, she died of an overdose," Brian said.

"She drank a glass of wine loaded with a lethal dose of Seconal and a small quantity of Soma Compound."

"Her own medicine?" Mina asked.

"I told you, it doesn't make sense. Not yet. We have her prescribed drug on the nightstand, but no Seconal in the house. Michael swears Paola never used it, and her doctor confirmed he never prescribed the drug." Lowering his voice, he continued. "Whoever killed her brought the Seconal and left with the empty capsules and the bottle. I intend to find that person or persons. I promise you that."

Mina wiped her eyes. When she lifted her head to thank the detective, she saw Michael standing in the archway.

"Who let you in?" *The front door was locked,*

wasn't it?

De Fiore took a step toward him, but Michael raised a hand and spoke. "Since you are all here, I thought it would be okay if I stopped by to get some of my things."

Mina bit back the words she was going to say when she saw his anguished eyes. Where was Adams when she needed him? "I guess that will be all right. Paco, will you go with Michael while he packs?"

Her heart like ice, she played the perfect hostess in what had been Michael's home, even offering him coffee when he came downstairs from packing.

De Fiore waited to say his good-byes until her brother-in-law was finished, then accompanied Michael down the walk. From the door, Mina watched him get in his old green sedan and follow Michael's black Corvette down the street, around the corner.

Later, after Brian and Paco had left, she felt guilty for ignoring that look of desperation in Michael's eyes. She wanted to hear a human voice, something alive and vital in the empty house.

She found Brian's number in Paola's handwriting under the S's.

"Mina!" He answered after her hello.

"I hope I'm not catching you at a bad time."

"Of course not. I'm glad you called. I felt funny about leaving tonight. I didn't know if you wanted to be alone."

"What are you doing?" *Should she tell him about the nightly phone calls?*

"Studying. I have a test coming up."

She heard a woman's voice in the background. "You've got company. I ought to let you go," she said.

"Thanks, Mom." Mina smiled at his emphasis on the word. "My mother spoils me. She just brought me a cup of hot cocoa."

"With marshmallows?"

Brian laughed. "No, no marshmallows. So now you know my weakness—hot cocoa." He must have covered the receiver with his hand, because the rest of what he said was muffled. "It's my friend, Mina Calvi. I will, good night, Mom. Sorry, Mina."

"Please, don't apologize. You know, I had never seen marshmallows until I came to America. At first I thought they were miniature meringues, until I touched them, of course. I should let you study, huh?" She didn't want to hang up.

"Are you afraid of being in the house alone? Do you want me to come over? I could bring my books."

Put on your red shoes—tell him about the calls.

"Thanks, but I may as well get used to it. It's nice of you to ask. I just wanted to hear a voice, and I thought of yours. I'd better go now."

"You can call me anytime, I'll be up late."

"Brian..." *Talk to him, he cares.*

"Yes?"

"Oh, nothing, it can wait. Good night. And thanks for being there."

CHAPTER 21

Mina's eyes flung open. In the darkness of her bedroom, the alarm clock showed twelve forty-five a.m.. Two hours of sleep, almost a miracle! Something had awakened her, what? She listened for unusual noises or strange creakings, but there were none. Could it be anticipation and fear for the one-thirty call? *Go back to sleep, Mina.*

She pulled the covers up to her chin and lay there awake for a while, eyes wide open. *Put on your red shoes*—Maybe she should phone Brian. To say what? "Hi, I'm scared; come hold my hand?" Forget it.

She sighed and slid a little further under the sheets. Michael's abrupt visit spooked her. She was sure the front door had been locked. How had he gotten into the house?

Her heart jumped. This time the noise was unmistakable—a creak from the stairs. Automatically, her hand searched for the light switch. No, that would mean giving away that she was awake.

She held her breath, her pulse pounding in her throat. *nine one one, dial nine one one, now.* Instead, she remained absolutely still. Time passed, when the sound didn't repeat itself, her heartbeat slowed and her breathing returned to normal.

Nothing to worry about, all the doors were locked. The emptiness of the house was getting to her. Maybe she should sell it. And then what? What was it that American say; *home is where you hang your hat*? Maybe she should buy a hat. Buy, sell, certainly that decision could wait until morning. Right now, she needed to get some sleep. A glass of warm milk would help.

Turning on the bedside light, she crawled out of bed. The room went dark. *Don't panic; don't panic.* She reached over and flipped the switch a few times, but the light was well and truly out. Great. A sense of urgency overcame her. Sweat dampened her nightshirt. It clung to her body like a shroud. She had to get her milk and rush back to bed before one-thirty. Yes, and she should be near a phone at all times *but,* she would *not* pick up that phone if it rang.

Enveloped by blackness and fear, Mina crept to the hall, clicked on the switch. A flicker, then darkness: another burnt-out light bulb? Two in one night? *Okay, God, is this a test?*

She had never changed a bulb in her life; she didn't even know where Paola kept them. The idea of selling the house was becoming more appealing by the minute.

A sound from the stairs, a creaking, like before. Mina jumped. This was ridiculous. Houses creaked—she had to get used to it. She just never noticed it when Paola was alive. Rationalization may be good at the office but it failed her completely in the pitch-dark hall. Even her body seemed to move at a slower pace, the only part of her working overtime was her heart walloping in her jittery chest. Standing still wasn't going to solve anything.

Mina slid her hands along the smooth wall, making her way to where the hall curved into the stairway. She searched for the switch to the chandelier; her fingertips met something warm, something human.

Mina screamed. Three night's worth of fear and frustration were crammed into that scream. A hand grabbed her wrist.

"Shhh, it's me."

The lights came on. Her brother-in-law stood on the top stair. His tie was askew, his hair disheveled.

"Michael, *maledizione*, what the hell are you doing here?"

"I didn't mean to startle you," Michael said.

"Well, you did. Let go of me." She jerked her arm out of his grasp. The strength of her voice surprised her; her fear vanished. "How did you get in?"

"Through the window."

"Tell me which window so I can lock it, and then get out."

"Mina," he said, his tone hopeless, "can we talk? Please."

He looked exhausted, defenseless. This was not the nasty, gutter-mouthed brother-in-law she was used to. Under her silent appraisal, he smoothed his hair, straightened his tie. She recognized that edginess, felt its kin under her own skin.

Instead of calling the cops, she sat on the edge

of the landing and stretched her sweatshirt to cover her knees. Michael hesitated a moment, then sat down too, keeping his distance.

"I want to know how you got in—and I mean both times." She couldn't bear to look at him. "Start talking."

"Both times? Oh, this afternoon. The front door was locked, but the kitchen door wasn't. I came in that way. And, while all of you were busy talking in the living room, I unlocked the window in the laundry room."

"You did what?"

"I didn't know you'd be here tonight. I thought maybe you'd spend the night at a friend's house. No one would ever have known."

Something in his voice forced her to glance at him. "Known what, Michael?"

He sucked his breath in, smothering a sob, then cleared his throat. When he spoke, his voice was barely a murmur. "I want to spend the night here, one last time."

"You've got to be kidding," she said. "Where?"

"You know." He pointed to Paola's room.

Was he crazy? She thought again of calling the cops. "What do you want?" *Stall until you figure out how to make him leave.*

"I want to stay, just for tonight. I won't touch anything and I'll never bother you again, I promise."

"I didn't know you were so sentimental." The man was a liar. She knew that. He was a thief and a cheater. *He could be a murderer.*

"Please, Mina."

He raised his eyes to hers. In his pain she found an echo of her own. "Just for tonight, huh?" she heard herself saying.

"Yes." He choked on the word. No, he was choking on his tears.

"The bed isn't made. It's still the same way—it's okay, I'll help you put on clean sheets."

"Thanks, I can handle it," he said.

"Do you know where Paola keeps...sorry, of course you do. Tonight only, right?"

"I swear." He got up and waited.

She didn't move, didn't say anything as he walked to the bedroom. Why was she being so weak? Let him stay after all he'd said and done?

We can all use some kindness at the beginning and at the end. It was a line from the play *Evita*. Was she being kind or stupid? The door clicked softly as it closed behind Michael.

She went downstairs, locked the laundry room window. On the way back up she listened, expecting to hear drawers opening and closing, the squeak of cupboards, but only silence came from Paola's room.

It was past one a.m. Very soon the phone would ring. Wait. Wait. Paola's princess phone was on the night table where Michael—yes! She would let the phone ring. Michael would pick it up and answer. *Si, si, good.*

Back in her room, she locked the door and went to bed, where she waited, tossing and turning, all kinds of what ifs whirling through her mind. Now that she had lost Paola, she was all alone in this world. No family, no close friends. In the dark, she checked her clock, her telephone. What would become of her? Maybe she should go back to Italy. The three-story *casa* flashed in her mind's eye. Mina sighed; maybe this was a good time for a Hail Mary.

She fell asleep shortly before sunrise. The phone never rang.

* * * * *

In the morning, Paola's bedroom door was wide open, the bathroom empty and the bed the same way it was before Michael's surprise visit. On the floor lay a folded blanket and a pillow.

Michael was gone. Better see what else was missing.

Mina opened and shut drawers, closets, doors. Nothing. She'd decided to give up on her search when she noticed the photograph missing from the dresser. It was a small silver frame with a picture of Paola and Michael taken at Yosemite, in happier times. Poor Michael. Where was he now? Did he have any money? Should she have offered him a job at West Coast Software? Maybe she could discuss that with Paco later on. After all, Michael was also alone.

Mina surveyed her casual clothes. Now that she was a businesswoman, she'd better dress the part, as Paola used to say. One suit—Italian design, navy blue, fitted—hung at the end of the closet, still in the plastic cleaner's bag. They had bought it for some occasion; she couldn't remember what, only that Paola had insisted. She stripped the flimsy plastic and took it off the hanger.

Beautiful garments hung in Paola's walk-in

closet. Mina knew she could have them altered for herself, but no. She could never wear them. They should be given to someone special.

Sadness returned. Mina stood there, the suit in her hand, staring at nothing until the clock chimed nine. Shaking herself, she finished dressing. She had to get going; lots of people were depending on her.

She parked in Paola's spot, aware of how odd the VW looked among the other automobiles. When she entered the front office, the phone was ringing. Where was Margo? Mina picked it up. "West Coast Software, may I help you?"

"Mina? Good morning," Adams said. "What's going on? The phone must have rung a dozen times."

"Margo is probably in the bathroom, attending to one of her beauty-related emergencies."

"I'm glad to hear your sense of humor is coming back. One moment, Mina." She heard him speak to someone else, his voice muffled. "I'm back. I've arranged for Cindy to stop by after she's finished here. She'll try to help you make some sense of the business' financial status. By the way, we canceled all the company credit cards and Michael's cellular phone. I thought you should know."

"Speaking of Michael, there's something I should tell you." She told him about the surprise visit the night before. He wasn't happy.

"Mina, really. You are leaving yourself open for bad situations. I don't want you to have anything else to do with Michael without my being present. You must learn to say no. Remember, he's still a suspect."

"*Si, si, lo so.* I know."

Adams continued, "Brian is having breakfast with De Fiore right now, hoping to get the latest news. Anyway, how does it feel to be in charge of the business?"

Startled by his abrupt change of tone, Mina fumbled. "Um, well, I don't know yet. You'll be the first person I'll tell when I figure it out." She lowered her voice. "Listen, Adams, about the Fernandez matter—"

"Don't worry, Mina. Have a good day, and call if you have a question about anything. I'm never too busy for you."

He hung up, leaving Mina puzzled. Maybe someone came into his office. That was the only thing that would explain his sudden breeziness.

The phone rang again. *Maledizione*, where was Margo?

Mina checked the ladies' room; empty. If she was out flirting with the workers, Mina would kill her.

The roar of machinery hit her before she opened the warehouse door. Margo, decked out in an orange polka-dot dress, stood in front of an idling forklift waving her arms and talking to Ishmael Fernandez, who sat in the driver's seat. The noise of the forklift drowned out her words and made Mina frown.

Ishmael noticed her and, without warning, shifted gears. The forklift began to move. Margo jumped back and saw Mina.

"Good morning," Margo pushed past her. "I had

to give Ishmael a list." She crossed the reception area quickly and answered the telephone. In spite of Margo's heavy make-up, Mina could tell she'd been crying, but she couldn't quite summon up the nerve to ask her why.

Paco came into the warehouse through the bay-door and saw her. He smiled and said, "Good morning, Mina. May I buy you a cup of coffee in our new office?"

Laughing, she held the door open for him. They went down the hall and into the office that Michael and Paola had shared. Paco poured the coffee and handed her a cup.

She took in the pleated trousers and white shirt under his open lab coat, "What, no tie?" Mina said.

Paco blushed.

"Did you have any problem opening up this morning?"

"No. I've opened the office before, you know." Paco said.

"True. However, you're now in charge of the whole business, including the security area." She pulled a wrinkled paper from her purse. "I'd better memorize these numbers before I lose them."

Paco closed his eyes, pretending he was pushing buttons while reciting. "Two, four, two, six." He sat back and picked up the phone from the desk. Without dialing, he spoke into it, "Good morning, American Alarm, this is West Coast Software, we are opening up for the day. I'm Paco Mendez, two, zero, one, eight."

"You mean you don't say, Paco Mendez, vice president?" Mina giggled.

He shook his head, his eyes mischievous. "Not that I wasn't tempted."

Mina motioned for him to hang up the phone, put a finger to her lips and pointed to the front office where eavesdropping Margo was probably busy listening. "Since you opened, I'll close. Okay?"

"You don't need to."

"I promised Adams I'd wait for Cindy. She's coming by after work to pick up some files." *Fernandez*, she mouthed.

Paco nodded. "Well, since you have to stay anyway, I'll let you close. My wife will be surprised to see me on time for dinner."

* * * * *

That evening, West Coast Software was too quiet with everyone gone. It made her nervous. For the hundredth time, she glanced into the parking lot. Very few cars left. What was keeping Cindy? Mina went back into her office, sat down and kicked off her shoes. How long would it take her feet to adjust to heels? A light knock on the front door sent her sprinting through the reception area in her stockinged feet.

By the time she recognized De Fiore through the glass pane, it was too late to go back into the office and pretend no one was there. Besides, Cindy might be right behind him. She sighed and opened the door.

"Good evening, detective," she said.

"Mina, I'm looking for Paco." He frowned when he said the name.

"Sorry, you just missed him."

"Was he going straight home?"

"I suppose. You can call his house, although he may not be there yet."

De Fiore stood as if debating with himself. "Since I'm here, I might as well take a look at the files." He strode into her office.

"What files?" she asked, following him.

"Relax." He flashed her a smile over his shoulder. "I just want to take a peek at the Fernandez' files."

"Haven't you done that already?" Mina said. He didn't answer. "Adams' secretary needs them. She's coming for them any minute."

He was already opening the file drawer. "I told you, I just want to take a peek."

"They ought to be in alphabetical order," she said. "There are so many of them and, what's worse, they're all related."

De Fiore fingered through the tabs, then stepped back and looked at the label on the drawer. "If I'm not mistaken, all the F's should be in here."

"That's right."

He rechecked every file carefully. When he was done, he slammed the drawer shut. "Dammit, I should have known. The Fernandez files are missing."

CHAPTER 22

"Gone, poof, disappeared." The minute she got home, Mina had called Paco. "Yes, all of them. Cindy and I searched the front office—nothing. All the Fernandez files are missing."

"And De Fiore wanted to see me?" Paco asked.

"That's what he said." Getting milk out of the refrigerator, Mina poured herself a glass, put it in the microwave and hit the timer.

"My wife was here all day, and I came straight home from the office," Paco said. "He never called or came over."

"I wouldn't worry about it. He knows how to find you." The microwave buzzer went off and she yawned. "It's been a long day, I'm going to bed. See you tomorrow—you are opening up, right?"

"Sure, I'll open. Have you heard anything from Michael? You want to make sure all your doors and windows are locked, Mina."

"Don't worry, I won't let the bogeyman get me. *Ciao."* The *bogey*man. Another great, untranslatable American expression.

After hanging up the phone, Mina sipped some milk from her glass. Why would anyone have taken those files? She put the milk back in the microwave, set the timer for one minute and stared at the rotating glass. What she really needed was a good night's sleep. Was last night the end of the red shoes caller? She closed her eyes, relaxing. The phone rang.

"Yes, hello."

"Hi Mina, this is Brian."

Her heart did a small pirouette. "Oh, *ciao*, how are you?"

"I'm fine, thank you." Her microwave buzzer went off. "Is someone at your door? Is it locked?" he asked.

"Yes to your last question, and no to the first." There was a long silence at the other end. "Hellooo, are you there? Hey, I didn't mean to be flippant, it's been a long day."

"It's okay," he said. "I don't know if it's too soon, but I was wondering if you might like to go to a movie?"

"Tonight?"

"No, of course not. Tomorrow, after work maybe? We could grab something to eat first."

"Sounds fine," she said. "Let's talk about it tomorrow afternoon, see how things are going. Okay?"

"Sure. Adams told me what happened last night. Are all your doors and windows locked?"

Oh, not him, too. "Yes, Brian, but I'll check them again, just in case."

"Want me to stay on the phone while you do that?"

"It's really sweet of you, but I don't think it's necessary." Mina didn't want to say goodnight, and she thought she sensed the same feeling at the other end of the line. For a moment they were silent.

"I'll see you tomorrow then, sleep well," he said.

"I will. *Buona notte*, Brian. See you tomorrow."
Sleep well, sure.

Because she'd promised, Mina toured the house, checking windows and locks, turning off the lights. Everything was quiet, peaceful. Upstairs, she paused in front of Paola's bedroom. The door was open, and Mina blew a kiss in the direction of the big empty bed.

Good night, Paola. I love you. I miss you. *Buona notte, Mamma,* wherever you are.

* * * * *

A black Corvette with tinted windows inched ahead in the fast lane. Could it be Michael? Mina maneuvered the Bug across two lanes of traffic. She got the finger from the driver she cut off in the middle lane, but she didn't care. The fast lane halted, and she finally caught up.

A glance through the dark glass revealed nothing. The driver must have noticed her maneuvering because he changed lanes in pursuit of the VW.

At first, Mina didn't pay too much attention. Apparently the driver wasn't giving up. Having the Corvette shadowing her rear bumper made her nervous. On impulse, she pulled out at the first available freeway exit and found herself headed for Irvine. The black car right behind hers.

Where was she?

The street sign read *Red Hill*. Oh, Okay. Now if she could figure out which direction to go, she'd be fine. She drove in the center lane while debating which way to turn. Both cars came to a halt, side by side, at a red light.

From the corner of the eye, Mina could see the passenger's side window of the Corvette sliding open. *Stay cool.*

"Hi, baaabe."*Baaabe? Would that be what Americans refer to as 'A wolf in sheep's clothing'?* Well, that middle age sheep-wolf could use better clothing and—a haircut. To compensate for his lack of hair on top, the well-fed man wore the back part of it in a long, oily ponytail.

The old Mina would have stuck out her tongue at him, then hit the gas. But this Mina was wearing a business suit and—high heels. So, she simply ignored him. He wasn't giving up that easy.

"Whatch you doing, baaabe?" He wiped sweat off his forehead with the back of his hand.

Mina played the deaf-mute. When the light turned green, the man retreated back to the driver's side. He turned up the volume of his car radio as the window closed.

"Put on your red shoes, let's dance—"

The music exploded in her head. *Oh, Dio Mio!*That song. The same song she heard on the phone, night after night.

"Mister, hey, wait."

The black Corvette was already vanishing to the left in a squeal of tires. Mina gunned her yellow rag top cutting off a motorist turning left. She wasn't rational. *She had to know.*

Now the car turned into what appeared to be an industrial park. Mina didn't know where they were headed. From behind one of the buildings, she could see a huge, colorful balloon floating in the sky. The kind used on promotional stints, like when they opened the new Albertson's in Mission Viejo.

The Corvette parked, the engine running. Mina pulled up right behind it. She got out of her car, strode up to the driver side, and tapped on the window. Ten seconds went by, then the glass glided open. The sheep-wolf looked surprised, gave her a silly smile. "Yesss—" He stared at her, in anticipation, a cigarette dangling from his mouth.

"Excuse me, is that the radio or a tape?"

His expression changed, "What the hell?" Without removing the cigarette he sneered"Tape? Tape? Yeah, this is a CD. Ever heard of CDs where you come from? You followed me here, babe, so don't give the music line."

She bit her tongue, tried again. "You were listening to a song." Mina hummed, "Put on your red shoes—"

"So?" He looked really ticked off.

She didn't care. "What's the title of the song? Who is singing? Where can I get it?" She blurted it all out without a breather.

She could tell by his glance he thought her to be a lunatic. He puffed on his cigarette, flicked the butt through the air, barely missing her.

"David Bowie, *Let's Dance*. This is California, not Bosnia. You can get the CD in any music store. Even at K-Mart." He looked at her as if she were dirt. "Hell, you may even get it over there," He pointed in the direction of the floating balloon. "Move your shitty car," he said and his window went up.

Mina got into her VW, backed up to let the Corvette pass and then, without giving it a thought, drove toward the balloon.

David Bowie, the English rocker? What was the meaning of it? Was there a connection between Bowie and Paola's death?

*Put on your red shoes...*Someone was trying to scare her, *trying?* No, someone had her scared to death. And she was going to find who that someone was.

Mina circled a large building and ended up by an electronically controlled gate that was open. A huge painted sign on the gate announced: FORT KNOCK. *Cute.*

Dozens of cars randomly parked had spilled out the strange mix of population that filled the area behind the gate. People walked around aimlessly, staring at—the grounds?

Never one for resisting temptation, Mina crossed the gate.

Upon closer scrutiny, the crowd wasn't looking at the grounds after all.

Tables covered with a variety of things were lined up across the length of the building. She finally realized what this was about, a self-storage business.

A young man with short, curly dark hair and soft brown eyes approached her; "You look lost, may I help you find whatever you are searching for?" *Searching, how appropriate.*

"What are you selling? I mean, you are selling, right?"

He had a nice smile, "You have an accent..." She nodded yes. "We are selling the contents of overdue rental spaces. We used to do it on weekends but then the competition from garage sales was hurting us. Now we do it on weekdays, twice a month."

"Oh, I'm probably at the wrong place, I happened by—do you have any CDs or tapes?"

"As a matter of fact we do. That way." He put his hand on her elbow, guiding her toward the corner end of the building. His touch annoyed her and the soles of her feet were starting to hurt. Damn shoes. She should be at the office. What got into her?

The place was set up in sections, like a regular store, and there seemed to be something for everyone. Used TV, stereos, books, clothing, and kitchen utensils, even a doghouse.

At the very end of the row of bay doors, there was a section for audio-visual and computer related products. Both sections were crowded with young people, some looked like students from nearby UCI, others could have been field workers or passer-by like herself.

Something caught her attention as she walked by the computer table.

Boxes, ordinary cardboard boxes, like the ones West Coast Software used to ship diskettes.

"Wait." She broke away from her guide and approached the table. The shipping labels from the boxes had been scratched out.

"People leave stuff like this behind?" She asked, surprised.

"Not really. The owner owns one of the largest discount-software stores in Los Angeles and from time to time he sends down a shipment for us to sell."

Mina picked up a diskette, "Are they any good?"

"Of course they are."

Still holding the disk in her right hand, she let her thumb slide lightly around, feeling each edge. Even before the impact began to hit her, she knew. The feeling rose from inside, rushed through her entire being. A gush of euphoria, quick and completely unexpected.

There it was, nearly invisible to the eyes. A tiny nick, the swipe of a blade. Paco's masterpiece. The missing diskettes.

"Are you okay?"

Before answering, Mina took a deep breath. She couldn't afford to expose herself. "How much?" She waved the disk in the young man's face.

"We sell them by the box," he smiled, "the more you buy, the less you pay, cool huh?"

"Whoa! I have a couple of friends who are looking for bargains like these. We could share. How many can we get?"

Now he laughed, "I thought you were looking for CDs."

"I can always get CDs. I'd rather get my friend here, see what kind of deal you'll give us."

"I'm not the one. You need to talk to my father. He's the manager. I'm just helping out."

Mina pulled another disk from the same box as the first one. She wanted to be sure while not getting the young helper suspicious. Her lips opened in a sexy smile while her finger went on reconnaissance mission. Now she was sure.

"I'll talk to my friend. We may be back. What time do you close?" It was hard to hide all the turmoil inside her. She kept on smiling, waved goodbye, and went back to her car. At a phone booth a hundred yards away, she dialed Brian's number.

With each ring, she renewed her plead to God; *per piacere, Dio Mio,* please, dear God, let him be there, let him pick up the damn phone.

He did, on the third ring.

* * * * *

It was close to ten o'clock when Mina arrived at West Coast Software. Inside, Paco sat at Margo's desk.

"I'm sorry to be late. Where's Margo?" She avoided looking Paco in the eyes, worried he may read the truth in her own.

"You mean she didn't call you? I already tried her apartment—no answer. This concerns me. I don't remember Margo ever missing a day of work."

"Would you like me to sit in for her?" *She wanted to be by the phone anyhow.*

"You'll have to. None of the Fernandezes came to work, either."

"Good riddance." Mina plopped her purse down on the floor as Paco rose from the receptionist's chair. It was going to be a great day after all. She smiled. And an even better evening.

"There isn't much to smile about. Think like an

owner, Mina. We're shorthanded." *If he only knew about the disks.*

"Sorry. I always thought the Fernandezes were just a bunch of leeches that kept their jobs because of Michael." She sat down in Margo's chair.

"Yes, Madame President, but with Margo, Ishmael, and the Fernandez sisters gone, it makes seven people missing in one day. And that's a problem."

The phone rang before she could answer him, and he walked away, shaking his head.

* * * * *

Mina was in the middle of a call when Paco came in from the warehouse around eleven-thirty. "One moment, I'll transfer you to shipping," she said, and punched the release button.

"Haven't you reached Margo yet?" he asked.

Mina dropped the receiver into the cradle. "I've been trying since I got here. I hate doing this."

"I'll see if I can get someone from the assembly line to relieve you, but I'm not sure any of them speak good enough English."

Mina leaned back in the chair and stretched. "Maybe we should get a temp, what do you think?"

"I don't know. It's expensive to use an agency." He looked at her. "Mina, are you sure you don't know where Margo is? You seem—you are—I have the feeling you are hiding something from me."

She wasn't going to blow it now. Act busy, preoccupied "—All the things I need to get done. I tried to go through the files, but this damn thing rings so much, I just keep running to pick it up."

Right on cue, the phone rang.

"See?" She punched the incoming line. "West Coast Software, may I help you?" When she recognized the voice on the other end, she looked up at Paco, pretending to be surprised. "Good morning to you too, Detective De Fiore. Yes, he's here. Can you hold please?" Depressing the hold button, she said. "He's on line two. He needs to speak to you at once."

Displeasure showed on Paco's face. "I'll take it in the office."

The UPS man came in for her signature, and she told him to take the delivery to the back. As the door closed behind him, Paco emerged from the office, beaming. "Mina, I've got to go to the police station."

"What for?" She lied.

"They think they've found some of the missing disks."

"Who?"

"The police. Sorry to leave you here like this, but I'll be back as soon as I can."

"What about someone to relieve me?" she yelled, but he was already out the door. Anticipating Paco's reaction once he knew the whole story, she let out a joyful, "All right!"

* * * * *

At four o'clock the workers went home, but still no sign of Paco. Mina hadn't heard from Brian since she left him at FORT KNOCK with De Fiore. If he expected her to go out to the movies with him now, he didn't know Italian women. He could have called.

No lunch, no breaks. She finally took the phone

off the hook and went to the ladies' room. No matter how broke the company was, she'd hire a temp for tomorrow.

When she came out of the restroom, a red-haired deliveryman stood inside the front door, his back turned to her. She cleared her throat, loudly. He turned and she saw the roses. Red roses, long-stemmed, beautiful.

Maybe Brian knew Italian women after all. She stepped forward.

"Hi," he said. "I'm delivering flowers for—" he checked his clipboard "—Margo Swift."

Mina's smile faded. "She isn't here."

"That's okay, can I leave them? You can give them to her, right?"

"Right." These gorgeous roses were for Margo? Unbelievable.

"Well, okay. I'll just leave them here." He put the green container with the flowers on the desk, giving her an expectant look that she chose to ignore.

After he left, she counted the roses: twelve. How corny. She walked around the desk and put the phone back on the hook. From this side, she saw there was a note with the flowers. She stood there a moment trying to resist, but it was too tempting. She reached for the card.

The front door opened, and Paco burst in. "You little witch, you knew it all along." He grabbed Mina's hand and pulled her around the desk, twirling her as if they were dancing. "We did it, we did it!"

"Paco, are you crazy?" His euphoria was

catching, and she laughed and twirled with him.

"We'll get the disks back as soon as the police are finished. Mina, we're in business!" He hugged her, and then twirled her again. "Next we find out where the original disk with the info is." He added.

She felt light headed. "Can you calm down long enough to tell me what happened after I left Brian and the cops at the storage place?"

He let her go and collapsed onto the couch. "The police found the man with our stolen disks."

"You mean the thief? It wasn't the young kid, was it?"

Paco paused. "Well, no. He didn't know anything about it. And the owner of the business...actually he's a victim, too. But he should have been more careful."

"Wait just a second, Paco. I'm going to put the phones on night service. Then I want you to tell me everything." It was actually two minutes before five o'clock, but she didn't care. At least she wouldn't need to answer the phone any more. She secured the switchboard and went back to Paco.

He'd calmed down a little, and spoke with his customary seriousness. "Well, it started with you going shopping. By the way, what were you doing there? Never mind. You are so smart. So you called Brian, he phoned De Fiore."

"Paco, I already know that part."

"How did you remember about my nicking the edges?" He didn't wait for her answer. "Well when the cops confiscated the disks, the manager told them to talk to the owner of the place. The man, an Iranian, also owns a large discount software store in

L.A."

"And?"

"And he was telling the truth," Paco was saying.

"Excuse me, Paco, who was telling the truth?"

"The Iranian. Boy, you think I have an accent, you should hear that man talk. Anyhow, he showed the police an invoice for the disks, proving he bought them from West Coast Software."

"You're kidding."

"No. He said Michael Davies made the arrangements over the telephone and a woman delivered the disks in our company van. He had to pay cash in order to get such a low price." Paco leaned his head back against the couch. "Do you know what a relief this is? And your mother." He took Mina's hand and patted it. "She would be so pleased, so proud of you."

Mina didn't trust herself to speak, so she nodded.

Paco noticed the roses for the first time. "Ooh, Mina, these are nice." He got up and went to the desk. "By the way, I have a message from Brian. He tried to call you several times but the phone was busy. He's still at the police station, talking to De Fiore."

"Yeah, I'm sure he has a sore finger from all that dialing. The flowers are for Margo," she said.

"Ahhh," he nodded. "For Margo? From whom?"

"I don't know. There's a card. Do you think something's happened to her? Maybe we should read it."

Paco shook his head. "It's not right. Oh, one more thing. De Fiore wanted me to tell you there's a warrant out for Michael."

"What for?"

"Selling stolen disks."

"Paco, when he made the deal he was still an owner of the company. They can't arrest him for stealing his own stuff."

"Over half of the disks were Takawa's. And there's more—the storeowner insisted that the woman who made the delivery was Rachel Fernandez. He identified her picture."

"Well, that's possible, isn't it?"

"Mina, the invoice is dated November twenty-fourth. Three weeks *after* her death."

CHAPTER 23

Her fingers drummed on the steering wheel to the beat of the rock music, but Mina's thoughts were still at West Coast Software. She and Paco had stayed late to clear up some of the paper work. When they'd finished, he made sure the building was secure, and they left for home.

But nothing felt right. All those little things that had gone wrong today—Margo's no-show, the missing files, the missing Fernandezes.

Not to mention Brian. Better not think about him. She last saw him standing by the gate of FORT KNOCK, waiting for De Fiore & Co. And as she was leaving, he blew her a kiss, saying; "Don't forget, pick a movie for tonight."

The excitement of finding the missing disks faded hours ago. All that was left was edginess and uncertainty.

Drive back to the office, that's what you should do. If she went home with all those unanswered questions, she would only feel worse.

It was seven o'clock and the traffic was an unbroken chain of fuzzy red and white lights tailgating into the dark. The Bristol exit sneaked up on her. Braking hard, amid blaring horns from irate drivers, she maneuvered to the off ramp.

West Coast Software's parking lot was deserted. Mina pulled her car up next to the entrance. She opened the front door, locked it behind her. After turning on the lights, she went to disarm the security system.

Sitting in the same chair where she'd spent most of her day, she stared at the flowers. *What's bugging me?* It was just a dozen red roses in a glass container.

The heat came on, blowing from the vent above the desk. The flowers, with their wired stems, didn't stir, but the card waved, taunting her.

She felt like a prowler when she reached for the envelope. A knock at the front door sent her heart to her throat in a single bound. Mina peeked around the roses to see Brian standing outside, motioning for her to open the door, a carryout pizza in his arms.

Without moving, she said, "What do you want, Starrs?"

He smiled and knocked again.

"I don't know why you expect me to let you in," she said, unlocking the door. "I've been stuck here all day. You don't call; you don't send flowers. You don't even tell me how it went down with the disks..."

He came in and put the pizza on the desk. All without a word.

Mina twisted the key in the lock, heard the deadbolt fall into place, and turned.

Oh, oh, there was a strange glint in his blue eyes.

"*Cosa,* what?" she said.

He walked to her, pushed her back against the glass doors and kissed her on the mouth.

For an instant her body stiffened, ready to fight back. Instead, she slipped her arms around his neck and parted her lips to taste the wetness of his tongue. He leaned into her, pressing her against the door with his body. The chill of the glass on her back, and his warmth, lent a fever to the kiss. When he finally let her go, they both gulped for air.

"I've wanted to do this all day long," he said, his mouth in her hair. He smoothed it back, slid his lips along her neck. "Do you know how much I wanted to come over last night?"

"It's a good thing you didn't," she whispered. "I needed the rest." She felt him chuckle, and moved her hands to the back of his head, her fingers lingering where his hair came to a point to meet his shirt collar. "I'm so mad at you."

"Yeah?" he said, and kissed her again until she thought the marrow of her bones would melt.

She didn't know how long they stood, bodies molded together. She didn't want to move. With her face against his chest, listening to the beat of his heart, she felt happy for the first time in days, and a little confused.

"I hope you like mushrooms," he murmured.

"Hmmm."

"And peppers."

"Si."

"And anchovies."

She put her hands on his chest and pushed back far enough to look in his eyes. "Brian, right now, Charlie the Tuna could be tap-dancing on that pizza, and I wouldn't have a clue."

That got her another kiss, and then he said, "I was kidding about the anchovies."

They sat on the couch with the pizza between them. Between bites, she told him about Margo and the missing files, and he told her about the disks, confirming what she knew from Paco.

Cold pizza never tasted so good.

"I'm glad I followed my instinct instead of my common sense," he said.

"What do you mean?"

"I got done about seven. No one answered the phone here. I should have gone home. Instead I bought the pizza and came over. When I saw your car out there, I knew it was fate."

"Well, you almost missed me. I got here right before you did." Mina told him about her impromptu freeway exit.

"Why'd you come back?"

She pointed to the flowers. "Those roses—," she said.

"I noticed them when I came in. So," he said, his tone casual, "who's giving you roses?"

Good, he's jealous. "They were delivered for Margo."

"Something wrong with that?" Brian asked.

Mina nodded, staring at the flowers. "Suppose I read the note—what would happen?"

He laughed. "We'd both know who sent the roses, and one of us—I'm not saying which one—would sleep better."

"Brian, you don't understand. It isn't just curiosity. I'm worried about Margo, and I feel there may be a clue in that note."

He walked to the desk and plucked the envelope from the plastic holder. It wasn't sealed, and he pulled out the small square card.

"Well?" Mina asked.

He handed her the note:

Sorry it had to end this way, Margo. Don't take it so hard and don't do anything stupid. Life's worth living. Honest!

It was unsigned.

They looked at each other. "Do you know where she lives?" Brian asked.

"I need to lock up and call the alarm company," she said.

"I'll get the car."

* * * * *

They drove up in front of the large, gated apartment complex on the corner of Edinger. Brian pulled his car up to the front and parked on the street.

"Number forty-three," Mina said.

"Should we tell the manager?" Brian asked.

"Tell him what? That we have a dozen roses and we're trying to find them a home?"

Steam rose from the lit pool as they walked the wide path, past the leasing office. At this time of night, with newly planted fast-growing shrubbery still in infancy stage, the enormous complex seemed like a cellblock: identical doors opening to identical spaces. *Residents Only,* warned the sign on the covered parking. Mina spotted Margo's car in stall number forty-three.

"Her car is here."

Brian scanned the numbered doors. "Do you remember which one is hers?"

"There," she pointed to the second unit from the end. Music blared from one of the apartments, getting louder as they got closer to the end. If Margo was having a party after all that Mina had gone through that day, she'd kill her.

By the time they saw the white numbers on Margo's door, Mina could hear that the music came from an apartment upstairs. With a glance at Brian, she pushed the doorbell, heard it chime inside.

After they'd waited a moment, Mina realized that the outside light wasn't lit. The window facing them was dark, too, and the drapes weren't pulled. She rang again.

Brian peered in the window, then knocked, softly at first, then louder.

Mina touched his arm. "Maybe you should get the manager. I can wait here, just in case."

He hesitated. "Promise me you aren't going to do something stupid."

"Like what?"

Shrugging off whatever was in his mind, he moved in the direction of the office, then seemed to have second thoughts. "I'll be right back. Don't try anything, okay?"

The minute he disappeared around the corner, she tried the doorknob. Nothing. Television P.I's always got doors open with a plastic card. She didn't even have her driver's license with her. Everything was in the car. *Maledizione.* She turned the doorknob again. This time she pressed her whole body against the door. It swung open. *Yes!* In spite of the darkness, Mina saw a large white form on the floor. Her mind jumped to the nearest conclusion: *Margo!*

Legs shaking, she stepped inside. Stale, uncirculated air reached her nostrils as she entered the apartment. She turned on the lights and let out a small gasp, blinking her eyes in the flash of brightness. The white form turned out to be a love seat.

"Margo," She called out, "Margo!" No answer.

Mina examined the room. At one end an opening on the wall seemed to lead to the kitchen. Two closed doors in front of her. The first one revealed a closet full of garments in plastic bags. The other— *would she dare?*

She swung it open, and then stopped.

Dozens of votive candles flickered in the dark. Their dancing flames bathed the walls in a quivering amber glow. The candles, in glass containers, were set in front of huge posters and small photographs. All showing an androgynous face, on an androgynous body. Man or woman? The name, always in large letters, left no doubt: David Bowie!

David Bowie? Mio Dio, but this is Margo's place. Yes, Margo's place. And Margo's body, clad in a white gown, lay in the center of the large bed, arms crossed, eyes closed. Shadows and lights streaked the stillness of her face, created the illusion of a smile on her silent lips.

"Margo." Mina's voice, hoarse, seemed to come from deep inside her.

"Mina!" Brian grasped her arm. "How did you get in? Is she dead?"

Mina couldn't move, couldn't talk. She thrust her head against his shoulder.

Gently he pushed her away, turned to look at her. "Stay here and don't touch anything." He walked around the bed. Mina watched him bend over and put his fingers against Margo's throat. She could see Margo's limp hair and her waxy, bare feet showing from underneath the gown.

Brian came back to her, took Mina's arm and dragged her into the living room. The smell of burnt candles lingering in her throat stirred childhood memories. Brian went straight to the phone.

Mina finally found her voice. "Is she dead?"

He shook his head no and dialed nine one one. "We need an ambulance immediately," he said into the phone. "I suspect a drug overdose—Yes, I'm guessing—My name is Brian Starrs—Correct—I'll wait. Mina, what's the address here?" He repeated the information, hung up then dialed again.

"Brian, is she going to be okay?" She started to sound like a CD skipping.

"Detective De Fiore, please," he said into the phone. "I see. Tell him—never mind. I'm sure he'll find out soon enough. Just tell him Brian Starrs called. Thank you." He replaced the phone in its cradle.

She took a step toward the bedroom. He grabbed her arm. "Mina, we'd better wait outside. There isn't much we can do, and I want to make sure we don't destroy evidence."

"What evidence?" asked De Fiore from the front

door.

Mina jumped. How long had he been there?

"That was quick, Dan," Brian said. "She's in there."

"In the bedroom?" The detective frowned.

Mina gulped. "How did you get here so quickly?

"ESP." De Fiore stepped in, followed by another plainclothes cop. A siren wailed in the distance. "You two stay put," he said from the bedroom threshold. "What—David Bowie? Never figured her for a Bowie fan." He turned to them, "What the hell are you doing here anyhow?"

"I'll tell you later," Brian said. Mina was still shaking and he put his arm around her. "It's going to be all right," he whispered.

The siren grew louder and louder. When the ambulance turned into the apartment complex, the place was glowing in red and white strobes of light. Mina heard hurried footsteps. Two men wearing white uniforms appeared at the door. Before they could speak, Brian pointed to the bedroom.

"Hey, is there something wrong?" a young man with spooky eyes and a beer-can in his hand appeared out of nowhere, and Mina jumped. *Where did he come from?*

"Get your paws away from that door, damn it!" De Fiore yelled from the bedroom.

"And who are you, Mister?" Spooky Eyes asked.

De Fiore walked right up to him and held his badge an inch from Spooky's eyes. "I'm the one who's supposed to ask the questions," he said.

"Who are you?"

"The upstairs neighbor," he said. A policeman in uniform appeared at the front door, and De Fiore spoke to him over the young man's shoulder.

"Sergeant, talk to this clown and then seal off the area," De Fiore said, "and tell someone to turn off that damn music."

"What are they doing?" Mina whispered to Brian.

He craned his neck to see in the room, and then mimicked an injection on the arm.

De Fiore glanced over at Brian, a deep furrow between his almond-shaped eyes. "You two wait in my car," he said.

"What for?" she said, and regretted it immediately. De Fiore gave her a strange look, and then turned his stare on Brian.

"Okay?"

"Of course," Brian answered. "We called the ambulance," he added.

"And my office," replied the detective. "I know, I know."

A commotion came from the bedroom. "Now," he said to Brian.

"Let's go, Mina." He took her arm and guided her to the door.

Outside, cops were everywhere, stretching yellow tape in a wide cordon in front of Margo's apartment. Clusters of people stood in the complex's common area, some in their nightclothes, some still dressed. Before Mina and Brian reached the pool, the ambulance attendants passed them carrying a stretcher: an oxygen mask hid Margo's face.

The men moved fast. Mina tried to keep up with them in spite of her high heels, but Brian held onto her arm, slowing her down.

"I want to know where they're taking her."

"Dan will tell us. Probably Fountain Valley Hospital. It's only a few blocks from here."

"Why was De Fiore mad at us?"

"He wasn't. That's just the way he reacts under stress."

"You know him that well?"

"Yeah. Look at you. You're all shaky. Are you angry? Cold? There's a windbreaker in my car."

They reached the front gate, now wide open. Police cars were parked on both sides, some on the sidewalk. De Fiore's green sedan was behind Brian's Mustang. That's how he'd known they were there as soon as he arrived.

Brian opened the unlocked back door of the detective's automobile.

"Can't we wait in your car?" she asked.

"Let's keep him happy." She climbed in, and he got in next to her, smiling. "Besides, I've never necked in a cop's car before, have you?" He saw the expression on her face. "Just kidding."

"Yeah, I'll bet," she said.

He put his arm around her shoulders and kissed her nose.

"Hey, there isn't any handle," she said, pointing to the smooth vinyl interior of the back door.

"That's why I'm keeping the door ajar," Brian said. "Patrol cars never have handles in the back. It prevents escapes."

"No wonder you wanted to get me in here." Before he could reply, she said, "Look, here he comes."

De Fiore stopped at the security gate to talk to the other policemen. He slapped one of the officers on the shoulder and started toward the car.

"Is he going to take us to the police station?" Mina asked.

"Ask him." Brian said.

De Fiore got in the driver's seat and sat sideways, looking at them, "Well?"

"Well, what? If you don't mind, I think I should go to the hospital where they took Margo," Mina said.

"She won't know the difference."

Mina swallowed hard, "Why, is she...dead?"

"I hope not. There are a few questions—"

"Is that all you care about? Questions?"

The detective slid his legs in, closed the door and started the engine.

"Where are you taking us?" she asked.

"Didn't you just say you wanted to go to the hospital to see Margo?"

"Yes, but—"

"Thanks, Dan, we'll take my car," Brian interrupted. He shoved the door open with his foot, got out and grabbed Mina's hand. "Come on, Mina. Fountain Valley Hospital, correct?"

"Correct," the detective said. Mina could tell De Fiore didn't like it, but Brian was already out of the car. "Margo will still be in the emergency room. I need to speak to you two. Let's meet in the coffee shop." He noticed Brian's arm around Mina's shoulder and smiled.

"See you there." Brian closed the car door. He paused an instant, then knocked on the driver's window. De Fiore rolled it down.

"What?"

"Thanks," Brian said.

The smile on De Fiore's lips widened.

* * * * *

The detective waited in the hospital lobby. "Forget the coffee shop," he said. "It's quieter in the ICU waiting room, and there are vending machines. Margo will be admitted there when they're through with her in Emergency."

"This wasn't a suicide attempt," Mina said as they started walking.

"Mina—" Brian said.

"You know it, too. I could tell what was going through your head when we read the note."

Sparks flew from De Fiore's eyes. "What note? Did you take something from the apartment?" *He might have been Oriental, but he reacted a lot like an Italian.*

"Please!" For the first time Brian raised his voice. "Let's wait until we sit down."

The sole occupant of the waiting room was a man slumped over in a chair, snoring softly. They sat down in the opposite corner.

"We didn't touch a thing, Dan, relax," Brian said before anyone else could start talking. "Okay Mina, tell him what you did from the moment you arrived at West Coast Software this morning. I'll go get the coffee."

By the time Brian came back with three

Styrofoam cups in a cardboard box, she was almost through with her story. She left out the part about David Bowie, and she didn't know why. Yet.

"We'll have to go get that card," De Fiore said. "Mina, you're going with me."

"I want to stay here. Take Brian."

"This isn't a multiple choice request. I need you for the alarm company."

"Give me a minute," Mina said. She got up, walked toward the ladies' room.

In a few minutes she was back. "De Fiore, Paco is on his way to West Coast Software. I asked him to meet you outside, by the front door. Okay?"

De Fiore gave her a dirty look. "I expect to find you here when I get back."

After he left, they sipped their coffee in silence. Until Margo was transferred up, all Mina could do was wait. Brian raised the coffee to his lips, and she studied his face.

She met him when—two weeks ago? He'd become such a part of her life; she couldn't remember when he wasn't there. How could she have known a nice guy would be so...nice?

"What made you tell nine-one-one that Margo overdosed?" she asked.

"There was an empty prescription bottle on the floor by her night table and the carpet was littered with capsules."

"Hmmm." She sipped her coffee. "I wonder how De Fiore got to Margo's so quickly."

"He didn't—it was a coincidence."

"When did he tell you that?"

"While you were gone." Brian stared straight

ahead, avoiding her eyes.

"What was he doing at Margo's?" she asked.

"After midnight, the night of Paola's death, a phone call was made from Michael's car phone to Margo's number. Margo's prescription for Seconal was renewed twice in the past few weeks. Fifty capsules in all."

"And?"

He shrugged.

Mina knelt in front of him. "Come on. You're keeping something from me."

He shook his head.

"Tell me!" Her stubby fingernails dug through the cloth of his trousers. "Tell me."

"De Fiore had come to arrest Margo for Paola's murder."

CHAPTER 24

In the dim light of the hospital room, Mina watched the miracle machines keeping Margo alive. Would she come out of the coma or would she float forever in the twilight zone of the living death? And what about her secrets? *Put on your red shoes*—She looked so helpless, so spent. Was she really the mind behind Rachel and Paola's death? *Why, why, why?*

A hand brushed her shoulder, and Mina looked up. "Adams!"

Glancing at Margo's colorless face beneath the oxygen mask, the lawyer shook his head.

"Let's go," he said, "It's past three in the morning. You need some rest." Mina followed him past the policeman sitting outside Margo's door, back to the ICU waiting room—now De Fiore's temporary headquarters.

The detective seemed the only one with any energy left. Looking at Mina he said, "Go home, kid. Get some sleep. We'll call you when there's news."

Her eyes searched the room for Brian.

"He went to the restroom," De Fiore said.

Right then Brian came in, smiled at her and lifted his hand to greet Adams.

"We need to get Mina out of here," Adams said.

She caught—a glance? No, it was a feeling at the pit of her stomach telling her something just passed between Adams and Brian. *Something—secretive—what ?*"My car's at West Coast Software," she said, hiding her thoughts.

"You're in no condition to drive anyway," Brian said.

"He has a point," Adams said. "Spend the night at my house, Mina. My daughter is away, you can stay in her room." *Here it is, that feeling again.*

She was so tired that even talking seemed a major effort. When Brian put his arm around her waist and guided her out of the waiting room, she didn't protest.

"I'll drive her," Brian said to Adams.

"Good, then we'll all have a nightcap; I sure could use one."

Adams went to get his car, and Mina followed Brian to the Mustang. Once they were rolling, she closed her eyes, sadness and a sense of doom loomed over her. She kept seeing Margo's pale face, the sweaty hair stuck to her scalp, showing the gray roots. A poster child for the fleetingness of life. All her assumptions about Margo's lack of depth and mental sophistication were crushed by this new twist. *Why would she phone and play David Bowie's song to her.* De Fiore found a phone call from Mina's home to Margo's place. Could calls from Margo to Mina's phone also be tracked? Who would she ask? Who could she trust? The pit of her stomach was full of doubts. Still, stress and the long day caught up with her. Mina heard Brian mumbling something about a policeman around the clock just before she nodded off.

When she opened her eyes, they had arrived at Adams' home. Before getting out of the car, Brian cupped her face in his hands and kissed her.

Her fatigue evaporated. She could trust *him*.

"What took you so long?" Adams asked.

"We stopped to neck," Brian grinned.

"Youth! Come in, my wife's upstairs sleeping. Let's go to the den."

He led them into the wood-paneled room, paused before his liquor cabinet. "Brian, you should try this brandy." He pulled out a bottle of Stock '84.

"That's Italian," Mina said.

"Paola brought it back for me on her last trip." He poured the brandy into a snifter, his blue eyes thoughtful. "Poor Paola, poor Margo, how terrible. To tell you the truth, I never thought Margo was all that bright. Hard to imagine her plotting all this." He shook his head. "Well, enough worrying for tonight." He handed the glass to Brian.

"Next?" Adams turned to Mina.

"What are you drinking?" she asked.

"Oh, I'll stay with the brandy. I know you like sweet liqueurs. How about a Brandy Alexander?"

"No, thanks. Maybe a little Crème de Menthe."

"One Crème de Menthe coming up."

He handed her the drink then sat at his desk. The three of them sipped in silence for a moment. Then Mina said, "Adams, do you have a picture of my father?"

Adams nearly choked on his brandy.

"I'd like to know what my father looks like,

that's all."

"I've never seen a picture of him." He put down his glass and dried the tears brought on by the cough.

"You told me you knew my father. I think it's time I met him too."

"Wait a minute, young lady. I may have said I know who he is, but I've never said that I knew him."

"What's his name? Where does he live? He is alive, isn't he?"

"Mina, it's late." He glanced at Brian, who looked uneasy.

"You're right," she said. "I should have been told about my father a long time ago."

"My God, with all the craziness that's going on, you want me to—"

"I need to know. Don't you see? My past is like a puzzle. I'm asking for the missing pieces so I can put it all together and maybe understand the present."

"Very well. Brian, could you excuse us?"

"No," Mina said on impulse, "I want him to stay."

Adams stared into his brandy for a moment. "Okay, Mina," He leaned back and closed his eyes. "You must understand, I'm telling you what Paola told me. This took place in a different time, a different culture."

With a sigh, he continued, "Paola was walking home from school—she was fourteen at the time—and took a shortcut through the churchyard. A sudden summer storm hit, and she stepped inside the recessed doorframe of the church bell-tower to wait for the rain to let up."

Images of the hundred years old *campanile* flashed in Mina's mind's eye. As a child, she remembered playing hide-and-seek in that same doorframe. Dear God! Adams' voice brought her back to reality.

"When she leaned against the door, it opened and she fell backward. Someone grabbed her, pulled her inside. The heavy door shut behind her, and all she got was a glimpse of a cassock.

"She never saw the face of the man in the priest's robe. She only remembered the wet dog smell permeating his clothing. They fought; she fell on the stone floor and blacked out.

"When she awoke, it was dark and she was lying in the thick bushes behind the tower. She ran home, hysterical. Her mother sent for the doctor, who examined her and knew immediately that she'd been raped. When she told them that a priest had done it, they thought she'd lost her mind. The parish priest was old and in bad health. At the time of the rape, he'd been administering the last sacraments to a dying woman.

"The only people who knew what happened were her mother, the doctor and the parish priest. Well, the rapist too.

"Paola refused to leave the house—wouldn't eat, wouldn't talk. Her mother began to think she was mentally ill. When she realized that Paola was pregnant, they used a cousin's illness as an excuse to move to Milan. The cousin died. A year later, Paola's mother married the cousin's widower and they adopted you. They went back to your mother's hometown and Paola came to the States, to my house. You know the rest." It seemed to Mina that Adams grew older and more tired-looking as he told the story. He pulled out a handkerchief, wiped his forehead and hands.

She closed her eyes and slumped in her chair. *Dio Mio,* she expected one of those Romeo-Giulietta made-for-TV affairs. Stories of love and lust, and betrayal. *I thought I was a love child.* Love child. *Try to translate that in Italian.* Mina laughed, a brief shriek of sound.

"Mina, are you okay?" Brian asked.

She nodded, wishing everyone would disappear. She tried to imagine how it must have been for her mother. What was it Paola had written? *A frightened young girl who couldn't even tell the truth, it being so inconceivable that everyone involved labeled me 'insane.'* God, how could you have let this happen? Tears rolled down Mina's cheeks.

"You said you knew who he was," she said to Adams. "I need to know."

Adams swallowed his brandy, put the empty glass on the table. "There isn't much to tell. When Paola went to Italy on her honeymoon, her mother gave her a letter that had been sent from India. No return address. It was from a missionary, Father Anthony something...I don't remember his last name. It's in my papers, at the office."

Mina didn't move. She waited for him to continue.

"This Father Anthony—he was seeking

forgiveness, from Paola. He was your father, Mina. In the letter—it's more a confession than a letter, really—he explained that he was a young seminarian, bicycling on his way to a nearby town to visit a friend. He got caught in the rain, sought shelter in the recessed entrance to the bell tower, just as Paola did. He never knew about you."

"What did my mother do?"

"About what?"

Mina stared straight into Adams' eyes. "About this...monster."

"You mean the priest? Nothing."

"Nothing?"

"You were doing fine with her parents. No one suspected who you were and, by the time she got the letter, she was married to Michael and happy. I don't think it mattered to her anymore."

"She should have shown it to those people who thought she was insane."

"My darling girl, Paola was better than that. You'd have been the one to pay the price, and she would have done anything to protect you." He got up from his chair. "I have a headache. I'm going to get some aspirin."

Mina wiped the moisture from her cheeks with the back of her hand, "You know, Paola was named after the parish's protecting saint; Saint Paul The Apostle. What a joke." She rested her head on Brian's chest.

The phone rang once and stopped. After a moment, Mina heard someone hurrying down the wooden stairs. Adams appeared, holding a sweater in his hands.

"What's going on?" Brian asked.

Before speaking, he swallowed twice. "That was Paco; something's happened."

"Margo?"

"No, Mina, it isn't Margo." He looked at Brian. "Something happened at West Coast Software. I need to go. The police are already on the premises."

"I'm going with you," Mina said.

"It isn't necessary, you know." Again he looked at Brian.

"Excuse me?" she said. "It is my business." She grabbed her jacket and purse. "Let's go, Starrs."

Adams sighed. "We'll take my car."

When they pulled into the company parking lot, Mina felt overwhelmed by déjà vu: the flashing lights of police cars, onlookers and an ambulance. Adams drove around to the back, parked behind De Fiore's car.

"Maybe you should wait in the car," he said, protectively.

"Not on your life."

They got out of his Lincoln and pushed through to where the ambulance, engine running, was parked in front of the open warehouse door.

Adams went to talk to a policeman. Mina saw a gurney being loaded into the back of the ambulance. She started toward it.

"Wait!" Brian grabbed her arm.

She wrenched her arm from his hand, but it was too late. The ambulance doors slammed, and it pulled through the crowd and out to the street.

"Why did you do that?" she snapped. She saw Paco walking out of the warehouse with De Fiore, and shouted, "What happened? Who is it this time?"

"Mr. Davies." Paco said. "He had a heart attack in the warehouse."

"Is he—?"

"He's alive," De Fiore said. "Go home." He turned his back on her and moved to the two policemen crouched on the ground outside the bay door.

"Paco, what was Michael doing here? Did you find him? Was he stealing? Is that why you called the police?"

"Mina, take it easy," Brian said. He called out to the detective, "Dan, can we go in the office?"

De Fiore waved his hand, still talking to the men searching the ground.

"What are they looking for?" she asked.

"Let's go inside," Brian said. "Are you coming, Paco?"

"Right behind you."

Inside, all the lights were on and the door to the storeroom was open. She could see the forklift, almost against the wall where the disks were stacked.

"Would you like some coffee?" Paco asked her.

"No. I want to know what's going on. Who called the police?"

"Night security guard," Paco said. "He was doing the rounds and he heard shouting coming from the warehouse. When he banged on the bay door, the voices stopped. He heard the roaring of an engine, got suspicious and called it in."

"Voices?"

"Yes, but according to the police, they found

only Michael, lying on the warehouse floor. I got here the same time as the ambulance."

"Was someone working the night shift?" Mina asked.

"No."

"Then how did Michael get in?"

Paco shook his head.

"I'm calling the alarm company. I want to know if they got a clearance call after you and De Fiore left," Mina said.

"Good idea," Brian said.

She ran into the front office. By the time they followed her a few minutes later, Mina had the information from the alarm company. "A man called in at twelve twenty-nine and gave Paco's clearance code," she said. "He had a heavy Spanish accent."

"It wasn't me."

Mina touched Paco's arm. "I know that," she said. "The question is how did someone get your code?"

"Good question," De Fiore said from the doorway. "Mina, can you join me for a minute?" Coming down the hall, he disappeared into Michael's old office, and she followed him.

"Do you know if your brother-in-law had a gun?"

"Yes, he kept one in his car."

"A .38 caliber revolver?"

"I don't know anything about guns. Besides, he has a permit. It's in his car. Where is his car? I didn't see it outside." But De Fiore was already on his way to the warehouse.

She followed him, and then stopped by the forklift. By the smell of exhaust she could tell it had been operated recently. No one was paying attention to her. She circled the machinery, checking the ground. Like the cops were doing outside. Light reflected from a tiny piece of metal caught under the tire. She covered with her foot. Pretending to scratch her ankle, she bent down, swiftly grabbed the shining thing and pulled. Nothing. She jerked hard, felt the metal snap. Her fist clamped around what felt like a chain, a piece of jewelry. Still scratching with her fingernail, she straightened up, plopped her hand in her pocket and went back to the office where Adams had joined Paco and Brian.

"What does De Fiore want with Michael's gun?" she asked the three men.

"They found it next to Michael," Adams said. "It had been fired and there was a trail of blood from the warehouse to the parking lot."

That explained why the cops were searching the ground.

"Michael shot somebody?" Paco asked. "Who?"

"That's what the police are trying to find out," Adams replied.

"Paco, was the forklift still running when the police arrived?" Mina asked.

He nodded.

"I think someone was trying to steal our disks by the carload, using the forklift," Mina said. "But where was Michael going to stash them, in his Corvette?" *Maybe it wasn't Michael.* "Suppose he surprised the intruder and shot him—maybe the thief took off in Michael's car? We're still one car short. The thief had to get here somehow. Unless, he or she came with Michael." She felt the chain in her pocket, a few links, smooth and flexible. *Did they hold the answers?*

"I have the feeling De Fiore has that figured," Adams said. "His men have checked the license plates of every car in the parking lot against a list of stolen vehicles."

"And?" Mina said.

"A van parked by the side of the back building matches a vehicle stolen in Long Beach earlier this evening. They're dusting it for prints now."

Paco stroked his mustache. "I'll bet—"

"What?" Brian asked.

"He bets," Mina finished, "that if they pick up the Corvette, they'll find Ishmael Fernandez in the driver's seat."

"Ishmael Fernandez doesn't exist." They all turned to De Fiore, who leaned against the doorframe, looking smug.

"Ishmael is Rachel and Sarah's brother," Mina said.

"There isn't a brother in the Fernandez clan."

"There must be a mistake," said Adams.

De Fiore shook his head.

"Aspetta, wait, you're making me crazy," Mina collapsed in the receptionist chair. "How do you know he isn't their brother? What's his name if—"

"How did you find out?" Brian asked.

With an amused glint in his eyes, De Fiore answered, "The old fashioned way: I ran a check on him. He has a rap sheet three feet long. Wanted in three states."

"Detective!" The voice came from the front office.

"Wait, wait." Mina got up from her chair.

"Sit down," De Fiore said. "I don't need an escort."

"I was going to use the ladies' room," she lied.

"Yeah, right. You pulled that on me in the hospital. Stay put." He left.

Brian got to his feet.

"Are you going out there?" Mina said.

He winked at her. "Dan didn't say anything about me not following him."

In the restroom, Mina sat down and leaned her cheek against the cool metal stall. The broken chain links found under the forklift glistened in her hand. Broken or not, it looked like Paola's chain. The same one Sarah wore around her ankle. How had it ended up in the warehouse? Most important—*when*?

Margo, the story of Paola's rape, then Michael, and now this. And Ishmael, or whatever his name was. *Basta*, enough!

If he wasn't a Fernandez, then — the smoldering look between Sarah and her so-called brother flashed before her mind's eye. *Maledizione*! He was her lover; they were in this together. Now if she only had an idea of what *this* was. Was Sarah in the warehouse tonight? Who brought her there, Michael or Ishmael?

No more wondering. Time to take action.

She opened the bathroom door and heard De Fiore's voice coming from the front office. Keeping the door ajar, she held her breath and listened.

He was talking on the telephone: "Let's assume he needs quick cash. No. He didn't take anything from the warehouse, and Davies' wallet was still in his back pocket. If he acted alone, he's driving around with a bullet in his body." A pause. "Maybe, but we won't know for sure until we find the Corvette."

There was another pause and then the detective said, "I bet he's already ditched it. Look, I don't think he's going to make a run for the border. Right, Sarah. Put out an APB on her too, will you?" He waited, "Ed, how are we doing with the witness? Great—Here or at the hospital. You too." He hung up and Mina heard his footsteps receding, then the sound of the front door opening and closing.

Holding her purse against her chest, she peeked out of the bathroom, then managed to tiptoe out of the building without being noticed.

The few cops in the front parking lot were busy with the van and the tow truck.

Of all the people involved, the one who probably knew the most about this mess was Margo. If she could talk to her, she might know how to find Ishmael and Sarah too. But Margo was still in coma and time was running out. Ishmael had to be stopped from crossing the border. Now.

Mina searched her handbag for the car keys. The door was unlocked as usual, but she needed the ignition key. She sneaked into the Bug quietly, hoping to drive out unnoticed.

A hand grasped her shoulder. Someone was in the back seat. "Where do you think you're going?"

"Maledizione! Brian, you scared me."

In spite of Brian's frown, Mina recognized the concern in his eyes. She couldn't lie to him. "I'm going to find Ishmael or whatever his name is."

For a moment, he seemed uncertain. Then he sighed, "Oh, and where would that be?"

Mina didn't answer. They drove out of the parking lot unnoticed.

* * * * *

"Which way are we going?" Brian asked when Mina turned right on Harbor.

"Trust me," she said, flooring the gas pedal.

He shook his head then sat back and kept quiet. Her eyes felt like sandpaper, and she rubbed them with her fist. God, she should probably call the hospital, see how Michael was doing. After all, he was family. *Extended family? Is that what it's called?*

Mina pulled onto the freeway. Brian was staring at her, she could tell.

How would he react when he found out she was heading home? Wait a minute, how was he going to get back? His car was still parked in Adams' driveway. She gave him an oblique glance.

The motion of the car began to lull her. Fighting to keep her eyes open, she turned on the radio. Wouldn't you know it? David Bowie's *Let's Dance* filled the car.

She told Brian about the phone calls. "Why didn't you tell me?" *Mamma mia.* He sounded like a guard dog. "What else have you been hiding?"

"I won't even respond to that," Mina said, scowling and getting off the freeway.

"Hey, you're going home. Good."

"I have this feeling...you know that saying...about returning to the scene of the crime..." She didn't want to say it was woman's intuition.

"De Fiore is right. You watch too much TV."

Maybe. But De Fiore and all his cops hadn't come up with any solution. Mina turned off the engine. "You can sleep on the couch."

Brian didn't answer. He was obviously upset. *About the couch or about her private manhunt?* They got out of the car. Darkness enveloped the house. "Strange, the outdoor lights are on a timer. I wonder what's wrong now." Mina said, remembering her last experience with the burned-out light bulbs.

Her voice sounded strained but she was past tired, past sleepy. Dead on her feet, she thought, but her mind was awake, sharper than ever before. She reached into the Bug and pushed the garage door opener. Nothing happened.

"Here, let me try," Brian said, he got the same result. "It must be a fuse. We'd better use the front door. Do you know where the fuse-box is?"

Can't he hear my heart pounding? I'm scared. Shaking her head, she walked to the front door, searched for the house key in her purse. Then tried to find the keyhole in the dark.

"Where's the moonlight when you need it?" Brian put his arms around her waist and kissed the back of her neck. *He doesn't have a clue about how I feel. Something is wrong and we are walking into it.*

When Mina finally got the door open, she

switched on the hall chandelier. "At least this one's working." She said softly, listening for unusual noises, creakings or whisperings.

Brian headed toward the kitchen. "The fuse-box is probably in the garage."

"Have fun. I'm going to change," she lied. Mina removed her shoes, and started climbing the big staircase.

Don't be a hero. Just do it. Wait for Brian, there is safety in numbers. Feel the fear and do it anyway. All the American clichés she so cherished flashed through her mind. She kept climbing. Slowly, listening for a tremor of sound. Carefully, looking for the faintest movement.

Her heart pumped blood with such force she knew she would be heard. Fear licked her ankles, drenched her body. One more step. When she reached the top and flipped on the light, nothing happened. Mina remembered she hadn't changed the light bulb.

An unfamiliar smell lingered in the dark hallway, filled her nostrils. Sweat? Yes, and cheap cologne. Halfway between the landing and Paola's bedroom door, she stopped dead.

Light from downstairs glinted on the doorknob of Paola's room as it turned. The hair rose on the back of her neck. Fear, she smelled fear. Hers or...a muffled sound came from behind her. She spun around and collided with a swiftly moving body.

Someone's feet became entangled with hers. She grabbed on to the stranger. Caught in a freeze-frame, they stood. For a split second, or an eternity. And Brian's cry reached her just as they fell backward. Together they tumbled, one step at the time.

Paola's million-dollar staircase.

Thump, thump, thump.

"Fifty-thou a step," she remembered Paola's voice.

Her mind was blank, her body weightless. Only her will sustained her. She hung on to the intruder, her nails ripped his shirt, clawed his torso.

Thump, thump, thump. Her head hit the wall just as the intruder's resistance relented.

"*Mamma...*" The pain grew intense, stopped her mind.

"Mina, Mina, answer me." Her eyes opened slowly, painfully, to see Brian's face. She felt his body shaking. Or was it hers? The marble floor felt cool against her legs, her head burned on Brian's lap.

"I'm okay, Brian." She couldn't move her head. "Ouch, my head hurts."

"That's good. If you feel the pain, it's a good sign."

"Gee, Brian, I'll remember that line. It may come handy some day."

From the corner of her eye, she could see a body sprawled on the white floor of the foyer, next to her.

"Is that—?" She pointed to the form clad in a Hawaiian shirt.

"Ishmael," Brian said. "I saw the Corvette when I went into the garage looking for the fuse box."

"He's dead, isn't he?" She choked on her words.

"I don't know, Mina. I've called De Fiore. And an ambulance." He glanced behind them. "You landed on top of him and he broke your fall."

Following his gaze, she noticed the blood—bright red against the white marble—trickling from Ishmael's head to the floor.

Her fingers grasped Brian's arm so hard her knuckles turned white. She felt nauseous.

Without letting her go, Brian stretched to check the man's pulse. When his head drooped between his shoulders, she knew Ishmael was dead. Did the fall kill him? Why was her life spared? She couldn't move, couldn't think. All these deaths—why? What brought Ishmael here ? How had she known?

Something in her mind clicked. *Grazie mamma*. For the first time, the picture came into focus.

"I'll get some ice for your head." Brian, helped her to sit up, headed for the kitchen. "Stay put, I'll be right back."

She had just heard him opening the refrigerator when a cry came from the top of the stairs, echoing through the silent house.

"Asesinos. Murderers!"

Mina looked up as Sarah flew down the steps. The girl's clothes were torn, and she wore one of Mina's towels as a sling around her left arm.

When she saw Mina, she stopped. A look of hatred distorted her features. It was so intense, Mina instinctively slid back. Sarah lifted her fist and shook it, inches from her face.

Mina pushed her away with both hands. "Don't you call me a murderer. What are you doing in my house?"

Mina didn't know Brian was next to her until he grabbed Sarah and pulled her away. The girl began to sob and fell to her knees like a rag doll.

Dark red spots appeared on her towel-sling. Michael's bullet, of course. Sarah crawled away from Mina, to Ishmael's body.

"Don't touch him!" Brian warned her.

Too late, Sarah had already lifted his head onto her lap. Blood spread across her legs and skirt as she sobbed and rocked back and forth, cradling his head in her arms.

A clear plastic bag fell out of Sarah's makeshift sling. In it, Mina recognized some of Paola's jewelry.

CHAPTER 25

De Fiore rubbed his hand over his face. Even from her seat on the other side of his desk, Mina could hear his beard scratching against his palm. He looked exhausted, but no more than she. Although she hadn't seen herself in a mirror lately, she felt spent.

Ten o'clock in the morning. Sitting here with Brian in De Fiore's bland cookie-cutter office, under the glare of fluorescent lights, it was hard for her to believe that last night's events weren't just a bad dream. But the painful soft lump on the back of her head was a good 'reality check'.

"What do you want to know first?" De Fiore asked. The man may have been up twenty-four hours, but his dark eyes weren't dulled.

"Who was he?" Mina said.

De Fiore didn't have to ask whom she meant. "Amado Corea. A coyote."

"A coyote?" she asked.

"That's what we call people who smuggle immigrants across the border—that's how he met the Fernandez girls," De Fiore said. "Has a rap sheet three feet long, and warrants in Texas and Arizona."

"I.N.S?" Brian asked.

"The Texas warrant is. In Arizona he's wanted for manslaughter. We just got the file last night." De Fiore leaned over and took a folder from the top of a stack on his file cabinet. Opening it, he browsed the papers and said, "It looks like during that last heat wave, our boy tried to cross the Sonora desert with a group of illegals. He got panicky when a helicopter started circling low and abandoned them. Two died before the rescue teams arrived." He slapped the file closed and tossed it back on top of the stack. "One was his own nephew, eight years old."

Brian turned to Mina. "When did Ishmael start at West Coast Software?"

"I'm not sure. It was one of those deals Michael liked to do behind Paola's back. After Paola..." At the sting of tears, she closed her eyes. God, she was so tired, she had no defenses left. "Anyway, the files were missing, so I don't know."

De Fiore spoke up. "It was after September, if that's what you're asking. He assumed the Ishmael Fernandez alias and, thanks to Rachel, got a job at West Coast Software."

"So what happened last night?" Brian asked.

"Wait a minute, back up just a little," Mina said. "Was Michael really stealing the diskettes? Or was that another little plan of Ishmael's? I mean, Amado's."

"No, according to Michael himself, he had been taking diskettes from the business for some time. He kept them in a rented storage unit a few miles away. He also hid the original Tawaka and he said it is in a safe place."

"Why on earth would he steal from his own business?" Brian said.

De Fiore leaned forward, his elbows on the desk. "This is the most bizarre part. Michael said he wanted to force Paola out of business so he could come to her rescue."

Typical Michael. Never walk a straight line when a crooked one was available. "He wanted to be her knight in shining armor," Mina said.

De Fiore shrugged. "Whatever. Anyway, Sarah said that after Paola died, Ishmael made sure she was always close to Michael. He was an easy target, close to the edge of a breakdown. When you entered the picture, Michael lost everything. Ishmael decided to cash in on what he could. First, he and Sarah loaded West Coast Software's truck with the stolen diskettes Michael had stashed away, and sold them to that Iranian in Los Angeles, Sarah posing as Rachel.

"His next step was to strip the company of the diskettes, sell them and split with Sarah. But when Michael found the rented storage empty and all the Fernandez's gone, he knew he'd been taken. He caught up with them last night in the warehouse, and confronted them."

"But how did they get Paco's identification number?" Brian asked. "The security company said they used his access code last night."

"I'm sure that was Margo. You know how she's always eavesdropping." Mina shifted on the hard chair. "I know Margo's a sucker for anything in pants, but I can't believe she was in league with that man. He was probably the one calling me up at night."

"Ah! I'm glad you mentioned that. There were indeed calls made from Margo's phone to your house. All around one o'clock in the morning. I understand you were being— serenaded—? Yes, that was another side of Amado's twisted mind. For what it's worth," De Fiore said, "I think Margo's just another of his victims."

"How is she?" Mina asked. "I called the hospital, but they wouldn't let me speak to her."

"She's very lucky. If she hadn't had such a high tolerance for Seconal, Ishmael's dose would have killed her." Brian yawned while he was talking, and De Fiore smiled. "Sorry the tale isn't exciting enough for you, Starrs."

"How about some of that industrial strength coffee you detectives live on?" Brian said.

"Sounds good," De Fiore responded, and before Mina could blink, he was gone.

"He didn't even ask me if I wanted some," she said.

To her surprise, he came back with three cups of black coffee. Mina took a sip and recoiled. "What's in this?"

De Fiore grinned. "The secret is letting it age."

Brian swallowed half the cup in one gulp. She stared at him in amazement. "It's an acquired taste of college students," he said. "Okay, Dan, back to last night. Michael confronted Ishmael and..."

"And recognized Paola's gold bracelet around Sarah's wrist. Michael swears Paola was wearing it the night she died. I guess he had suspicions about Paola's death, and that just confirmed it. He literally ripped it off her, and started waving his gun around. He and Ishmael really got into it, but when they heard someone banging on the bay door, they stopped fighting."

"Then how did Michael get hurt?" Mina asked while the tip of her fingers searched deep in her pocket. *Withholding evidence.* Found it. Her fist closed tenderly around the broken chain. *Holding on to memories.* She smiled at De Fiore who kept on talking.

"Ishmael tried to pin him against the wall with the forklift. When Michael fell to his knees, the gun went off and hit Sarah in the arm. Ishmael panicked, grabbed Sarah and they drove off in Michael's Corvette."

"And they went to Mina's," Brian finished.

Mina tucked her legs under her. The police station evidently didn't believe in a heater. "Why take a chance on my house, just for Paola's jewelry?"

"I doubt if they knew you were still living there," De Fiore said. "Don't forget that they drove away in Michael's car. Ishmael had all his keys. Not knowing the locks were changed, he probably thought he could get into the house without any problem. Instead, he had to force his way through the garage."

Remembering Ishmael's body on the cold marble floor, Mina shivered. How long would that haunt her? She looked at her watch. "I've got to get back to the office."

* * * * *

She and Brian rode for a while in silence, his

hand resting comfortingly on her arm. Her head hurt, especially the tender spot on the right temple. With only those two catnaps the night before—Brian didn't even have that. She couldn't imagine how he felt. "I called the hospital," she said. "Michael's going to make it."

She could feel his gaze on her profile. "How does that make *you* feel?"

Shrugging, she pulled into West Coast Software's parking lot. "I don't feel vengeful, if that's what you mean. Things sped out of his control. He'll suffer from that more than I could ever punish him."

They got out of the car and walked to the entrance. A surprise awaited them when Brian pushed open West Coast Software's front door.

"Good morning, may I help you?" asked a trim young lady sitting behind the desk. Her red hair was held back with a clasp, and her dress was neat and professional.

Mina was so used to Margo's flamboyance that the woman looked out of place. She hesitated before extending her hand. "Hi, I'm Mina Calvi."

At the sound of her voice, Paco poked his head out of the office. "You're back," he said. "Have you met Diana?"

"I'm sorry, Miss Calvi." The receptionist looked embarrassed. "My name is Diana Mason, I'm a temp."

"You'd better come in here. You too, Brian. There's news," Paco said.

The phones were ringing as Brian closed the office door behind them. Mina sat at the desk.

"Coffee?" asked Paco.

"No, thanks, I already drank plenty."

"Me too," Brian said.

Paco sat at Mina's side. "I hope this is all behind us, Mina. De Fiore called and filled me in. I still can't get over it. Who could have guessed, especially about Ishmael—or Amado—what an evil man. Mrs. Davies was very intuitive. She never liked him."

There was a tap at the door. "Yes?" Paco and Mina said in concert.

Diana peeked around the corner of the door. "There is a Mr. Adams to—"

Adams pulled back the door and came into the office before Diana could finish her sentence.

"It's all right," Mina said to the receptionist. "Hi, Adams."

"Well, where did you two disappear to last night?" Adams asked.

"It's a long story," Brian said.

"I'll bet. Lots of things have been happening. I guess I just missed you at the police station."

"What were you doing there?" Mina asked.

Adams pulled up a chair, sat down and sighed. "Did you know Sarah asked me to represent her?"

"You must be joking," Mina said. "What nerve!"

"Well, it's understandable. She doesn't know anyone else."

"Next you'll be telling us she's innocent," Brian said.

"No, and I explained to her I'm not a criminal lawyer. But she is cooperating, so to speak."

"Oh, please, you're breaking my heart," Mina said.

"Well, anyway," Adams continued, "she's scared and she sounds sincere—most of the time. She told us the whole sordid story."

Mina tried to smile at him, but her eyes filled with tears. She was afraid of what Adams would say next, but wanted to hear it. The question was: Would she be able to handle it?

"Can you talk about Sarah's statement or do we have to wait until it becomes official?" Brian asked Adams.

"Oh, the reporters were there. It will probably make the noon newscast."

"What did Sarah say about—Margo?" Mina's soul screamed Paola, but her lips couldn't say it.

"More or less what we all suspected; Margo's only sin was to fall for Ishmael's lies. He used her to get information and when she finally caught on, he tried to kill her and make it look like suicide. The roses were to cover his tracks. His plan from the beginning was to get Michael to marry Rachel. Margo must have told him about the Davies' pre-nuptial agreement. So our resourceful young man planned the chocolate filling to get rid of Paola. Sarah swears that neither she nor Rachel knew of it. We already know how Rachel got the candy." He cast a glance toward Paco, who was rubbing his moustache.

"It wasn't your fault, Paco," Mina said.

"Thank you, Mina," Paco mumbled without looking at her.

"Rachel had a key to the warehouse and the

loft," Adams continued. "She used to meet Michael there after business hours. And Michael gave her Paola's security number. Nice, huh? As for her pregnancy, Rachel was a very—popular girl. Mina, are you okay?"

She rubbed her eyes, but didn't look up. "Yes, please go on." Brian got up and came to stand behind her chair, resting his hands on her shoulders.

"There isn't much more," Adams said.

"Adams," her voice was like a cry.

"You should tell her what you know, Adams," Brian said, "Better you than a stranger."

"You're right." The lawyer seemed to search for words. "When Rachel died, something happened to Michael. Maybe it was when he heard about her pregnancy. He knew he couldn't have been the father. Or maybe he really loved Paola and decided to win her back. Anyway, he tried to break away from the Fernandez clan, but Ishmael wouldn't let him. Sarah was always there, telling him what Ishmael wanted Michael to hear. The night of Paola's death, that evening before Thanksgiving, Sarah persuaded Michael to spend the weekend with her. Sarah says he stopped by the house to get some clothes while she waited in his car, in the garage.

"When he got to the bedroom, Paola must have confronted him about the missing disks and told him she'd filed for divorce." He spread his hands apart in a dismissive gesture. "I'm just guessing here. All Sarah knows is that they were arguing loudly enough for her to hear them. Using his car phone, she called Ishmael, who was spending the night at Margo's. Sarah says she just wanted to get out of there quick. But she made the mistake of telling Ishmael about Paola's threat to divorce Michael."

The longer Adams talked, the more colorless his face became. "After coaxing Margo into taking a large dose of Seconal, Ishmael took her car and left. He also took her prescription bottle, but she didn't discover that until much later. Because of the drug, she really had no idea how long he was gone."

Paco let out a long sigh and covered his face with his hands. "Poor Mrs. Davies. She deserved better than that—how could they? And for what? Money?"

Mina kept her eyes closed. She would not cry, not now. But she had to know.

"The Fernandezes didn't know how much trouble West Coast Software was in," Adams continued. "In their eyes, Michael was a millionaire. He never did or said anything to make them think differently. Remember how he used to spend, trying to impress those girls?"

"Could we please get back to the subject?" Mina said.

"What do you want to know, Mina?" Brian's voice was gentle.

"Did Paola suffer?"

"I don't think so, Mina," Adams began, his voice scratchy. He cleared his throat. "In the time it took Ishmael to drive from Fountain Valley to Mission Viejo, Michael had gone back to the car with a bottle of whiskey, drunk it, and passed out. When Ishmael got there, he and Sarah went up to

Paola's room. The bedroom door was open. Paola seemed to be asleep—she'd probably taken the Soma Compound earlier. I guess she'd been complaining about her back all day. After the fight with Michael, she may have taken a couple more tablets or drunk some wine; we'll never know for sure. Anyway, Paola woke up. In the dark—in her drowsiness—she mistook Sarah for Mina and said she was thirsty. Ishmael went to the night table, dumped the Seconal in a glass of wine, and handed it to Sarah. Barely conscious, Paola drank it all. It was over in less than twenty minutes.

"Sarah insists that Paola was still breathing when they left and that she didn't realize the dose was lethal. She swears she never saw the suicide note, which, by the way, was typed on Margo's typewriter. She and Ishmael wiped their fingerprints off the glass and drove off in Margo's car."

Laughter came from the front office, where Diana was answering the phone. Young, carefree laughter.

"Stop it, make her stop it," Mina cried.

Brian knelt and pulled her close. "It's okay to cry, Mina. Don't fight it."

She didn't know how long she sobbed in his arms, her tears soaking his shirt. Paco pulled some tissues from the desk and handed them to her, his rough hand caressing her head. "I need to get back to work."

"Paco's right," Brian said. "Someone has to run the business."

Adams checked his watch. "Mina, dear, I'm due in court in thirty-five minutes. Where did I leave my briefcase?"

Mina stood and hugged him. "Thank you, Adams, I know how hard it must have been for you to tell me about her death. *Grazie."*

"You're welcome, darling."

"I'll walk you to your car." she said.

"Me, too. I need some fresh air," Brian said. She slipped her arm around his waist, and he hugged her, kissing the top of her head.

They all walked into the front office. The receptionist swiveled in her chair, smiled and extended a box, filled with candies wrapped in gold foil.

"Chocolate, anyone?"

The End

BOSOM BODIES
is the second book of the Mina's Adventures series:

Italian-born Mina Calvi has a way of finding trouble, but when she offers to help a friend by moonlighting at Bosom Bodies restaurant, it's trouble that finds her. The body of the restaurant manager is discovered on the beach, a hit and run victim, and Mina's VW Bug is impounded as the vehicle used in the crime. Stunned beyond belief, Mina is suddenly up to her ears in assault, betrayal, smuggling and murder. Now the police are watching her. The mob is targeting her. And who comes riding to her rescue on a metal steed—none other than the cook at Bosom Bodies, the mysterious Diego. Is he more than a bad cook and a good lover? Is he protecting her, or setting her up? Scared, clueless and on her own, Mina struggles to reclaim her life and stay two steps ahead of the those stalking her, but it's a treacherous path and she's losing ground fast.

Chapter 1 of Bosom Bodies

Employees must wash hands before returning to work. Mina stared at the sign posted on the mirror above the sink. She still couldn't grasp the fact she was one of them, *the employees.*

How could she have let Ginger, her yoga instructor, talk her into doing this? How? They weren't even really good friends. From yoga to waitressing at Bosom Bodies? She glanced at the curly red wig, the thick, fake lashes fluttering like butterfly wings. The image looking back from the mirror was a full size version of that doll. What was it called? Orphan Annie? No, not that one, oh, Raggedy Ann. Mina's eyes moved to her black top, stretched to the max over her foam-padded bra. This was no ordinary padding. The falsies had foam nipples to create the illusion of bona fide implants. *Viva l'America*. Two large, sparkly Bs marked *the spots*. According to the marketing people, the Bs stood for Bosom Bodies. Mina had her own version, Big Boobs! And to make sure everyone noticed them, the letters were imbedded with pretentious rhinestones. The kind Paola used to call, "circus diamonds."

"If Paola saw me like this..." She said it out loud. It had been over a year since her mother's death. Mina still found herself talking to her and thinking of her as she did when she believed Paola was her sister.

"There you are." One of the other waitresses peeked in the bathroom door. "People are hungry. Orders are getting cold. What's your problem? Wanna get fired your first day on the job?"

"*Magari*. I wish," Mina mumbled. She checked her red mini skirt, adjusted the uncomfortable top with the nametag that read "Ginger" and went to serve those hungry people. Barbara, the manager, hired Ginger, the real Ginger/yoga instructor, and since she hadn't started working yet, no one else knew what Ginger looked like. The only person aware of the switch was Barbara, and she already clocked out for the evening. Two more days and Mina's career as a redhead, big-busted waitress at Bosom Bodies would be over because Ginger would be back from her impromptu honeymoon. She didn't know how Barbara would explain the new Ginger to the rest of the staff, and she didn't care to know. The last time Mina waited tables was fourteen months earlier in October 1989. Before Paola's death, before Mina met Brian. She wasn't going to think about Brian now.

Her high heels clicked on the concrete floors of the smoke-filled restaurant. The loud music and the chattering noise could cover up cannon fire, never mind the annoying shoes. Round tables, higher than regular dining tables, with stools to match, occupied most of the large room. The rest of the space was taken by a well stocked bar. Men of all ages, shapes and means warmed most of the seats. They must all come for the food, Mina thought as she stretched on her toes to be able to hear the orders. Even in high heels, she was the shortest waitress there, and the least busty, the least giggly and, at twenty-four, probably the least young. Then again, she wasn't depending on the generosity of these men to make rent.

"Ginger, psst," Angelina beckoned from the other side of the glass separating the kitchen from the main room, "I put your plates here to keep them warm. Take them."

Angelina's English was marginal, but her intention to help Mina/Ginger was clear enough. She was the only ally in this whole place. Mina suspected it had to do with the accent, sort of a bonding factor. Angelina sounded Latina and probably had cultural similarities to Mina's Italian background. She looked so young to Mina. How did she end up here? In this…restaurant? Mina could see past Angelina's sweet smile. She could read the sadness and uncertainty in the young woman's eyes. They reminded her of her own eyes, her own feelings those many years ago when she first stepped off that plane at Los Angeles International.

She grabbed the warm plates and tried to make sense of the orders. She couldn't read her own handwriting. *That's what using computers will do to you!* Eyes watching her? She turned around. The kitchen helper, a short dark-haired man, was looking at her. His name was Diego. The girls talked about him, calling him the silent type. Mina wasn't even sure he understood English. Something about his piercing eyes made her uncomfortable.

She gave Angelina a smile of thanks and scooted to her assigned tables.

It was nearly midnight by the time she walked out of Bosom Bodies.

Only Diego, a cashier named Lisa, and Mina remained. Angelina and another waitress left a few minutes earlier. Due to corporate policy, Mina had to change clothes before leaving, so she looked even more silly with the idiotic wig and fake lashes wearing her jeans and the Ultrasuede coat, which was Paola's last gift. She was thankful she didn't know a soul on this side of town and aimed to keep it that way.

Her ragtop Bug was parked at the back of the building inside the fenced area reserved for *the employees*. There was that funny word again.

Enough rain drizzled from the night sky to allow December to be taken seriously even in Southern California.

Mina noticed something peculiar about her car. Maybe it was the reflection from the streetlight, but the car looked lopsided.

"Hurry up," Lisa the cashier said. "I need to lock the gate, I'm already late. The sitter will charge me overtime."

"Hey, I'm sorry. I think I have a flat tire." Mina walked around her car and, sure enough, it was the front tire, passenger side—as flat as her chest beneath the padding.

She could call Triple A. Her membership was current, wasn't it? It would take time, and Lisa wanted her out of there. She opened the hood and remembered the spare tire was sitting in the warehouse of West Coast Software where Mina left it to make room for moving boxes. That was last week. She had forgotten about the tire.

"*Maledizione!*" She slammed the hood close.

The male voice came from behind her. "So you're Italian."

Mina turned. Diego stood looking down at the flat tire. She was surprised at his perfect English, no accent, yet he understood Italian? Italian swear words. *How about that?*

"Lisa, go ahead, go home. I'll lock the gate as soon as we take care of Ginger's car." Mina stopped herself short of explaining her name wasn't Ginger. She bit her lip and avoided his eyes. The man made her feel self-conscious. How old was he? And what did she care? Lisa started the engine of her small, beat-up truck, waved to Diego, ignoring Mina and drove off in a blast of unmuffled engine and Michael Bolton's falsetto.

"Do you have a spare tire?" Diego asked.

"If I did, I would have already taken care of this."

"Oh, you change your own tires? In the dark, while it rains?"

She hated him. Smart-ass. That was one American expression she found fascinating and mostly to the point, especially on this occasion. How would that translate into Italian? Not very well. Smart *furbo*. Ass.

"Do you want a ride home?" Was he talking to her?

She looked around. The only vehicle left in the fenced space was her Volkswagen with the flat tire. "A ride? On your shoulders?"

"Suit yourself. Your car will be safe until tomorrow, but there aren't any cabs around here." He glanced at her heels. The streetlights played hide and seek with his expression. Even so, she knew he smirked. "See you tomorrow," he said.

Mina watched him walk to the side of the building. She didn't know what to do. The damp wig itched. Her leaden feet ached. She wasn't used to being on her feet for so many hours. All her prickliness left her. She wanted to sit in her car and wait for the sun to come up or this restaurant from hell to open, so she could use a phone. Who would she call? Brian was on a flight to Europe with his loony mother, and Mina hadn't dared tell Paco about moonlighting as a waitress in this place. *Maledizione.*

The rhythmic engine growl preceded him as Diego cruised around the corner on a shiny monster Harley.

"Last chance." He looked even smaller on that huge thing. He revved up the engine and waited. Mina approached him, still unsure. He steadied the bike by firmly planting both feet on the pavement. He wore fancy black boots. Who was this Diego, really? A substitute for a honeymooning cook?

"I don't have an extra helmet." He strapped his under his chin. "How far do you live? I don't want to get a ticket because you aren't wearing one."

"I'm wearing a wig. It'll soften the blow if I fall."

He didn't smile.

She moved up beside the motorcycle and sent a mental thanks to the corporate policy that made her change clothes. She could never straddle that metal horse wearing a short skirt. Even with her jeans, she had trouble. Her legs were too short and she had to lean on Diego's back to get on.

"Do you need anything from your car? Is it locked?"

"No and no."

"What do you mean? You didn't lock the car?"

"I never lock the car. Just go. Let's get it over with it. I'll have someone come over in the morning and fix the tire. Go."

He turned and clicked the padlock on the gate without getting off the bike. "Yes, ma'am, but tomorrow is Sunday. Most places will be closed."

She shrugged in the dark as he steered through the front parking lot. The instant they reached the road they gained speed. The bike glided under a canopy of twinkling holiday lights decorating the streets. A whiff of wind lifted her wig. Damn! She held on to Diego's waist with one arm while trying to keep the wig from flying off her head with the other. Diego patted her hand. Mina sensed he did it just to annoy her. He must have picked up on her discomfort. Soon they crossed the bridge and were in Newport Beach.

"Okay, you can drop me off just up the hill." She yelled into his back. She had no idea if he could hear her with that helmet.

"What hill?" He heard her. Good.

"Bayside Condominiums."

He whistled. "You live there?"

"Your Harley would look right at home in the garage." She remembered a magazine article about Elizabeth Taylor having a Harley-Davison. She felt pretty sure Ms. Taylor didn't play with cheap toys. "You can let me off at the gate, thanks."

He removed his hand from hers, made a sharp turn to the left and stopped the bike with the motor running. "*Buona notte,*" he said without turning his head.

Jerk. She struggled but got off the shiny machine without too much huffing and puffing. She knew her wig was askew. She pulled it off, tucked it in her pocket, and hurried to the gate. She waved to the old man minding the gate when she walked by. Her hair felt glued to her scalp after all the time spent wearing that wig. One set of the fake eyelashes were stuck shut. She tried to open her eye, but it only fluttered. The guard winked back.

About the Author

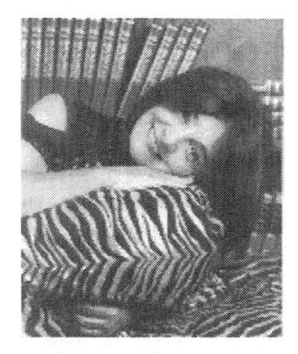

Maria Grazia Swan was born in Italy, but this rolling stone has definitely gathered no moss. She lived in Belgium, France, Germany, in beautiful Orange County, California where she raised her family, and is currently at home in Phoenix, Arizona—but stay tuned for weekly updates of *Where in the World is Maria Grazia Swan?*

As a young girl, her vivid imagination predestined her to be a writer. She won her first literary award at the age of fourteen while living in Belgium. As a young woman Maria returned to Italy to design for—ooh-la-la—haute couture. Once in the U.S. and after years of concentrating on family, she tackled real estate. These days her time is devoted to her deepest passions: writing and helping people find happiness.

Maria loves travel, opera, good books, hiking, and intelligent movies (if she can find one, that is). When asked about her idea of a perfect evening, she favors stimulating conversation, spicy Italian food and perfectly chilled Prosecco—but then, who doesn't?

Maria has written short stories for anthologies, articles for high profile magazines and numerous blogs tackling love and life. She engaged her editorial and non-fiction skills for *Boomer Babes: Tales of Love and Lust in the Later Years.* Her romantic suspense novels *Love Thy Sister* and *Bosom Bodies* are available at Amazon.com.

Website: http://www.mariagrazia.tv
Contact Maria: mariagswan@gmail.com
-or-
touch base with her on Facebook.